MURDER IN THE MIST

Recent Titles by Amy Myers from Severn House

MURDER IN THE QUEEN'S BOUDOIR
MURDER WITH MAJESTY
THE WICKENHAM MURDERS
MURDER IN FRIDAY STREET
MURDER IN HELL'S CORNER
MURDER AND THE GOLDEN GOBLET

Writing as Harriet Hudson

APPLEMERE SUMMER
CATCHING THE SUNLIGHT
QUINN
SONGS OF SPRING
THE STATIONMASTER'S DAUGHTER
TOMORROW'S GARDEN
TO MY OWN DESIRE
THE WINDY HILL
WINTER ROSES

MURDER IN THE MIST

A MARSH & DAUGHTER MYSTERY

Amy Myers

This first world edition published 2008
in Great Britain and the USA by
SEVERN HOUSE PUBLISHERS LTD of
9–15 High Street, Sutton, Surrey, England, SM1 1DF.

British Library Cataloguing in Publication Data

Myers, Amy, 1938-
  Murder in the mist
  1. Marsh, Peter (Fictitious character) - Fiction 2. Marsh,
  Georgia (Fictitious character) - Fiction 3. Private
  investigators - England - Kent - Fiction 4. Fathers and
  daughters - Fiction 5. Detective and mystery stories
  I. Title
  823.9'14[F]

  ISBN-13: 978-0-7278-6658-5   (cased)

All Severn House titles are printed on acid-free paper.

Typeset by Palimpsest Book Production Ltd.,
Grangemouth, Stirlingshire, Scotland.
Printed and bound in Great Britain by
MPG Books Ltd., Bodmin, Cornwall.

Author's Note

Kent has many literary connections, but the Fernbourne Five are fictional, even though they have become so established in my own mind that I expect to find Fernbourne and the King's Head ready to greet me (or otherwise, as you will see after reading this novel) whenever I go to the part of Kent that Jane Austen knew so well. Three of the Fernbourne Five wrote poetry, amongst their other talents, but this is not a talent of my own. The short quotations from their work that appear in this novel, therefore, are either my own, which fall sadly short of what the Five could have produced, or adaptations based on two poems by Edward Thomas and one by Benjamin Gough, a nineteenth-century Kentish poet.

I would like to thank Amanda Stewart and Sheena Craig at Severn House for their help over this novel, together with the rest of the impressive Severn House team. As always, my thanks go also to Dorothy Lumley of the Dorian Literary Agency for her unwavering support and guidance.

One

'Poisonous, of course,' Peter remarked.
     'You're thinking of larkspur,' Georgia pointed out. 'That's love-in-a-mist. Look at it.' There were pockets of tiny blue flowers as far as she could see, and here and there in this wilderness of a garden a stray poppy or hollyhock peered through the tangle of weeds.

'Whichever it is, we're still lost,' her father said crossly.

'This is Kent, not the Australian outback,' she joked. 'And we're merely temporarily mislaid.'

An understatement. They had come through a maze of lanes, most of which were single track with occasional passing places – if they could be called that, since they seemed to begrudge having to yield an inch more than necessary. This particular lane appeared to have given up completely on its purpose in this world; ahead, it degenerated into a grass track across a field, and so turning into this gateway was their only option.

On a late August day, the silence and beauty of the fields and woods around them were a tranquil contrast to taking the A2 back via Canterbury to their homes. Rather too tranquil if you were lost, however, and for no apparent reason the still-ness here was beginning to get to Georgia. It should be a rural idyll, but somehow it fell short of that. Idylls drew you towards them, but this garden was sending a different message. It was signalling 'leave me alone; stop right there'.

It had once been lovingly tended, but now flowers fought for air and on closer examination even the mass of blue love-in-a-mist that had first caught Georgia's eye looked frail, as though another year would see them disappear too.

As a child love-in-a-mist had been her favourite flower, and in defiance of her instinct to get the hell out of here, she got out of the car and walked over to look at them. She was aware of Peter's disapproving eye, however. Too late, she recalled how fond Elena had been of love-in-a-mist, and no doubt her father was recalling that too. Her mother was living in France with her second husband, and few such English country flowers would adorn her garden there.

Beyond the garden Georgia glimpsed the peg-tiled roof of the house, which must lie tucked behind the sprawling shroud of laurels. 'I'm going to take a look,' she shouted over to Peter. 'Someone *might* be living there.'

'I'll come,' was the unexpected reply, and he promptly began to manoeuvre himself into his wheelchair. She and Peter were returning from a visit to his sister Gwen, and had driven over in Peter's adapted car.

The path curved round to the house and as they approached it, Georgia saw that it was larger than she had first thought, although it still ranked as a cottage. The nearer they got, the stronger her impression that it was unlived in became. A climbing rose over the red brick struggled in its death throes with ivy as it fought for possession of the front of the house. A cobwebbed nameplate by the door announced that this was Shaw Cottage. The latticed windows looked bare and, peering through them, she could see no furniture or carpets. There were radiators, however, and the house looked in reasonable repair, with no broken windows or rotten wood. It would fetch a tidy sum on the market – so why was it left empty? A legacy dispute, perhaps?

Having negotiated their way round the outside of the house, which proved to be an unusual L-shape, Georgia left Peter nosing about at the rear, and decided to push her way through the overgrown sloped garden to see what lay at its foot. Her initial instinct put aside, she felt almost indignant at the thought of this garden left to its own devices. There were signs that it received the occasional attention, perhaps with weeds and grass being scythed, but it had been without tender loving care for many a year. Once this had been a lawn, and once this could have been a path she was stumbling along. Every so often there was the occasional clump of love-in-a-mist, as if marking the way, and yet she felt she was journeying into the unknown.

Like Rick, she thought with a shiver. Her brother had disappeared in France on a warm late summer's day such as this, thirteen years ago, when he was twenty-one, and there had been no clue since as to what had happened to him.

The trees and bushes she could see at the foot of the slope suggested a stream. As she grew nearer she saw that she was right and the water was running rather than trickling. There were overhanging willows, and by the stepping stones that led to the far bank was another patch of love-in-a-mist, preening itself in the sunshine. Across the stream there were woods, undergrowth at first and then a dense mass of trees and bushes. Perhaps in spring there might be bluebells but the woods looked too thick even for them to flourish. At one point they came right down almost to the stream's edge, with a large oak tree stretching its boughs out towards her.

And then it happened. Her stomach seemed to turn over, and despite the sun she was shivering with irrational fear. It must have been thinking about Rick, she tried to tell herself. Both she and Peter still had such reactions to his disappearance, as the past reached out its powerful hand. But these willows and that oak tree had nothing to do with Rick. Shakespeare's Ophelia had drowned herself in such a place. 'There is a willow grows aslant a brook . . .' Not here though; no one could have drowned here, surely. And yet . . . She couldn't follow the thought through and hurried blindly back to join Peter, as if the stream and trees were actively pushing her from their presence.

'You're as white as a sheet.' Peter looked concerned.

'Yes.' She had to force herself to continue. 'There's a stream down there.'

'So?' And when she couldn't continue, he added gently, 'Georgia, *tell* me.'

'Something awful must have happened there.' At least her father would understand what she meant by this.

A silence. 'Can I get this prison down there?' he grunted.

She shook her head. The ground was too rough for wheelchairs.

'Are there fingerprints?' he asked.

She felt relieved now that Peter had put her irrational fear into words – *their* words. Such 'fingerprints on time', their code for the stamp left on the atmosphere by violent crimes or injustice in the places where they had occurred, were the key to their working partnership. If they both reacted in a similar way, they looked into it further in the hope of providing some sort of resolution to unfinished business – for that was surely what these cries from the past implied. Such resolution depended on facts, however, not tenuous theory, not least because Marsh & Daughter recorded them in a series of true-crime books.

Many such fingerprints proved groundless, and this stream, she now told herself, must surely be one of those. Perhaps it was seeing the love-in-a-mist that had brought back memories of her mother so strongly and it was that, rather than the stream, that had upset her. But she suspected this wasn't the answer. Somehow this neglected garden had touched her on the raw and the fact that it was wheelchair inaccessible made it all the worse as Peter would be unable to confirm it.

Inaccessible? She should have known better. She'd only turned away for a moment, and there he was lurching towards the stream. Knowing that he would hate her interference, she forced herself to wait, expecting a grumpy request for help at any moment. It didn't come though, and it seemed an unbearably long time before he reappeared up the gentle slope.

'Gold medal performance,' she called out. A weak joke in a wobbly voice and she was hardly surprised that he didn't respond.

All he said as he reached her was: 'You were right, Georgia. Something very much amiss there. I wonder—'

'What?' she cut in more sharply than she had meant to. Had the tenuous connection with Elena occurred to him too? He had not seen her since she walked out after the accident that had paralysed him, and Rick's disappearance. Georgia herself had only met her on one or two rather stilted occasions.

'Where are we?' he asked, looking surprised. 'Let's look at that map again. It's large-scale, so this house and stream should be marked.'

She felt safer once back in the car, although she knew that was ridiculous. Apart from the stream, what threat was there from a neglected house? There was an active burglar alarm winking, so there must be a caretaker of some sort, although who would hear the alarm in this remote place?

Peter was studying the map. 'Chillenden, Adisham, Goodnestone – and Godmersham not that far. We're in Jane Austen territory. Her brother married a daughter of the family living at Goodnestone Park, didn't he? And then they lived at Godmersham? Jane was always popping over on jaunts.'

'I doubt if she'd have lingered here long,' Georgia said with feeling. 'Let's get going.'

'We seem to be here.' Peter's finger stabbed the map triumphantly. 'We took a farm track instead of the lane. If we go back to this fork –' he showed her – 'we can go on to the village of Fernbourne. Now why should we know that name?'

At first it meant nothing to her. Kent was like that; it had its public face and its private face, and the latter had countless byways leading to tiny communities still so far off the beaten track that she had not even heard of them. Nevertheless there was something about the name that was beginning to ring a bell.

'The Fernbourne Five!' she exclaimed.

'Quite,' Peter said smugly. 'Hoo-ha in the press. They seem to be going through a revival.'

'Of what?' Georgia asked. Then that too came back to her. 'Weren't they a sort of Bloomsbury Group in the late 1930s?'

'Right. And it went on after the war too, through the late forties, lingering into the fifties. Then the group must have fallen out of favour, because I don't recall much after that, until recently. One or two of Gavin Hunt's novels have been reissued, *Fanfare* and *Shadows*. Read them? Dilemmas of the young living through the war.'

'Like Hemingway's *A Farewell to Arms*?'

'In a way, though Hunt's were about the Spanish Civil War. Deep philosophical delvings. And not long ago I remember reading reviews of an exhibition of Clemence Gale's work at the Academy. She's chiefly a portrait painter, and was married to Hunt.'

'Did they have such interesting and varied private lives as the Bloomsbury Group?'

'Not sure. But something's nagging at my mind – it'll come to me. I was too busy growing up to take much notice myself in the 1950s, and it's not a side they stressed at the exhibition, from the reviews I read.'

'Is this the road to Fernbourne?' she asked, peering at the almost invisible signpost.

'The physical or the figurative one?'

So Peter was assuming that the cottage was something to

do with the village, perhaps even the Fernbourne Five. 'The physical one will do for the moment,' she answered. 'It's more likely to have a cup of tea available.'

'Done. Although . . .' He hesitated. 'Fernbourne looks less than a mile as the crow flies, but it looks a lot further than that by car. Do we want to do this?'

So now it was Peter who was holding back.

'Why not? Someone might know about that cottage, and neither of us can resist unanswered questions,' she replied lightly. This was a hard card to play, in view of the black hole of doubt still dogging them after Rick's disappearance. Nevertheless, Georgia told herself, if she grasped this nettle firmly, it might help staunch the deeper wounds. After all, that's what Marsh & Daughter was all about: dealing with unfinished business to compensate for not being able to find the answer to Rick's.

Perhaps Peter thought the same, because he nodded without comment. Once he was driving – or rather bumping – back along the track to the point where they had gone wrong, she felt better, and the journey with golden fields on either side of the unfenced road began to have the feel of a progress rather than a retreat.

Fernbourne proved to be a small and sleepy village. Even though it had a church, it still looked only the size of a hamlet, and didn't even possess a sign to indicate its name as they entered it. The road bypassed the centre of Fernbourne, which consisted of a gravelled square off to one side. The road itself was lined with cottages and a village shop, which possessed a post office sign, a rarity now. Perhaps the village was so buried that it had escaped notice. It was even possible for Peter to park easily so that they could explore the interesting square. This was pleasingly uniform with red-brick eighteenth-century cottages, a pub, church and formidable gates to a drive that presumably led to the village's Big House, whatever form that might take.

'Pub or shop first?' Peter asked.

'Shop,' Georgia decided. Shops could give you the feel of a community.

Its post office section had a firm 'closed' sign on it, so Fernbourne hadn't escaped that modern tendency; it was part-time service only. The food section was well stocked – and for the well-heeled from the look of it, Georgia thought, spotting some of the prices. Nevertheless it carried a good general spread of both luxuries and basics, and she decided to stock up for dinner that evening.

Time to open up discussion as she took her purchases to the counter. Peter was clutching a purchase of his own – a book, entitled *The Freedom Seekers*, which mystified her until she read the subtitle: 'The Story of the Fernbourne Five'.

'We were almost lost for good on the way here,' she began. The woman behind the counter, a fading blonde with a worried look and a false smile, which sat oddly together, began to add up Georgia's purchases.

'Easy for strangers to do round these lanes,' was the perfunctory and loaded reply, as if such foolish people drove through the village at their peril.

Georgia decided to establish her credentials as a true-born Kentish citizen. 'We're only from Haden Shaw, the far side of Canterbury, but it's amazing how quickly one can get lost. In our village all roads lead promptly to the A20 or the A2.'

'I daresay.'

Not promising, and Peter took over. On the basis that it's harder to be rude to someone in a wheelchair, he often rushed in where Georgia feared to tread.

'We saw a most attractive house out in the wilds. Shaw Cottage, I think it was called.'

He was fixed by a steady glance. 'What about it?'

'It seems to be empty. Is it for sale, do you know?'

He was eyed narrowly, to Georgia's amusement, as though any information given might lead to Peter whizzing off straightaway to vandalize any remaining assets.

'Not to my knowledge.'

'Is there a caretaker?'

'That'll be twelve pounds fifty.'

That ended the conversation, especially as the door to the private quarters opened and a young girl in jeans and flashy tank top marched through the shop, displaying the confidence and condescension bestowed by youth and beauty – extreme beauty in this case. Long blonde hair framed an exquisite oval face, from which dark blue eyes looked disdainfully upon the world.

'See you, Mum.'

'Got yer mobile, Emma?' enquired her mother.

'Yeah.' A heavy sigh.

'Then use it. Your pa will pick you up.'

'Adam's bringing me home.'

'Your dad said . . .' But the girl had already gone.

The brief encounter must have humanized her mother, since as Peter paid for his book, she volunteered, 'Mrs Elfie's place, that was. Keep away, that's my advice. Most do.'

'Why's that? Ghosts?' Georgia enquired, but a sour look was the only answer.

'I'm shaken, not just stirred,' Georgia admitted ruefully as Peter manoeuvred the wheelchair outside. 'This Mrs Elfie must have been as weird as her name.'

'Then a drink is most certainly in order.' Peter set off for the pub in determined fashion. Georgia hesitated, aware that they were still being assessed through the shop window by Emma's mum, but followed him to the square and into the King's Head. The flowering baskets hanging outside had made the place look more promising than the interior proved. The public bar was dark, given over to a snooker table, slot machine and in one corner an ancient game of Devil among the Tailors. The licensee was one Robert Laycock, so a bronze plaque over the door read.

'I wonder if they know World War Two's over?' Peter whispered, making his way to the other bar. This luckily proved far more welcoming and opened out into a restaurant area on the far side of the pub. There was no one behind the bar, but a door opened almost immediately, and a man of seventy-odd appeared. He was hardly beaming, but Georgia was relieved that at least he hadn't emerged with all guns blazing. He should be pleased to see custom; there couldn't be much trade around at four o'clock on a weekday afternoon, even if it was still the holiday period.

'What can I get you?' He sounded pleasant enough, which was encouraging. As he supplied them with their drinks, he added, 'Just passing through, are you?'

A casual question, but Georgia noticed that his eyes went from one to the other as though he were more interested in their reply than his tone suggested.

Why not plunge in, she thought, slightly surprised that she had even considered not doing so. What had they to hide?

'We're interested in the Fernbourne Five,' she said as Peter obligingly flourished his newly acquired book. 'We thought we'd see the village they worked in, but we landed up on the wrong road at Shaw Cottage.'

'Mrs Elfie's place.'

Another man, much younger – his son, perhaps – had come in through the door to the private quarters. One of the two was presumably the landlord – her guess would be the new arrival. The hair was brown and thicker than his father's but the faces looked much the same. She decided she would rather get on the wrong side of the son than the father.

'Not hard to lose your way round there, is it, Dad?' the newcomer continued.

Dad polished a glass by way of answer.

'Was she part of the Fernbourne group?' Georgia asked brightly, taking a wild guess and hitting an unexpected bullseye.

A prompt reply from Dad to this one. 'Best ask the board about that.'

'The board?' Peter queried.

'The Fernbourne Trust. You'll be reading all about the group in that book of yours.'

Even the son looked slightly surprised at the note of churlishness in his father's voice and obviously decided he needed to step in. 'Matthew Hunt, who wrote that book, he's the chair of the board. You've missed him though. Went up to London today, he did.'

Well, well, volunteering information, Georgia thought. Time to persevere. 'So is Shaw Cottage anything to do with the Fernbourne Five's story?'

'That's the manor you want,' was his prompt reply. 'Not that old place.'

The son glanced at him. 'There's interest growing in the Fernbourne Five again. You're the second this week. Trade's looking up. Come back in a year or two.' He laughed as Georgia blinked. 'The manor,' he continued. 'The trust is making it into an arts centre, isn't it, Dad? Opening next year, and that will put us on the map.'

'For what that's worth,' Dad muttered.

'Survival, Dad, and you know it.' He nodded to them. 'Bob Laycock's the name. And Dad is Ted.'

'Still remembered round here, they are, Mr Hunt and his wife.' Ted seemed to find his voice, even though it sounded more of a threat than a chatty comment.

'That's Clemence Gale. She's still alive, isn't she?' Peter pressed on.

'I meant his first wife, Mrs Elfie.' Ted grudgingly grew more expansive. 'She was a lovely lady. My dad was gardener up at the manor. They called her Elfie, though her name was Ella. Loved flowers, she did, and wrote and illustrated books for children, under her maiden name Ella Lane. She was Mrs Elfie to us. My father said she was like an elf herself.'

'Lived with Birdie Field,' Bob added.

This drew a dark look from his father, Georgia noticed. Odd. What could be so secret about this, save that presumably it was after she left Gavin Hunt? And who was Birdie Field?

'Did Elfie own Shaw Cottage?' Peter asked.

This was received in silence by Ted, but Bob seemed happy enough to answer. 'Mrs Elfie was divorced from Mr Hunt. Miss Birdie asked her to come to live with her.'

'It's coming back to me,' Peter remarked, with a look Georgia knew well. The bloodhound had just been given the scent. 'There was a great love affair, wasn't there?' he continued. 'Elfie was married to Gavin Hunt, but fell in love with one of the others in the group. She had to choose between him and her child.'

'Mr Matthew, yes,' Bob agreed.

'And she chose to stay with Matthew?'

'Yes,' Bob said casually. 'So Alwyn Field topped himself. Hanged himself from a branch over the stream in the garden.'

'So that was it,' Georgia said, unaccountably depressed, when they returned to the car. 'It must have been Alwyn's suicide that caused the weird atmosphere by the stream. He killed himself over his unfulfilled love affair with Elfie Lane.'

'Possibly. Presumably he was this Miss Birdie's brother. Look, why don't you check out the churchyard before we go? You might find Alwyn Field's grave, and perhaps Elfie's.'

So she was right: Peter *did* have a scent in his nostrils. From which direction? she wondered, She knew better than to press him, so despite her misgivings she set off for the church. Beyond it, there were thick woods, perhaps part of the manor estate. Together with the yew trees in the church-yard, they looked tranquil enough – unlike those at Shaw Cottage. A quick scout around would present no problem and would please Peter.

Passing through the lychgate, she almost bumped into an embracing couple just inside it. She recognized that blonde hair: it was Emma from the shop, wrapped in the arms of the famous Adam, presumably. Love's young dream. The couple unwillingly parted at her arrival, glaring at her in a way that was becoming familiar in this village.

'Gotta go, Sean,' Georgia heard the girl say. Beauty then passed on her way. So the lover wasn't Adam. Another eternal triangle in Fernbourne, she wondered, amused. What would Adam make of this? Where was he? She suspected she knew, because in the church porch another young man was loitering. He flushed when he saw her, but had obviously been watching the couple at the lychgate. Being young was tough, and it always was, she thought, remembering her own youthful passion for Zac. She'd made the mistake of marrying him, and she only hoped that Emma was making the right choice here.

She had no luck finding Elfie's grave, and it took a little time to find Alwyn's, since it didn't seem to be amongst the main block of forties and fifties tombstones. As a suicide – even if with the usual caveat of 'balance of mind being disturbed' – she suspected his grave might be separated from his peers, cruel though that seemed from today's perspec-tive. She tracked it down eventually in a corner, half hidden by bushes, and she found she wasn't alone in her mission. A good-looking man in his late twenties was already there. He was dark-haired, casually dressed, and looked at her with an inquisitiveness that suggested more than a passing interest.

Good, she thought, smiling at him. 'Do you know anything about Alwyn Field?'

'Some. What in particular?' he countered.

'About Shaw Cottage,' she answered promptly, conscious that he was watching her keenly, as if she were trespassing on his private patch.

'Why?'

There seemed no harm in telling him – omitting the fingerprints on time, of course.

He listened, then nodded his head. 'The great love affair.
You know about that?' he asked.

'Yes, though I don't understand why Alwyn hanged himself.
If Elfie came to live with him at the cottage, there must have
been some ongoing relationship.'

'Elfie didn't move in with Birdie until after he had died.'

Georgia blinked. 'That's strange, isn't it?'

'I think so. I'm Damien Trent by the way.'

'Georgia Marsh.'

'Of Marsh and Daughter? You write books, don't you?'

There was definitely more than casual interest now. 'Yes.'

'Is this going to be one?'

'I doubt it.' She decided to err on the side of caution. 'We're
only passing through. And you?'

'Journalist. My dad's just died,' he added abruptly. 'Staying
here a few days.'

This too seemed odd, but she supposed it was his reason
for getting away in the aftermath of the funeral. The tombstone was plain: 'Alwyn Field, poet and philosopher, 1912 to
1949. Greatly loved.' Underneath were two lines of verse.

> Could the Piper not have stayed for me?
> I heard his music too.

'Do you know what that means?' she asked.

'It's from one of his poems, so his sister told me yesterday.'

Georgia did a double-take. 'She's alive? She must be a fair
age.'

'Birdie's over ninety and in a home, but she's still got all
her marbles.'

'Was she part of the Fernbourne Five group?' He shook his
head, and so she asked, 'Then who was the fifth member after
Clemence, Gavin, Elfie and Alwyn?' Immediately the words
were out she remembered the answer herself, but he spoke
first.

'That, as Hamlet said, is surely the question. It was Roy
Sandford. Poet, essayist, artist, philosopher. The bright
flame of the five, snuffed out in an air raid in 1941 aged
twenty-eight.'

'And what's the question about that?'

He regarded her seriously. 'I wish I knew.'

'You mean this could be a new case?' Luke looked worried.

Though Georgia loved and lived with him, there were times when their relationship was necessarily delicate, as he was Marsh & Daughter's publisher. Medlars, their home for the last year, was only a mile or two from Haden Shaw where she worked, but by mutual assent her work was distanced as far as possible from the converted oast house office in Medlars' forecourt. She was breaking the rules by raising a matter of business during the evening.

'Don't you fancy a book about a Kentish Bloomsbury Group?' she asked.

'What's the crime?'

Georgia stared at him, then began to laugh. She'd forgotten that tiny detail. 'I haven't the faintest idea. None that we can see yet, except that technically in 1949 suicide was a crime. A suicide and a love affair are all we have to go on.' Except for the fingerprints on time that Peter and she had sensed, and Luke wasn't privy to that approach. 'You're still frowning. Why don't you like the idea?'

'The usual reason. I don't fancy libel suits, and you said that one or two of the group are still alive.'

'Unlikely to sue at their age.'

'My love, it doesn't work like that,' Luke said ruefully, 'and you know it.'

She did. 'Anyway, there's no case and therefore no book.'

And nor would there be, she tried to convince herself. She couldn't stop thinking about the Fernbourne Five, however, and found a pretext to sneak off to her laptop after supper and search the Internet. The results were interesting. Gavin Hunt, novelist, had ten novels to his name and a mass of awards, born 1908 and died 1988. Married twice, first to Ella Lane, second to Clemence Gale, with one child by each marriage, respectively Matthew and Jane Elizabeth.

The best picture of Gavin she could find (as Peter had rightly marched off with Matthew Hunt's book) showed him with windswept hair, laughing into the camera, more the outdoor type than the academic. As for Elfie, Georgia could see why she got her nickname. She had a mass of hair, delicate, almost elfin features, and such of her illustrations as were shown on the Fernbourne Five website had a fey quality to them, as did her children's stories. No J.K. Rowling at work here. Her style might not be modern, but it had great attraction. And, Georgia noticed, in one of the watercolour illustrations a mass of love-in-a-mist was a major feature. Had she, and not Birdie or Alwyn, planted them at Shaw Cottage? And if so did that mean anything other than that she liked the flower?

Clemence looked a different sort of woman altogether. More sturdy, down to earth. Her portraits seemed straightforward at first, until one studied them. Reviews of her work mentioned her use of symbolism, and there were indefinable aspects about the way the subjects were placed or where they were looking that suggested another dimension to them.

She found less about Roy and Alwyn, save that both were poets. Roy's greatest work was to be found in *The Flight of the Soul*, a collection published in 1942 to which Alwyn had also contributed. In addition Roy had written two pre-war collections and a detective story. Alwyn had published one collection before the war and one after, and he too had written a mystery novel, which seemed to have had good reviews, though it had never been reprinted. Nor had *The Flight of the Soul*.

'Odd, wouldn't you say?' Georgia asked Peter the next day, when she reached their office. 'The Fernbourne Five's reputation seems to have been as a group rather than as individuals.'

'Except for Clemence Gale,' Peter pointed out. 'And two of them died before they could really get under way.'

Their office was in Peter's home in Haden Shaw. Before Georgia had moved in with Luke, she had lived next door to Peter, and she still used the house occasionally as an office, or to put up friends. She was reluctant to sell it, but was uneasily aware that it was becoming an unspoken issue between her and Luke. To sell it announced clearly that she was ready for marriage and commitment, a decision she kept postponing, not through misgivings about Luke, but through memories of the failure of her previous marriage.

'The oddest thing for me,' Peter continued, 'is that Matthew Hunt's book *The Freedom Seekers* – and the website – ascribe the authorship of *The Flight of the Soul* mainly to Roy Sandford, with some input from Alwyn, but when I checked *The Times Literary Supplement* to see the reviews on publication, sole authorship was ascribed to Alwyn Field. No mention at all of this Roy Sandford.'

'Really?' She frowned. 'A mistake?' It seemed unlikely for such an informed source.

'The *TLS* doesn't make mistakes. So . . .' Peter was deliberately taking his time, to her annoyance.

'Tell me,' she said sweetly.

'I looked at the *Times* back issues CD. Further study of Alwyn Field reveals that hopeless love for Elfie might not have been the only reason for his suicide. In late 1948 a plagiarism charge was lodged against Alwyn on the grounds that *The Flight of the Soul* was chiefly Roy Sandford's work, and not that of Alwyn Field. There's no mention of its coming to court, so it was probably settled, but there must have been a lot of gossip.'

Poor man, Georgia thought. The author's great fear. A plagiarism charge was easily made, but so rarely disproved without stigma. A whole authorship issue was unusual however. What on earth had happened there?

'That's another reason for his suicide and our reaction to that place. There's nothing to investigate.' She registered with some surprise that she was relieved.

'Sure?'

She considered this. 'Ninety per cent.'

'Stick with the other ten per cent. Why isn't the village proud of the Fernbourne Five? They don't seem too eager to welcome visitors, but why not? Matthew Hunt's book must surely be aimed at spreading the reputation of the Five, not damping it down.'

He was right, and it *was* odd. 'I take it you want to ask some awkward questions?'

'I do,' Peter said happily. 'I'll drive.'

It was clear something was wrong as they turned the corner. A police incident van was evidence of that, even if the police cordon round the lychgate hadn't betrayed it. It could hardly bear any relevance to their mission, Georgia tried to tell herself, even as her stomach lurched with foreboding.

It was quickly justified when she saw Detective Chief Inspector Mike Gilroy stepping down from the incident van in the square. Mike had been Peter's sergeant in his own police days before the accident had put an end to them, and now he was a friendly – usually – source for help. In theory this help went both ways, but it was heavily weighted in favour of Mike helping Peter.

Mike's poker face didn't change when he saw their car draw up, and he strode over to them. 'Just happened to be here, did you?'

Peter ignored this. 'What's the case?'

Georgia held her breath. *Please, please Mike, say it's a mugging, say it's a theft, say it's anything but something involving the Fernbourne Five.*

She had banked on this visit resolving loose ends, not opening up a new and more terrifying prospect.

'Man staying at the pub. Found shot at the back of the churchyard.'

'Not Damien Trent?' Georgia asked in alarm. 'Late twenties, dark, quite tall?'

Mike looked at her stonily. 'Yes.'

Two

'It's just coincidence, Mike,' Peter added pacifyingly, after he had explained why they were so fortuitously at his crime scene.

Georgia kept silent. She wasn't so sure. Mike seemed uncommonly eager to wrest the story – such as it was – from them, and he had informed them that their coincidences had a habit of entwining themselves into his cases rather too often.

'You'd better have a look, Georgia,' he told her matter-of-factly, nevertheless.

'Is the body . . .?'

'No. He was found five hours ago and the scene lads and doc have finished with him.'

She was both relieved and annoyed with herself for being so craven. Churchyards and corpses held memories for her of a previous case, and now the same prospect hung over her once again.

In fact the scene of the actual crime turned out not to be in the churchyard itself, but in the woods some twenty yards away on its far side. As she approached, the site became immediately apparent by the tent, and the number of white-suited SOCOs moving around. This footpath was clearly a well used one, which suggested it might eventually end up at the manor house.

'There's no doubt about its being Damien, I suppose?' she asked Mike as he stopped on the last SOCO 'stepping stone' to the tent.

'Not much. Identified by the licensee at the pub, but a relation is on his way to double-check. Trent booked in at the King's Head three days ago, and was supposed to be leaving today. He was shot. Feeble attempt to make it look like suicide by leaving the gun at his side.'

'Is accident ruled out?'

'Pretty nearly. Poaching by night is out of fashion anyway, so I doubt if he got in the way of a man and a pheasant. He was killed roughly between nine p.m. and midnight.'

'Gun?'

'Smith and Wesson.'

'Registered to?'

'Unregistered. There was a lot of noise in the village last night. Party and music at the pub. Could have masked the shot.'

Georgia looked round. The path disappeared into the thick woodland. Where could Damien have been going or, more likely, coming from? This would be a creepy choice of route from the manor late at night, and so why bother when its driveway would have been so convenient for the pub? She tried in vain to suppress the question of whether his death had any relevance to Alwyn Field, whose tombstone was close by.

'Do you want to talk here, or rejoin Peter?' Mike asked.

No doubt about that – the latter. Peter had gone to the pub to wait for them and it was a bad sign that Mike wasn't making the usual 'Marsh and Daughter's fancy ideas aren't needed here' noises.

The pub itself was full, no doubt after word had spread of the murder, and Peter had remained in the garden where there was less chance of being overheard.

Mike pounced for the kill straightaway. 'Right. So you sniffed a case for Marsh and Daughter?'

He wasn't usually so aggressive. Perhaps even as a DCI he didn't like to be reminded of his days as Peter's sergeant. No, Georgia couldn't believe that Mike was as petty as that. Probably his wife or children were presenting problems, though that too was unlikely from what she knew of them. Besides, Mike was a skilled performer in keeping his life compartmentalized. It was more likely that this case looked to Mike as if it might be a tricky one, and the suggestion it was a 'Marsh' sort of case would, alas, only make it trickier in his eyes.

During his work with Peter in the Kent Police, Mike had once explained to her that some incidents informally became categorized as 'Marsh cases', and it was only later that, accentuated by Rick's disappearance, Peter himself had begun to assess his vague hunches as attributable to fingerprints on time. Mike, for all his apparent straightforward approach to his work, had a keen sense that if something worked, it worked – and Peter's hunches had often fitted that bill. It's what had made them a good team until Peter's accident had put an end to it. Now the combination did not work so well.

'Not really.' Georgia tried to answer Mike's accusation. 'It was Shaw Cottage that intrigued us, and that's some way from the village. It was only later we discovered it had a link to the Fernbourne Five arts group. That's all,' she finished lamely, aware it still didn't sound convincing. The truth often didn't, she thought crossly.

'So you immediately rushed off to see this tombstone, where you met Damien Trent. Why?'

Why not, would be the natural reply, but Georgia suppressed it. 'Idle curiosity. Nothing more.'

Mike loosened up. 'Tell me again what Damien Trent said to you.'

She related the conversation as clearly as she could remember it.

'A journalist,' he repeated. 'Sure of that?'

'Positive.'

'Would it surprise you to know that when the police broke the news to his mother, she said he worked at Gatwick Airport?'

Georgia was taken aback. Surely not. Damien had behaved like a journalist – though how one could define that, she wasn't sure. 'He could have been a freelancer.'

'He could,' agreed Mike, 'but if so he kept remarkably quiet about it. No one seems to know what he was doing in Fernbourne. The name meant nothing to his mother. His home was in the Haywards Heath area and neither she nor his girl-friend knew he was here, let alone why. He'd said he was taking a few days off to see some old friends on the south coast.'

'Did he live with this girlfriend?' Georgia asked practically. A live-in partner would probably be better informed.

'No.'

Pity. She, more than the mother, might have known why he had such an interest in the Fernbourne Five, Georgia thought. Maybe he'd just been reading about them and, real-izing he was nearby, drove in to investigate their home territory. This explanation didn't satisfy her, as it would have been odd to book in for three days on a mere whim. Nevertheless, it didn't seem long enough to stir up any reason for his murder involving the Five. If there was a link, she would be furious with herself for not pushing for more information from Damien – not least because she might have prevented his death. Or, it occurred to her belatedly, she might have shared it, if there were such a connection. And she could still. The thought was not pleasant.

'Is there still a doubt that it was murder?' Peter asked.

'Just possible, I suppose.'

'Even if poaching is old hat, he might have disturbed badger hunters or some other nocturnal activity.'

'If you count drugs as nocturnal activity, that's more likely to be on the cards. The churchyard is, or was, a favoured spot for deals. Even so, why leave the gun?'

Peter grunted. He liked to leave no stone unturned. 'Is it certain that Trent has no contacts here?' he probed. Georgia held her breath, but fortunately Mike seemed to be giving them leeway.

'We're not far enough into it yet. He did ask whether a Joe Baker was still alive, and there are still Bakers in the village. One owns the village shop.'

'Emma's mum?' Georgia queried. At least there was a line of enquiry that was nothing to do with the Fernbourne Five.

Mike grinned. 'It must be a hard fate being known as that young lady's mum. No, is the answer. Mum's only a Baker by marriage and her husband Ken is the legal owner. This Joe Baker turns out to have been his grandfather's brother and died in the 1980s – although with such a common name there might have been other Joes. Ken says he was in his early twenties when Joe died. He knew him, of course, but only as a jolly uncle figure. He asked Trent if he was a long-lost relative, and Damien said he was looking into it. Hardly likely to have led to his death, is it?'

'But it fits Damien's statement to me that his father had recently died,' Georgia said thankfully. If this had been a family history search for Damien, that meant his death could be one step further from the Fernbourne Five, lessening her responsibility over not probing further.

Mike took his departure, leaving them in the garden. 'What next?' Georgia asked Peter after he had gone.

'Another pint, as you're driving.'

She went in to fulfil his request and emerged bearing the drinks, reflecting on pub gardens in general, now that the question of Damien Trent seemed to have receded as something in which they might be deeply involved. Pub gardens could often tell as much about the pub and its clientele as the interior. This one was more of a problem as the interior was somewhat neglected, whereas this garden was neatly mown, clipped and weeded. No love-in-a-mist would dare to seed itself here and spring up expecting to be welcomed. Neat begonias, dahlias and French marigolds formed the army of flowers disciplined here into strict regimental order. Was this Bob Laycock's wife's domain? Or Ted's? And if so, what did that tell her about Ted? Nothing, she answered herself cheerfully, as she placed Peter's pint and her own decorous fruit juice on the table.

'Do we take this further or do what Mike clearly wishes and clear out?' she asked hopefully on her return to Peter. 'We could just put the Fernbourne Five on the shelf.'

There were a lot of such files on the shelf – or more literally nowadays in the computer. What remained in the shelf files were newspaper cuttings, Internet printouts, photographs and other paraphernalia of cases that might one day develop, but which lacked the vital key to whether they progressed or not.

'What about Alwyn Field?' Peter asked. 'We can't abandon him.'

'A troubled end for a troubled life. We've nothing more to go on.'

'Except curiosity,' Peter pointed out.

'Which killed the cat.'

He grinned at her. 'But the cat has nine lives.'

Georgia spent the intervening weekend after Damien's death reading *The Freedom Seekers*. It would be one step forward in combating her reservations about this case – if a case it was. Even though it looked as though it had nothing to do with Damien Trent, she still had an uneasy feeling of responsibility, illogical though it seemed.

As she and Peter turned into the manor drive on the Monday afternoon, she had managed to put Damien temporarily aside, in favour of keeping a clear mind over the Fernbourne Five, particularly Clemence Gale. Peter often left such spadework meetings to her, but on this occasion he had been insistent on coming himself. When she asked why, he had merely replied vaguely, 'It's the way in.'

'To the manor perhaps, not necessarily to Shaw Cottage,' she had argued. 'Are you shifting emphasis?'

He had looked worried. 'Let's agree that it's a side gateway to Alwyn Field.'

This was some gateway, she now thought. Whoever designed the manor had built in the maximum potential for impressing the newcomer through this curved driveway; it was bordered with huge rhododendrons, so that when Peter rounded yet another bend the house was revealed in all its glory.

And glory it was. In front of them was a magnificent brick building of three storeys, the same red brick as the rest of the village cottages and the school. This building, however, had a stone portico and matching window ledges, and its shape suggested there had been later extensions.

From her photographs Clemence Gale looked a formidable lady, but Peter had told Georgia that Clemence had sounded most welcoming on the telephone and she had even suggested Matthew Hunt should be present today. Peter wasn't surprised at that. He'd given their reason for the visit as general interest after having read Matthew's book, but Marsh & Daughter's occupation could well have been known to them.

'Hence the reception committee,' Peter had commented. 'They'll probably be lined up on the front steps to greet us.'

Clemence Gale was now in her late eighties, and was still actively painting, according to Peter. She'd made a passing reference on the telephone to 'studio time'. There proved to be no reception committee lined up on the front steps, only a ramp for the wheelchair and the door opened by Clemence's daughter, Janie Hunt, as she introduced herself. She looked in her late forties, and a throwback to the 1970s in her style of dress, with dangling earrings amid long wild hair, floating long skirt and sandals. She seemed friendly, however, despite the anxiety lines Georgia could see on her face, and her smile was valiantly fighting those. An interesting woman, Georgia thought, and obviously her mother's carer, but what else?

'Come in. I hope the ramp holds up,' Janie joked.

'I'm not that heavy,' Peter said cheerfully as he embarked on the journey up. It held.

So far, so good. The house seemed welcoming too; its polished floors and carpets didn't clash with its atmosphere of run-down comfort. Georgia could see this was a home, not just a house, and the paintings and objects in this large entrance hall suggested a random selection that pleased its owner rather than one to impress visitors. Janie led the way into a large room on the left, where four long sofas were set in a square with a low table in the middle. Clemence Gale, as her photographs suggested, was a short, impressive lady with grey cropped hair and clad in an array of clothes that offered nothing to fashion. She was not seated but leaned heavily on her stick, and her determined lively face made the idea of a carer somewhat redundant. At her side was Matthew Hunt, who looked a well-preserved seventy-something, with a mop of curly well groomed white hair, suntanned face, lithe figure, and an air of being leader of the pack. This was, as Peter had expected, the modern face of the Fernbourne Five on display.

'Clemence tells me you've read my little book, and hence your interest in the Fernbourne Five. Excellent, especially as I've been reading yours,' Matthew began with polished flattery. 'The one about the Spitfires and the Battle of Britain. I spent many days in my childhood lying on the lawn watching dog fights in the air by day and sleeping in Anderson shelters by night.'

'You were a WAAF, if I recall correctly, Mrs Hunt.' Georgia turned to Clemence after suitable murmurs of appreciation all round.

'I was called up in late 1942. I was a driver at RAF Manston. It's left me with a long standing aversion to black shoes, thick stockings and blue-grey heavy skirts,' agreed Clemence, waving to Georgia to sit down, and following suit. There was a glint in her eye which suggested that she knew exactly how Georgia was summing up this formal welcome.

She tried to imagine what it would be like to be painted by Clemence, suspecting those keen eyes would probe further into one's psyche than might be comfortable. Janie took her position at her mother's side while Matthew sat in lonely state on one of the other sofas, one arm casually draped along its back. Oh, yes, the leader of the pack all right.

'Your interest in the Fernbourne Five was sparked off not so much by my humble book as by Shaw Cottage, so I hear,' he observed.

Peter laughed. 'Glad to hear that Fernbourne has the usual efficient village communication system. Yes, you're right. The cottage is a sad place, isn't it?'

'Empty houses always are,' remarked Janie.

'Shaw Cottage isn't empty,' Clemence said firmly. 'It's full of memories.'

'Of Alwyn Field?' Peter leapt in. 'Yet he doesn't seem prominent in your book, Matthew.'

'Or in the group, Mr Marsh,' was the soft rejoinder. 'Poor Alwyn never felt that he measured up to the rest of you, did he, Clemence? He was wrong, of course. He was very gifted. My mother would not have loved him otherwise. And, of course,' Matthew moved on, 'Clemence meant the cottage has memories of her too.'

'You don't mind talking about that aspect?' Georgia asked. She had been surprised to find there was plenty about Elfie and Alwyn's affair in *The Freedom Seekers*. No shirking the issue, even though Elfie had been Matthew's mother.

'Of course not,' was Matthew's reply. 'It's a major part of the Fernbourne Five story. I have little personal memory of the affair to upset me. My mother rarely talked to me about it, but it's a necessary factor if you are to understand the Fernbourne Five.'

'Did you live in Shaw Cottage with your mother?' Georgia asked.

'No. I saw her, of course, but lived at the manor. I was at boarding school and only in Fernbourne for holidays. In due course Clemence came to live here.' A smile in her direction. 'And then I had two mothers.'

Georgia saw Clemence glance at him, but her expression was unreadable. And expressions could be misinterpreted, she reminded herself, as the danger was that one would see what one wanted to see. But what would that be in this case, she wondered. Love, or just the bonds created by the past?

'I should explain,' Clemence said, 'that Gavin and Elfie's parting was by mutual consent. After that, in due course, he came to love me. Elfie had moved out by then, she and Gavin were divorced and in due course we married. I remained on good terms with Elfie too – naturally, because she was one of the group and so was I.'

'She moved into Shaw Cottage after Alwyn died, didn't she?' Georgia still thought that strange.

'After she had satisfied herself that I was happy at boarding school,' Matthew picked up smoothly. 'Before that she devoted herself here to her writing and illustrations. She had given up the chance of a happy married life with Alwyn. It is a remarkable story and her work was very fine, even if not in today's fashion. If you read her books and poems and look carefully at the illustrations, you can glimpse sadness behind them as well as the magic and charm. She had a knack of combining all the elements of the child's world together; the magic, the music, the fantasy, the quest for the unknown, the unexplained on the one hand and everyday life and realities on the other. The fun and quirkiness of her work, plus a world to which one can relate, often remind me of the Harry Potter books.'

Not the impression that Georgia had received so far. It sounded too sweet for words, Georgia thought, and yet perhaps she was only judging from hindsight. Children's books did have those elements then, and sometimes still did, though in different form.

'What sort of person was she?' she asked.

Matthew considered this. 'She was my mother, so that's hard for me to answer. Let's say she wasn't like me.'

Clemence laughed and took over. 'Elfie and I were chalk and cheese too, if that's any guide. Elfie was, as her nickname suggests, very much an other-worldly person. The realities of life left her bewildered. She needed to be looked after, but unfortunately Gavin required this too, and eventually the two clashed too much. This makes her sound a selfish person, but I assure you she wasn't. She was loving, gentle and unselfish, a fairy story in herself.'

'And no wicked witches around?' Georgia couldn't help asking. This still sounded too good to be true, and perhaps Janie realized it because she broke in with her own opinion.

'Every fairy tale has its darker side. Elfie's certainly did. After all, she did have to give up Alwyn to look after Matthew.'

'That wasn't *so* dark a fate,' Matthew laughed, but with none too friendly a glance at his half-sister.

'Her happiness disappeared with that decision,' Janie stubbornly maintained.

'With Elfie,' Matthew rejoined, 'her dreams were her happiness, and who knows what *they* were?'

'Oh, come on, Matthew,' Janie snorted. 'How can you say that?'

Georgia thought Matthew might point out that Janie wasn't in a position to know; she wasn't even born then. But he didn't. All he replied was, 'In her way, she was happy.'

'You're her son, you would say that.'

'Matthew might be right, Janie,' Clemence contributed to this sibling clash. 'Elfie lived in her own work and her garden. You know how many of her illustrations stemmed from the garden at Shaw Cottage. Did you know she planted it for Alwyn, Georgia? Birdie was no gardener. And before you ask, Elfie began it before Alwyn died. Although she wasn't living there, she'd come to tend the garden and no doubt while away some hours in his company.'

Georgia felt a shiver. Elfie's garden. The love-in-a-mist. No wonder that after Alwyn died Elfie couldn't bear to leave it.

'It's so neglected now,' Georgia said. 'That's sad. Who owns the cottage now?'

'Birdie,' Clemence replied promptly. 'She's kept it although she's living permanently in the home.'

'It would upset Birdie too much to see it sold,' Matthew explained. 'It's her last link with Alwyn and Elfie. We promised that whatever happened we wouldn't sell it to pay her fees or anything ghastly like that. We all help out with those.'

'We?' This seemed an exceptionally generous thought – especially for the leader of the pack.

'The Fernbourne Trust. It's left to us in her will.'

So that explained it. 'Because she never married?'

Matthew looked surprised. 'But she did. Didn't I include that in the book? Perhaps not. I was concentrating on the Five, and Birdie wasn't one of them. She married the local vicar in the early fifties, the Reverend Timothy Atkin. She moved into the vicarage and Elfie stayed on at Shaw Cottage. The idea was that the vicar and Birdie could retire there, but he died before that point. Birdie moved back there after his death and her son Christopher is on the board of the trust.'

Birdie seemed an ambivalent figure, Georgia thought. Very much *not* one of the Five in one way, and yet firmly attached to them financially. She wondered why Christopher didn't live in Shaw Cottage now. Presumably because it would only be a temporary home until the trust took it over. Didn't he mind his heritage being directed elsewhere?

'The trust's plans are to convert this house to an arts centre, not just a memorial to the Five,' Clemence explained. 'An active one, of course, with art classes, craft-making sessions, and creative writing courses as well as its being a permanent place to display the Five's work. I've moved into the coach house, where I have my studio, so that the manor can be entirely devoted to the Five. Janie lives here as chief custodian.'

'And chief cook and bottle-washer.' Janie laughed dismissively, although clearly pleased at her mother's acknowledgement.

'In honour of Elfie,' Clemence continued. 'Children and their artistic needs will be given special attention. You see, we plan the manor to be far more than just a testament to what the Five achieved in the past. We were the starting point. The manor will continue that work. That's what the trust is all about.'

'With all five of the group's work represented?' Peter asked innocently. 'Including Alwyn's?'

A slight pause. 'Of course,' said Matthew.

'But what about the plagiarism charge against him?'

If Peter had thought to shake him, he failed. Matthew laughed. 'Oh dear, that old chestnut. Let me explain.'

'I know it didn't reach court. I wondered what the real story was.'

'One can rarely know the *real* story about anything,' Matthew informed them. 'In this case, however, one can. There was no juicy scandal, I'm afraid. It was a pure mistake. Roy was living at Shaw Cottage for a year or two and asked Alwyn to contribute one or two already published poems of his own work to *The Flight of the Soul*. It was wartime, and so some of Roy's poems dealt with that as he was on active service in the RAF. He therefore wanted Alwyn to provide another viewpoint, which he could provide as he had been rejected for military service. The publishers somehow managed to attribute the whole collection to Alwyn however, and as by this time

Roy was dead and Alwyn teaching at a school in Wales, it
went through by mistake. Its instant success resulted in the
entire edition selling out, the publishers folded and the book
remained out of print. Roy's parents had no idea that he was
intending to publish such a collection, but the story leaked
out a year or so after the war and they naturally raised a hulla-
baloo. Alwyn had been appalled when he first saw the mistake
on his return to Kent, but by that time the book was printed.
There was nothing he could do, except not reprint it. By such
mistakes the course of history can be turned.'

Georgia thought about Damien's comments about Roy, and
the story still seemed unsatisfactory to her, but perhaps wartime
conditions didn't allow for formal apologies, reprints and so
on, particularly if the publishers no longer existed. Matthew
was going no further on the subject. His body language made
that quite clear. 'What was Roy like?' she asked, curious to
see if his description fitted Damien's.

She saw a glance pass between Clemence and Matthew, but
it was the latter who answered – of course. 'Roy was . . . well,
take a dash of Richard Hillary, with a pint or two of Rupert
Brooke, add a spoonful of Alexander the Great plus a good
dose of his unique personality and there you have Roy.' He
laughed at his own wit, but Peter didn't. Matthew was beginning to get on his wick, Georgia realized. Urbane gentlemen
always did. Strip off the polish and you find the stain, he
remarked from time to time, regardless of its technical inac-
curacy.

Fortunately, Clemence stepped in. 'Would you like to see
my portrait of him? There's a reproduction of it in Matthew's
book but the oil original reveals more of the personality.'

'I'd like that,' Peter answered.

'It's in the room across the hall. Most of my work is in the
coach house where I live, but we have just created what we
call the Fernbourne Five Room, for fairly obvious reasons, as
you'll see.'

'Can you manage, Mum?' Janie asked solicitously, as
Clemence struggled to her feet.

'Of course, Janie,' Clemence replied with dignity. 'The
trouble with getting old,' she commented ruefully, 'is that the
essential *you* gradually takes on a new dimension. The original identity begins to acquire an old person's patina little by

little and as the years go by the latter smothers the former in everyone's mind – except one's own, alas. In my deep soul, believe me, Peter, I'm eighteen years old and a new member of the Fernbourne Five. I remember my first day with them – in fact, I can show you. I painted the scene.'

She led the way – with Janie's help despite Clemence's protestations – across the hall, and with Peter and Georgia behind her and Matthew quickly sliding to the front of the group, Clemence indicated the large oil painting facing them on the opposite wall.

'Here,' she said. 'My first day, although painted I admit from memory some years later.'

Nevertheless, Georgia was impressed. Clemence had caught the atmosphere, or at least *an* atmosphere, stored in her memory of that first day. It was set in this very room judging by the windows and view outside. A man of about thirty was portrayed at one end of the long window seat – Gavin Hunt presumably, since in the painting the focus was on him. Elfie sat on the floor at his feet, hugging her knees, and two youths in their twenties lounged casually in armchairs. One, with legs stretched out before him, was fair-haired, and with a weak face – no, Georgia decided that she was wrong. It wasn't weak but neutral, almost closed off. He reminded her of the film star who played Ashley in *Gone with the Wind*, Leslie Howard. That must be Alwyn. The other chair's occupant was presumably Roy Sandford. No lounging for this one. He might be sitting casually, but he was tensed up, as if ready to shoot off at any moment. He was darker, better-looking and supremely confident. And there, reflected in the large mirror over the mantelpiece in the painting, was surely Clemence herself, standing at the doorway, watching.

Did this group painting add up to more than the sum of the individual portraits hung around the room? Perhaps it did, for these looked five distinct personalities, and that impression was surely given because only Clemence herself had her eyes on the rest of the group. The other four were intent on their own thoughts, avoiding her or any other's eyes.

As for the other portraits, the half-length study of Gavin in his library reaching out for a book suggested the academic rather than the outdoor man his son had portrayed in *The Freedom Seekers*. The portrait of Elfie reminded Georgia of

Watts' painting of his wife, the young Ellen Terry, caught at
a moment of fleeting joy. Clemence had depicted her in a
garden – Shaw Cottage? It wasn't over prettified, and captured
her character, so far as Clemence saw it at any rate. There
was a sense that Elfie might choose to wander deeper into
that mysterious garden at any moment, although these portraits
were all drawn before the war, so Clemence told them.

Georgia remembered what Peter had once said to her: the
past is merely the present in different clothes. Looking at the
faces illustrated, she could believe this, as if at a moment's
notice they could spring from their portraits and relive all their
conflicts, traumas and hidden lives.

Alwyn's portrait hung next to Elfie's, almost a companion
piece, for that too was in a garden. But his was different. His
gentle face stared out starkly at the viewer, as though he had
little connection with the garden – or world – that he was
standing in. Again, it wasn't weak, but it wasn't one to cope
with life's problems. Roy was the opposite. Clemence had
chosen to paint him on the tennis court with racket in hand,
clearly victorious, with his defeated partner – unidentifiable
– a solitary figure in the background. Roy was laughing at
life, and inviting the world to share his joke. Or was it just
his confidence that Clemence portrayed? Had war changed
that? Had it changed them all?

'You're known for your use of symbolism, aren't you, Mrs
Hunt?' Peter said. 'Were you using it in these portraits?'

Clemence looked disconcerted. 'What a viewer considers
symbolism could merely be the painter's need for shape or colour.'

'Is that so in these paintings?' Peter persevered.

Clemence didn't answer directly. 'I don't believe I know
the answer to that. It depends on what you mean by symbolism.
Do you know the work of Lavinia Fontana?' she asked.

The name meant nothing to Georgia, but Peter nodded.

'Judged to be the first professional woman artist,' Clemence
continued. 'She worked in Bologna in Renaissance Italy, in
the late sixteenth century. A hero of mine. She had a mastery
of subtle symbolism. Everyone knows that pet dogs equal
faithfulness, or a book on the table signifies literary interests,
but I don't mean that kind of symbolism. Fontana uses such
devices, but also goes further. Her self-portrait in 1577 was
a masterpiece of subtle symbolism as well, more than a mere

reproduction of what she saw in the mirror. It explained her own character, her determination to be her own person rather than a commodity at the disposal of husband or father.'

'Are we looking for any such approach in these paintings?' Clemence looked amused. 'Decide for yourself.'

'Not now regrettably,' Matthew interjected smoothly. 'It's time for the meeting, Clemence. Janie's just gone to let them in.' He turned to Peter and Georgia. 'You must forgive us. Our trustees' meeting is today, and it's an important one. We're in the thick of fund-raising and applications for grants and so forth. As we want to open next June, it's rather urgent.'

'This is when the dull work gets done,' Clemence said ruefully. 'Would you care to meet our fellow trustees before you leave?'

'I would,' said Peter promptly, and Georgia agreed, although she noticed that Matthew did not look pleased.

Clemence led them back across the hall to the room they had left earlier, which now held two newcomers besides Janie. One was a smart, rather cross-looking woman in her forties who looked as if she'd be more at home in the Savoy, and the other was a tall, large-boned stocky man.

'Molly,' Clemence addressed the new arrival, 'let me introduce Georgia Marsh and her father Peter. They're interested in our project and the Fernbourne Five. Molly Sandford.'

The cross look disappeared into one of interest. 'True-crime books? Frost and Co?'

'You're well informed,' Peter said, obviously highly impressed.

'I'm a Londoner, but I'm in the trade. I'm a literary agent. Roy Sandford was my great-uncle and I handle his work.'

Despite Molly's rapid change of mood, Georgia decided she wouldn't like to be in a book auction bidding against her.

'And, Georgia, this is Christopher Atkin, Birdie Field's son,' Clemence said. 'Meet Georgia and Peter Marsh, Christopher.'

Their hands were shaken by the stocky man, surprisingly rather weakly. Looking at him more closely, Georgia decided his benign face didn't fit with the tough image his appearance at first suggested. 'I'm here on my mother's behalf,' he explained almost apologetically.

There was another ring at the bell and Janie dutifully disappeared, returning with a familiar face, which took Georgia aback through its sheer unexpectedness in this context.

'Oh, there you are, Ted,' Matthew said jokingly. 'We wondered where you were.'

'Least far to come, last to arrive,' Ted Laycock said flatly, staring at Georgia as though he'd never seen her before.

Ted Laycock. Mr Non-Cooperation himself, on the board? Curiouser and curiouser, she thought, considering he was the one who didn't want to talk about the Fernbourne Five. She was conscious that they were all still standing and quickly picked up the signal that it was time for the Marshes to depart.

'A remarkable show of unity, don't you think?' Peter remarked as they reached the car.

'Shall we go to the pub to recover?'

'Excellent idea. Especially now we know the Laycocks are part and parcel of the trust.'

'So what's remarkable about their unity?' she asked, having found a quiet corner and fetched drinks, and still reeling from the fact that stonewaller Ted was part and parcel of a group ostensibly dedicated to furthering study of the Five.

'They were *too* unified.'

'Over what?' Georgia asked cautiously.

'Alwyn Field, Elfie and the love affair. The love-story-of-the-century line.'

'Just because it's dramatic, we don't need to doubt it,' she said fairly. 'Or even doubt Alwyn's suicide.' Even as she said it, she felt disloyal to Damien's memory. He had questions over the Fernbourne Five, which suggested there were indeed some that needed answering.

'It doesn't fit our usual pattern,' Peter admitted crossly. 'Marsh and Daughter cases usually involve unfinished business, but surely suicide involves a decision *taken*. And so why the fingerprints at that stream?'

Georgia considered this. 'If the reasons behind the suicide were unjust, then isn't that the same thing? They could still leave traces behind.'

'Would the village have cared about Alwyn Field pinching poems? It certainly cares about something.'

'The Elfie Lane story?'

'Perhaps.' A pause, and then inevitably came the words Georgia had been dreading. 'Suppose Field's death wasn't suicide?'

Three

To hear her own misgivings voiced was giving them an unwelcome push forward although an invisible notice-board was clearly marked 'Don't go there'.

'Do we have one scrap of evidence for that?' Georgia asked matter-of-factly. 'It's not like you to theorize on no solid facts at all.' She wondered if Peter was casting round for some peg to justify looking into this case further. Did he too feel something was owed to Damien Trent? 'What's set you on that track?'

He continued to fiddle with his half pint of shandy, and when eventually he answered, the reply was the last thing she had expected. 'Your mother,' he replied simply.

The shock jolted her into silence for a moment, but then she managed to ask, 'How does Elena come into this?' She was uncomfortably aware that her mother had been in her mind several times in the last few days, but she hadn't made the connection.

'You really want to know?'

'I must.' She couldn't remember the last time Peter had openly spoken of his ex-wife. It was a bad sign.

'That painting of Elfie,' he explained awkwardly. 'It reminded me of her. Didn't you think so?' He looked at her in appeal.

Handle this with kid gloves, she told herself. Very soft kid gloves. Both she and Peter needed care where the subject of Elena was concerned. 'There was a slight physical resemblance,' she conceded as casually as she could. 'Elfie was slender, blonde and seems to have had that faraway look that Elena has at her dottier moments. But basically Elena is practical and Elfie hardly looked that.' Practical was a good word for what more truthfully could be described as a hard core of selfishness. Charming she might be, but in the end Elena would get what Elena wanted, no matter the devastation she left in her wake. Georgia always had to monitor her judgements on Elena, to divorce her objective opinion of her mother from the emotional resentment caused by her leaving them at the time when she was most needed. Elena couldn't cope, so Elena hadn't tried, but had blithely left them to sort it out themselves.

Georgia had been in her mid-twenties at that time, and had struggled hard to see Elena's point of view. Her son had disappeared, her husband was in a wheelchair, and her daughter newly divorced after a disastrous marriage to a con man. It must have seemed to her that there was no way out but flight. Nevertheless Georgia always came back to the same point. They had all faced the same problem as to how to struggle back to everyday life. Had Elena looked hard enough for the path forward or was she really too fragile to cope? The answers always came back in the negative. That was what tore Georgia in two whenever she thought of it now.

Had Elfie had this core of selfishness too? Apparently not from the descriptions of her, and even in her portrait there seemed a frailty that Elena's photographs failed to convey. Nor did Elfie get what she most wanted. She must have agonized over her dilemma too, but accepted that she had no choice but to stay with Gavin and Matthew.

'Elfie was the trapped butterfly,' Georgia added, gambling on its likely effect. 'Elena just fluttered on her own merry way.'

Luckily Peter cheered up. 'That's very lyrical of you, Georgia.'

'How does it affect Alwyn Field's death?'

'I suppose I feel I should look into it for Elfie's sake, just as I would have done for Elena,' Peter ended with a shame-faced glance at her.

'We should be doing it for Alwyn's sake, not Elfie's. But there is nothing in Alwyn's story to take us forward.'

'Except Damien Trent.'

Blast Peter, she thought crossly. He would pick on her Achilles heel. 'He came here to talk to Joe Baker, probably for family reasons.'

'Point dismissed. If good old Joe were so important to Trent, he would have known before he came that Joe had long departed. There are such things as death certificates, the internet and family research. And at the very least Trent would have known what generation Joe came from and be able to calculate whether he was likely still to be living aged a hundred and five or whatever.'

'True,' she admitted reluctantly. 'And I admit Damien had seen Birdie Field, as well as Joe, which fits in with his interest in Alwyn.'

'He had, you said, more than a passing interest in Field. He might have been just a fan of his work or of the Fernbourne Five as a whole, but if so why didn't he spread the word more widely that this was his reason for being here? Who else did he visit apart from Birdie Field?' The tapping fingers on the arm of his wheelchair began: a sure sign of frustration. 'We need to know more about Field's death. I'll ask Mike if he can put in a request for the inquest report. He won't begrudge me that.'

Unless it trod on his ground, she thought, as she went inside to pay for their drinks. The sun was still shining but sinking fast, and she and Peter had had the garden to themselves. When she came back, however, she saw that Peter was deep in conversation with an elderly woman who had seated herself at the table. An unusually clad one, Georgia noticed. A pink woolly hat with blue bobbles adorned her white hair, and a bright red jacket with orange trousers and blue blouse completed her outfit. Her face was tanned and wrinkled, but it looked extremely happy. She beamed at Georgia.

'Alice Laycock, Georgia,' Peter introduced her. 'Ted's wife.'

Georgia's immediate thought was that this garden couldn't be attributable to her; it was more likely to be Ted's precise handiwork. Alice looked a few years older than Ted, and as if she might have taken a step back from the worries of everyday life.

'Here for supper are you?' Alice enquired. 'Doreen turns a good chip, does Doreen.'

'Doreen's Bob's wife,' Peter explained. Typical, thought Georgia, amused. She'd only been away for a couple of minutes and already he had the family sorted out. On their earlier visit with Mike, there had been too much going on for Peter to indulge in his normal pursuit of making himself completely at home, but he was making up for it now. A shout from the doorway distracted them.

'Gran, Mum wants you.'

When there was no sign of a response, the young man slouched unwillingly towards them. He was a good-looking lad in his late teens – and Georgia recognized him. Last time she had seen him, he was lurking in a church porch, with his face contorted with jealousy over Emma Baker.

'Like hell she does,' volunteered Alice happily. 'She thinks I annoy the customers. Aren't annoying you, am I?'

'By no means,' Peter assured her – truthfully, Georgia knew. He always related to eccentricity, which he claimed was often the truth uncomfortably presented.

'Tell your ma I'm busy, Adam. Met him, have you?' Alice winked at her.

'No,' Georgia smiled, as the self-conscious lad was forced to nod to them. 'But I've seen you. You're a friend of Emma Baker's, aren't you?' He blushed red and mumbled something.

'Was.' Alice cheerfully put her foot in it. 'That Sean's messing around with her now, ain't he? Up to his old ways, is he? You're not snorting again, are you?'

Georgia hastily intervened, seeing Adam's embarrassment. 'She'll see sense,' she said with more assurance than she felt. She had been referring to Emma, but to her dismay she realized she had been ambiguous.

'No I damn well won't,' Alice said gleefully. 'Bang, bang, *bang.*' She brought her fist down on the table. 'He'll get himself rough music, he will. You mark my words.'

Adam's embarrassment turned to gentleness rather than annoyance. 'Come on, Gran. Mum's got your supper ready.'

If she were Emma, Georgia thought, she knew which swain she would pick. But then would she have made the same choice at seventeen or eighteen? And what was this about drugs? It tied in with what Mike had been saying about the area behind the church being used for dealing. Was that Sean's 'old ways'?

'What do you mean about rough music?' Georgia asked, intending to lead on to the drugs, but Alice was off on her own track.

'Did Sean have anything to do with that killing, young man?' she asked.

'Dunno, Gran,' was Adam's stonewall reply.

'He's in trouble, ain't he?'

Adam glanced at Peter and Georgia. 'Yeah. Sort of.'

'Village business, that is. We could've coped till that daft Trent man came here. Strangers are always trouble. Comes of sticking your noses in where they're not wanted.' She grinned at Peter, but there was no warmth in the smile now.

By the time Georgia reached Medlars, it was past eight o'clock and she was in a mood to expect problems. Peter had already snapped her head off for insisting on checking that his carer Margaret had left supper ready for him. He was not a child, he yelled at her, thereby making her feel like one.

Luke was nowhere to be seen, and Georgia prepared their own evening meal, still fuming without any outlet. Finally at gone eight o'clock she was forced to go across to the oast house where he had his office. It was only a stone's throw from their front door but sacrosanct land so far as unnecessary intrusion was concerned. The staff had long since gone home, but Luke was poring over a set of proofs in the office, and hardly looked up as she came in.

'Is anything wrong?' she asked fatuously, trying to sound calm and sympathetic.

'Only the usual.'

'Which is?'

'We're in overdraft again.'

'The company or us?' This was unexpected and definitely deflating. Nothing like a dose of depression to dampen irritation.

'They're beginning to be suspiciously similar,' he grunted. 'The company for the moment, but that will have a knock-on effect. No salary for me, and no royalties for you in October unless we buck our ideas up.'

'I'd love to buck, but how?' This was looking like really bad news.

Normally Luke would have laughed, but not today. That was hardly surprising, considering he still had a mortgage on Medlars, and the higher interest rates weren't helping.

'Is there a magic bullet?' she asked.

'A bestseller or two would help.'

So now was not the time even to discuss another Marsh & Daughter case, she realized, otherwise the dreaded word 'contract' would emerge at some point, only to be refused. 'How bad is it?' she asked.

'The bank has given me an overdraft for three months – at a price. Everything rests on autumn sales and prompt payments.' He grimaced. 'Not the rose garden I promised you, is it?'

'There's one way out of course, to tide us over.' The words were out of her mouth before she had thought them through. Now all she could do was wait for the fall-out.

Inevitably, Luke realized immediately what this way out was. 'That's entirely your decision, but it shouldn't be made only because we need the money.'

Oh, hell, she'd walked into the quagmire head-on. The ball was back in her court: should she sell her house in Haden Shaw? Cutting her lifeboat adrift would inevitably bring up the question of marriage again. And *that* decision was even harder to make.

He obviously read her expression correctly for he continued wryly. 'Let me help, my love. Think of capital gains. Would it be sensible to sell it? House prices have gone up a lot since you bought it.'

'It would help us out of our present hole.'

Luke agreed. 'Especially if we married.'

'Either way,' she said too quickly, appalled that marriage was back on the agenda so quickly.

He sighed. 'Keep the house.' He didn't add 'as an escape route' but it was implicit.

'I could rent it.' It was a good straw to clutch.

'Compromise has never suited you, Georgia. Or me,' he added.

Stalemate.

Determinedly, she pushed domestic matters to the back of her mind, telling herself correctly, if unconvincingly, that injection of capital wasn't the basic answer to their problems.

On her next visit three days later her former house felt reproachful at her treachery. It was waiting for her like a pair of well-worn slippers, and she lingered over her mail – increasingly little – before she went next door to the Marsh & Daughter office. Of course, she thought, as Peter now slept on the ground floor there was a spare room upstairs. Two in fact. She could use one of those . . .

She dragged her mind back to the Fernbourne Five, wondering if they worried about mortgages too. That was the trouble with the past: what survived were the memorable high-lights. Even diaries recorded only clues to someone's everyday living problems, but how did one know they were true and not loaded in one direction or another? She thought back to her childhood, and her memory persistently threw up happy days of family picnics. Were they the rosy glow created by present longing or had they really existed? The latter surely, but then what had happened to the unhappy niggles and prob-lems that must have occurred?

'Ah, there you are, Georgia.' Peter greeted her arrival in the office, and then promptly demanded to know her progress.

'Not much further forward,' she confessed. 'The local papers report the death on the lines of "man found dead by hanging" or "suspected suicide of local poet", but there were no inter-views with Hunt or Elfie as there would be nowadays.'

'I did better,' Peter said smugly. 'No *Times* obituary, which is unusual, and no word from Mike yet on the inquest report, but the press reports are most interesting. It wasn't a verdict of suicide, with or without the balance of the mind being disturbed. It was an open verdict, which means there must have been some kind of police investigation. And that isn't mentioned in Matthew Hunt's book.'

Georgia was annoyed with herself for missing this. 'Mike will be delighted to hear that. Do we infer that it might have been murder disguised as suicide?'

'It's possible.'

'Wouldn't more than one person have to have been involved if it were murder? It would be too difficult to manage it other-wise, even if he were strangled before being suspended.' Plain words, but to Georgia they immediately brought back a sick-ening image of that peaceful stream and tree. The thought of what might have happened there one summer's day long ago became frighteningly real, and merged with Damien's death in her mind.

He regarded her wryly. 'Do you envisage the rest of the Five murdering Alwyn for letting the side down over the plagiarism?'

'Four,' she amended. 'Roy was long dead by then.' She had found out further details after speaking to Damien. 'He had died

in the Café de Paris during an air raid on Saturday, the eighth
of March 1941. And it's not such a crazy idea. It would explain
the lack of mention in *The Freedom Seekers*.'

'You don't think Birdie would have noticed all this activity
at her home? Anything about her in the local reports, by the
way?'

'Yes. Alwyn died on the twenty-first of May 1949. It was
a Saturday. Birdie was away for the weekend visiting their
parents, and came back to find the body; he'd been dead over
twenty-four hours by then.'

Peter reached for *The Freedom Seekers*. 'Matthew might
be short on detail about the inquest, but I seem to remember
he waxed lyrical over the suicide notes. Yes – here we are.
There were two, one for Elfie and one for Birdie, and both
consisting only of short extracts from his verse. Elfie's read:

> "Only you
> Will mourn my passing soul,
> Only you,
> Have loved the whole of me."

'And this was Birdie's,' he added.

> "I cannot limp beyond the mountain
> Into paradise.
> The door was closed when up I came.
> The music melted."'

Peter pondered. 'Does this get us any further?'

'It might do. Birdie's was from the same poem as on Alwyn's
tombstone,' Georgia said. 'I looked it up. It was from a poem
called "The Piper".'

'Perhaps after Browning's "The Pied Piper of Hamelin"?
It fits. Only in Browning's poem, it's physical limping, as the
last of the village children fails to reach the mountain before
the door closes on the Piper and all his friends. In Alwyn's
case the limping is emotional.' Peter paused. 'In view of this
open verdict, I take it we're limping onwards in this case?'

'Yes,' she agreed. There seemed no choice, even though
Peter now seemed to have reservations too. If Damien Trent
had been following this track, they had a duty to Mike to

pursue it, as well as assuaging her nagging sense of responsibility. Irrational perhaps, but it was still there.

'Matthew first? No, bad plan. In his book he states flatly that Alwyn killed himself. He's hardly likely to contradict that at this stage. Clemence is the better bet. How about a woman-to-woman talk?'

'I don't see her as a womanly chat sort of person. But I'll have a go.'

'Janie is at the hairdresser's,' Clemence announced, straight-faced – which was clearly why she had suggested Monday afternoon rather than the weekend to Georgia. 'How about a nice nip of whisky in the garden?'

'Perhaps a nip of tea instead, in the interests of driving home, and a rain-check on the whisky,' Georgia amended.

'Done.'

Georgia carried the tray down to a small walled garden in the manor grounds. It was a pleasant spot, reminiscent of Sissinghurst Castle gardens, and she thought the great gardener Victoria Sackville West would have approved of it, especially in this September sunshine. There was a vine loaded with ripening grapes running riot over the arbour that sheltered the bench to which Clemence had led her; pears ripened against the warm red brick of the wall, and the garden itself was still full of colour. Various statues peered out of the greenery at points along the paths. At right angles to the bench a life-sized warm stone sculpture of a man on a seat regarded them, a folded newspaper on his knee.

'That's Gavin,' Clemence said matter-of-factly. 'I do, or rather did, some sculpture work and it's a friendly face to have around me here. It was his house after all, and in a way it still is since Matthew inherits after my death.'

'Not the trust?'

'That didn't exist when Gavin died. It was very much the family thing with him. Janie was otherwise provided for, and Matthew got the house. He'll lease it to the trust on a peppercorn rent. His house in the village goes to his wife and children, of course. There are two sons, and three grand-children. The oldest, Sean, is nineteen now.'

'Sean?' Georgia exclaimed. 'Would he be a friend of Emma Baker?'

'Ah. You *are* getting to know our village. Yes, she's his latest conquest – unless it's the other way around. She's a heartbreaker, that one. Rather a problem is our Sean. A rebel, but he'll grow out of it. At present he fancies himself as the boss amongst the village youth. He dropped out of university and now he's supposed to be doing an IT course to work in his father's firm. He seems to have a lot of time on his hands unfortunately, and he's not the only one. Even a rebel can't rouse saints. Still, I shouldn't be bothering you with this blot on our picturesque village. Cheers.'

Clemence, thought Georgia, probably did or said nothing without a reason and so what lay behind this? She was not going to get sidetracked, however. 'I have a difficult question for you.'

'I'm used to those.' Clemence's eyes flickered. 'About the Fernbourne Five, of course. What is it?'

'Alwyn Field. Is there any chance that he could have been murdered? The inquest recorded an open verdict.'

She had obviously taken Clemence by surprise, as though this were a completely new idea, but she recovered quickly. 'In theory it could equally well have been an accident. After all, some people got their sexual thrills in the same variety of ways as today,' she said briskly. 'However, I don't see Alwyn risking his life like that, and as for murder, well, there was no doubt about its being suicide amongst us. For good reason. Alwyn was in deep depression having realized that Elfie could never be his. Tragic doomed love affairs are splendid for Pre-Raphaelite art, but not quite so much fun in real life. And then,' she continued, 'there was the plagiarism charge, which was somewhat more complicated than Matthew told you. Alwyn played a much more positive role than Matthew implied. Matthew wasn't there, of course, but I was. After Roy died, I believe Alwyn deliberately decided to claim ownership of all the poems, not just the couple he had already published. I had felt a little sorry for him because before the war his own work had languished beside Roy's. His detective novel had a phase of popularity after the war, as did his new collection, *A Mourning in Spring*. Unfortunately they have both sunk without trace since then.

'After the war, when Alwyn suggested a reprint of *The*

Flight of the Soul, it all came to light,' Clemence continued. 'Gavin had always been surprised by the strength of the poems in that collection, compared with Alwyn's former style. Then he found the originals in Roy's handwriting when some of his papers left behind at Shaw Cottage were taken up to the manor. Alwyn had no answer to that; he was unable to produce any handwritten originals of his own, only the typewritten copies. He blustered for a while, refusing to admit what he'd done, but the evidence was all too clear.'

'A terrible story,' Georgia agreed. 'What was he like as a person? He comes over as a dreamy poet, victim of a love affair, but you knew him as a friend and colleague. Why did Elfie love him? There must have been a definite rapport between them to bring them together, yet at present it seems like a Hollywood romance without a cause.'

Clemence looked blank for a moment, almost cold, and Georgia wondered if she'd gone too far. 'Time reduces everything to Hollywood stereotypes,' she replied flatly.

'I don't agree,' Georgia said firmly. 'You must remember the real Alwyn, at your discussions and everyday dealings. Was he sulky, good-humoured, funny, selfish, untidy, tidy? Could you paint a picture with words for me?'

'Oh, Georgia,' Clemence answered regretfully. 'If only we could pour out every single recollection in a heap and let people like you sift through the results. Instead we have to select. I select as a painter, both consciously and subconsciously. I can't paint everything I see or believe about someone. I paint what I think is the essence, which no doubt thereby acquires a layer of myself as well.'

She began to look tired, and Georgia remembered how old she was. It was easy to forget, as Clemence was such an energetic and forthright presence.

'Alwyn laughed,' Clemence offered at last. 'We had an innocence in those days, a silly sense of humour, harking back to P. G. Wodehouse days, I suppose. That's what made it all the harder as war clouds gathered. Alwyn liked puns,' she added vaguely. 'They're unpopular now, in this non-verbal age, when the eye has taken over from the voice. But he and Gavin leapt on them as eagerly as on the crosswords . . .' She broke off. 'I'm not doing very well, am I?'

'Did you *like* him?' Georgia asked, still puzzled.

'Of course. We couldn't have worked together if we didn't like and respect each other.'

'And Roy? Did you like him?'

'That's an easy one. *Everyone* liked Roy. Alwyn probably suffered because of that. He was in his shade as a poet. When Roy was killed . . .' For a moment she looked her full age.

'Was that on active service?'

'Yes and no. He was in the RAF at Biggin Hill at that time, with 609 Squadron; he had a forty-eight-hour pass that weekend and that's how he came to be in London at the Café de Paris. It was in Coventry Street, near Piccadilly, underneath a cinema, which should have protected it, but by an architectural fluke failed to do so. The Café de Paris was *the* most glamorous spot in London for the youth of society – which in those days included lots of young officers. A friend of Gavin's had been one of the survivors, and told him that night was a particularly glittering one. The dancing had just begun and the band was playing "Oh, Johnny"' . . . She broke off. 'Now where is this going, Georgia?' she shot at her. 'We're getting away from Alwyn. Are you intent on proving that someone faked his suicide? I can think of no reason that anyone would have bothered.'

Taken aback, Georgia replied without thinking. 'He can't have won friends over his love affair with Elfie.'

'Are you suggesting *Gavin* killed him?' Clemence looked outraged, but gradually calmed down. 'The idea is ridiculous. Elfie had stayed with Gavin and he'd had over ten years to get used to the idea that Elfie was or had been in love with Alwyn. You may think of it as a Hollywood romance, but it was very real at the time. I watched its progress.'

'But what brought them together, apart from, presumably, sex? Hindsight must surely suggest something.'

Clemence looked at her steadily, as if considering whether this deserved an answer. 'I suppose you could say it comes down to the medieval four elements: earth, air, water and fire. Gavin was a creature of the earth, as I am. Alwyn was of the air and so was Elfie.'

That was reasonable, Georgia thought, even if it got her no further. And that, she thought ruefully, could be because there was no further to get.

Clemence was still watching her closely. 'Gavin might have

loathed Alwyn when Elfie first fell for him, but hardly later. He'd won the battle, and had no reason to kill him.'

'And no one would do so over the plagiarism charge?'

'Roy would have been the only one to feel murderous, and he was dead.'

Back to square one, and possibly, Georgia thought, knocked out of the game. One last throw. 'What about Birdie? Do you mind if I talk to her?'

'Why should I mind?' Clemence whipped back. 'I'm not her keeper. If anyone is, it's Christopher. I should ask him to take you there. He likes being included in things. Oh, and Georgia,' she added, seeing her rise to leave, 'don't be surprised if Birdie informs you *I* murdered Alwyn. She does tend to get bees in her little bonnet nowadays, and I'm not her favourite person.'

Was this a sign that not all relations were harmonious in the Fernbourne Trust circle, Georgia wondered? She remembered that in the Fernbourne Room there had been no portrait of Birdie. She wasn't one of the Five, despite the fact that according to Matthew's book she had artistic talent. So what had that been like for Birdie? Talented but not sufficiently to be in the group, on the outskirts but not part of it. Would she be devoted to the Five's memory or, as the outsider, might she break the united façade of the trust, if façade it was? Would Birdie be longing to tell hidden secrets or even more determined to keep the flame alive?

Four

The only obstacle to Georgia's plans to see Birdie Field had been Christopher Atkin, not entirely to her surprise. At first he had flatly refused to allow her to see his mother, although he could give no reason such as poor health. Then he had had a change of heart, and telephoned to say that she could come over on Saturday afternoon. Luke had groaned at the intrusion into their weekend, but she couldn't miss the opportunity.

Christopher seemed amiable enough today, fortunately. She found the cottage in a lane just off the main street, a hundred yards away from the square and on the opposite side. It was a small, uninspiring nineteenth-century building with a neat but equally uninspiring garden. From what little she saw of the interior – the hallway – it looked the bachelor pad it was. Tidy, dull, and somewhat soulless. A large stuffed bird in a glass case on a table by an old-fashioned coat stand stared out at her with lacklustre eyes.

'Dad's hobby,' Christopher said briefly, which conjured up a weird picture of vicarage life in an earlier decade. His own was carpet-making and toy soldiers, he told her with pride, and the woolly rug she was standing on was obviously an example of the former.

'We can take the footpath,' he told her, giving her no choice. This, he explained, was a short cut to the retirement home.

Georgia didn't mind walking. The day was fine and she was a dab hand at karate if he decided to protect the Five's secrets by force. She wondered why that notion had occurred to her, until she remembered that Damien Trent had been killed on just such a footpath. In the event, Christopher proved to be the great big softy of the group, obviously devoted to his mother and her welfare. Talking wasn't his strong point, and she had to make most of the conversation, while he ambled at his own pace, examining hedgerows and flora as he went.

'You have everything you need for life in this village,' she commented. 'Church, surgery, school, post office and retirement home.'

He looked at her doubtfully, as if wondering whether her observation was as light-hearted as it seemed. 'Mum's happy there.'

'I'm sure she is,' Georgia said hastily, and he beamed. She wondered how much actual use he was on the trust board. All committees needed a listener, and willing pairs of hands were a must, even if they were slow. Christopher would provide both services, she guessed, whereas Ted Laycock was more of a force to be reckoned with.

'I'm to be doorman at the new arts centre,' he told her proudly, when she mentioned the trust. 'Matthew said you wanted to write a book about us, but he's written one. Did you know that?'

'Yes, and it's a good one,' she agreed. 'At the moment we don't know whether we will write one, but it wouldn't be the same as Matthew's. We're just interested in the Fernbourne Five, like Damien Trent,' she added experimentally to see what resulted.

That did receive a reaction. 'He's the dead man. We reckon it was drugs. That Nick Baker.'

'Is that Emma's father?'

'No.' He looked amazed at her ignorance. 'Her older brother. Had up for dealing. He's out now.'

'Was Sean Hunt involved?'

'Don't know,' was all Christopher offered on that score. 'Get the village a bad name, drugs do. Drink's one thing, drugs another.'

'Have you lived in Fernbourne all your life?'

'Yes,' he said, stooping to admire a butterfly. 'That's a Red Admiral, that is. I look after Mum. And work at a garden centre near Sittingbourne till I start work at the manor.'

Christopher could only be in his early fifties, she thought, so retirement would be a way off yet. 'Did you ever live at Shaw Cottage?' she asked.

'Went there when Dad died. Then I got my own house. Suits me better.'

'Didn't you like the cottage?'

He thought about this. 'Not with that Mrs Elfie there.'

'Didn't you like her?'

'Yes.' He seemed doubtful though. 'Funny lady. Always out in the garden, but didn't want no help. Said it was hers, but it wasn't. It was Mum's, so I went and got my own house and garden.'

After a quarter of an hour he pointed out a gate ahead in the hedgerow. 'There it is. That's where Mum lives. Use this path every day, I do. Bring Mum's clothes, sweeties, magazines.'

'Will your mother feel like talking about the old days?'

'Don't know,' he said simply. 'Some days she does, some days she doesn't.'

The retirement home was a large but unspectacular Victorian house with a modern annexe. Georgia followed Christopher into the back door of the main house, and was pleasantly surprised at how light and smell-free it was, even though it was necessarily warm. She crossed her fingers that Birdie would not be in the home's communal room, in which talking always tended to be difficult, in her experience, as so many pairs of curious eyes were fixed upon the visitors. Fortunately Christopher was walking past the general lounge, and then turned up a flight of stairs to the first floor. Birdie's room was on a corner at the end of the corridor and Christopher peered round the half-open door.

'Visitor, Mum,' he called out. 'Wants to know about Shaw Cottage, she does.'

Birdie Field, or Atkin as she legally was, lived up to her forename. She must always have been a small woman, Georgia thought, but now she seemed tiny, sitting in a large armchair by the window with only her head peeping out from an otherwise all-encompassing blanket for extra warmth. Her silver hair was elegantly waved, which suggested a woman fully in command of her life, despite the restricting circumstances. Her features were sharp, her nose almost beak-like, and her eyes were as bright as buttons, despite her physical frailty. They were busy summing Georgia up with great suspicion.

'What about it?' she snapped.

Was this a good or a bad day, Georgia wondered? 'It's a lovely house,' she began tentatively.

'Is it?'

'Especially the garden,' Georgia persevered, under that unwavering gaze.

'She did that.'

'Elfie Lane?'

Her eyes gleamed. 'That's what she called herself, Mrs High and Mighty Hunt.'

'You liked her though. You invited her to live with you.'

'How did you know that?' The eyes gleamed like a falcon spotting prey.

'The licensee of the King's Head told me.' She was glad she wasn't forced to mention Clemence's name. 'My father and I are interested in the Fernbourne Five. You must have been very proud of your association with them.' She was aware that this last comment was a hostage to fortune, but Birdie merely stared at her. It was Christopher who replied.

'We are. It will be nice when the manor opens next year. Mum will be at the opening, won't you, Mum? You're making a speech.'

'Depends on whether the pearly gates open for me first. I'm ninety-one.' She looked at them triumphantly.

'And still hale and hearty,' said Christopher. He looked upset, as though the merest mention of her eventual departure was too much to bear.

'It must have been a great loss to you, as well as a shock, when your brother died,' Georgia said gently. 'Do you mind if we talk about him?'

'Why should I?' she countered. 'He was one of the Five, wasn't he?'

'He was,' Christopher confirmed anxiously.

'You must have loved him very much, especially as you had lived with him so long.'

'Must I?'

Georgia almost gave up. This was getting nowhere, but fortunately Christopher took a hand. 'Now then, Mother, don't tease the lady. She's read Matthew's book.'

'Then she doesn't need to talk to me.'

'I'd like to know what Alwyn was like,' Georgia began again, aware she was making a pig's dinner of this interview.

'He killed himself. That's what he was like,' Birdie told

her, glancing at Christopher almost like a child taunting its mother.

'Because of his love for Elfie, and the charge that he put his own name to Roy Sandford's work?'

The eyes flickered. 'Rough music,' she announced.

Exactly what Alice Laycock had said in the pub garden, and now the words began to ring a bell with her. 'What does that mean?' she asked Christopher, who shifted uneasily in his seat. Neither answered her, and she tried a different tack. 'Was Alwyn often depressed?' she asked Birdie.

'Of course he was. Wouldn't you be? Loving that stupid woman.'

'Mother,' Christopher said warningly. 'Mrs Elfie wasn't daft, you know that.'

Birdie stirred under the blanket, and apparently heeded whatever her son was implying, because when she next spoke it was in a lilting monotone. 'She was a pretty little thing, and so fond of that garden of ours. I was no use at it, so she had it all to herself. Always there she was. "Love needs its gentle mist." She wrote that. Or was it my Roy?'

She looked at Georgia, who suspected that Birdie knew quite well what she was saying. And what was this 'my' Roy about?

'Now there was a man,' Birdie continued more normally, and with sudden warmth in her voice. 'I loved him. So long ago. "All the bells of heaven would ring, For you, my love, and me." He wrote that for me,' she ended sadly.

Birdie in love with Roy Sandford? Of course, Georgia remembered, there had been a brief implication of it in Matthew's book. Roy had lived with Birdie and Alwyn for some years, she remembered. As Birdie's lover or as a lodger?

Then Birdie was off on another track. 'I met that Damien Trent. They say he's dead too. Rough music, I daresay. Then came the war. Alwyn was turned down and became a teacher. My Roy went into the air force.' A pause. 'Elfie, well, she had a child to look after so she didn't do war work. I did though.' Georgia detected a note of satisfaction that she was getting one over Elfie. 'I was single then, so off I went to do my bit at the Kent and Canterbury Hospital.'

'What about your parents? Were they living with you then?'

She thought for a while. 'Not with us,' she said finally. 'They moved to London while the war was on. Dad's war job. He'd been through the first war in the trenches, and then he was called back for the second; said London was worse than the trenches during the Blitz. I was visiting them when Alwyn died. After the war they stayed where they were.'

'The lady thinks Uncle Alwyn might have been murdered, Mum,' Christopher said bluntly.

How on earth could he know that? Georgia wondered. She hadn't told him so. It seemed the village gossip hotline wasn't the only one in existence. The trust had one too. What was Birdie going to make of this? Would she launch into a diatribe about Clemence being responsible?

Birdie stared at her, then, to Georgia's amazement, instead of looking shocked, she cackled. 'Murdered? They were the Fernbourne Five, not the Mafia.'

When Georgia joined Peter on the Monday morning, he seemed more interested in the Internet than hearing about Birdie. 'Except that she's making a speech at the manor opening next year about Roy Sandford, there's not much new,' she told him. 'She was in love with him. She doesn't think Alwyn was murdered.'

Peter was obviously dying to get going on Suspects Anonymous, the computer software designed by her cousin Charlie Bone for keeping track of their evidence in their cases. Until there was a case, however, there could be little data to feed in.

'Because of the united front again?' he asked, whirling his wheelchair round to greet her.

'That depends whether it's unified because of some conspiracy between them, or whether it's simply the truth. If the former, I don't see any way to crack it; if the latter, there's no need. Incidentally, do the words "rough music" mean anything to you?'

'Of course.' Peter looked smug. 'And they should to you. Friday Street was a variant of rough music. What brought that up?'

How stupid of her to forget. Friday Street was the scene of an earlier case, in which villagers played music in the streets to indicate an injustice done. Rough music was the opposite of this. Villagers would take to the streets to bang saucepans, iron pans, or washboards outside the home of someone deemed not fit to be a villager.

'Your turn to forget,' she said. 'Alice Laycock mentioned it and Birdie Field did too.'

'A coincidence, do you think? Or is it something to do with Alwyn Field?' Peter looked interested. 'Do you think he could have been the victim of it? If so, it's possible that that's what drove him over the edge.'

'But if so,' Georgia pointed out, 'that simply confirms the suicide verdict.'

Boxed into a corner, Peter took the easy way out. 'We're doing too much theorizing. Let's go back to the scene of the crime – not poor Damien Trent's, but Alwyn Field's. There's nothing like the actual scene for helping the mind to focus. I've already fixed it in fact – for tomorrow. Matthew was somewhat grudgingly agreeable, and said we could pick up the key from the pub. I had to insist it was on Mike's orders.'

Georgia hoped that one wouldn't come home to roost – or that Ted Laycock wouldn't have ideas of his own when they requested the key. In the event, he didn't, but his silence as he handed it over on the Tuesday afternoon spoke volumes of disapproval. The weather held the edge of autumn chilliness now, which made the cottage and garden seem even more forlorn than on their earlier visit. The love-in-a-mist was little in evidence now, and the poppies had vanished altogether, giving way to Michaelmas daisies fighting for survival amongst nettles.

'Cottage first,' Peter decreed. 'You'll probably have to do most of it though.'

In fact getting the wheelchair inside was not difficult, owing to the width of the eighteenth-century doorway. Georgia could see the cottage was as empty of contents as their earlier peeks through the window had suggested, and though clean enough it smelled musty. She couldn't see Clemence coming round with a brush and pan but someone must do it. Janie probably, or else they paid for help from the village.

She walked through the hallway into the large kitchen, trying to conjure up a picture of Birdie, Alwyn and Roy eating here. Or perhaps they ate in state in the dining room with its peeling striped wallpaper. To her disappointment, however, nothing spoke of the past here, and indeed she had to bear in mind that it had been over fifty years since Alwyn had lived here. As she went upstairs, each step creaked in protest at un-accustomed work, and her footsteps echoed because of the lack of carpet.

The cottage seemed larger on the first floor than down-stairs, with four bedrooms and a 1950s bathroom which had once been smart with its avocado suite; above the first floor, the eaves space had been converted into a large studio. For all of them, she wondered, or just Roy and Alwyn? Large windows, probably inserted in the days before listed building regulations, made it light and a pleasant place to work, she imagined. She could see the two of them working here – and of course Birdie.

She returned to the first floor to nose around the bedrooms. She wouldn't mind betting that Birdie had the best one, which was tucked away on its own round a corner at one end of the passageway, making the cottage L-shaped. It had a splendid view over the garden – or what would have been splendid when the garden was lovingly tended. Did Roy tiptoe round here night after night? Perhaps he didn't return Birdie's love.

Perhaps was a useless word, Georgia decided, looking out on the wilderness beneath. It absolved you from having to put further thought into something – although at the moment that would have been welcome, so close to the place where Alwyn Field had died. Instead, she needed to grasp the nettle firmly – and there were plenty out there to grasp, she thought ruefully.

An ivy-covered fountain was just about visible in the middle of what had been the lawn beyond the stone terrace and steps, and on the left a high rockery delineated the end of the lawn. On the right were the remains of the path she and Peter had struggled down on their first visit, and she shivered at the memory. It was time to join Peter again.

'Unpleasant, isn't it?' he remarked as she reached him.

He was right. Although nothing like the atmosphere at the stream, this part of the garden was far less appealing than

Elfie's front garden, perhaps because the band of dark trees across the stream looked so formidable.

'I had a call from Mike, while you were gallivanting all over the house. The police investigation led nowhere. Alwyn Field was thoroughly unpopular all round, with his colleagues, with his family and the village, but no one would seem to have had reason for murder and nothing more turned up in the way of evidence to suggest it was.'

'Didn't you find that curious?' Georgia asked. 'Like the trust, it's a united front.'

'Possibly. Mike says the reason for the open verdict was an amount of alcohol in his body, plus sedatives. That could have been a way to keep him quiet, as there wasn't much deep haemorrhaging or bruising, which could indicate a forceful strangling. But it could be the opposite. There was nothing found at the scene in the way of trace evidence. The rope was thick clothesline of the kind used by much of the village.'

'Another impasse then, just as the jury found. So do we go on, or stop?'

'We never stop. We merely pause,' Peter said grandly. 'But in this case, onwards. In Stella Gibbons' immortal words, I still think there's something nasty in the woodshed.'

'For woodshed, read stream,' Georgia said more bravely than she felt. 'I'll go down there again. There might be something about the layout of exactly where it happened that might help.'

She had hoped Peter might demur, but he didn't, and so she picked her way through the brambles and overgrown grass to the point she had reached before. The willows, the stream, the tree that reached its branches over it – everything seemed to have stilled around her, as if waiting for her next move. The fingerprints remained, she was in no doubt of that. Alwyn had died here, either as a helpless victim or glad to leave the troubles of his life. She felt prickles of tension in her spine, as if the stillness around her was about to break into something more terrifying. Perhaps it was Alwyn's desperation reaching over the years. But it could be more than that. It almost felt as if something or someone were watching her. She wanted to turn and run but pride prevented her.

But neither could she go across those stepping stones. The woods on the far side were presenting themselves as a dark mass of threat, and the stream had turned itself into a formidable obstacle. Fingerprints were becoming claws and there was no way this Little Red Riding Hood was going forward to find Grannie; she knew when it was time to retreat and leave the wolves to themselves. As if on cue, she thought she heard a quiet whistling coming from the woods. Her imagination? She listened, and heard nothing. Even as she turned to stumble up the slope to where Peter was waiting, however, she could have sworn she heard it again.

'Still there?' Peter called out to her.

He meant fingerprints, of course. Nothing else, and the stifled cry she had inadvertently let out seemed ridiculous in the security of the fading sun on the terrace. The anxiety in his voice gave her a reason to return that she gratefully clutched.

'It's stupid,' she said to Peter, when she reached the terrace, 'but I felt I was being watched.'

He didn't laugh. 'Is that so stupid? Suppose you are – suppose we are? Let's get out of here.'

Being taken seriously made her feel worse, however, and she followed the wheelchair back to the car in silence. It had been nothing, she told herself; the mere product of an over-active imagination. 'There isn't a note on the car reading "Keep Away", is there?' she tried to joke, as Peter leaned forward to open the car door.

'No,' Peter said gravely. 'But someone's been here. We didn't lock up, and my stuff on the back seat looks as if it's been moved.'

So her panic could have been justified after all. She swallowed, trying to stop feeling like a kid scared of the dark. 'Anything missing?' she asked. 'The computer's there?'

'I didn't bring it, luckily. Someone's just curious, perhaps, or giving us a gentle warning. Which means there really is something nasty in the woodshed.'

'That Alwyn was murdered as an extension of being a victim of rough music?'

'If so, what gave rise to that, Georgia? Is it likely the village would be so upset by a love affair between two adults, even though it was the lady of the manor and a poet concerned?'

'No.'

'Or over Alwyn plagiarizing a dead man's work?'

'No. So that means . . .'

'There's something else.'

Five

'Georgia?'

Luke's sudden exclamation made her jump, abandoning her lowly position as table-setter. Luke was by far the better cook, and was currently mid stir-fry for supper. She was ready for it, if only to take her mind off the events of the afternoon at Shaw Cottage.

'Molly Sandford,' he continued, 'came to see me this morning. She's a literary agent, and says she's met you.'

'What on earth did she want?' she asked uneasily. This seemed a remarkable coincidence. She had deliberately refrained from telling Luke more about the manor and the Fernbourne Five, partly because he had business worries of his own, and partly because Luke was their publisher, not their mentor. She played momentarily with the idea of Molly being the watcher in the woods, but she couldn't see those smart London designer shoes stumbling through Kentish undergrowth. Peering into cars perhaps . . .

Luke looked mildly surprised. 'I'm a publisher. She had a couple of projects about the Fernbourne Five that she thought might interest me.'

Georgia was immediately suspicious. 'What projects?'

Luke merely raised an eyebrow to indicate she was off limits. 'Why?'

What on earth to say now? Nothing but the truth, she supposed, weak though it sounded. 'Peter and I have just decided to tackle them as our next case.'

Luke looked startled, then remembered the stir-fry and pulled it off the heat. 'I thought you'd abandoned that idea. So it's on again. What's the angle?'

She could hardly answer that Marsh & Daughter didn't yet know. 'Trade secret,' she said lightly.

He eyed her thoughtfully. 'So's mine.'

Her heart sank. 'There might be a clash here, Luke.' How could she and Peter cast doubt on the established legend of the Five, of which Alwyn's death was a part, but on the other hand, what would be the point of repeating it?

'No clash for you,' he pointed out. 'Only for me, if I couldn't publish both. But, on the whole,' he added comfortingly, perhaps reading her stricken expression correctly, 'that's unlikely to happen.'

Was it? 'You're not thinking, Luke,' she said, trying to sound professional and only succeeding in producing a sort of doleful squeak. 'Marsh and Daughter books usually turn accepted fact upside down. That's their whole point.'

He laughed. 'True, but a juicy scandal might spice up the sales all round. Look, the only concrete proposition is reprints of some of the Five's work to coincide with this big do they're having next year. Hunt's novels have recently been reprinted, so the trust wants the others to be represented too. There is another project as yet under wraps, however. Satisfied?'

'I'm afraid not.' She played the only card left in her hand. 'Did you know there was a plagiarism issue over *The Flight of the Soul*?'

She lost the gamble. 'Yes,' Luke said somewhat coolly. 'All settled, I gather.'

'Not for Marsh and Daughter.' She was getting in too far. She knew it, but couldn't stop herself. Her words hardly made sense even to her, especially as she and Peter hadn't yet fully examined this issue. Indeed they'd almost bypassed it, taking the plagiarism as established fact. The only doubt seemed to be in the degree of Alwyn's duplicity. But if Marsh & Daughter took a different line to the trust's, what then? It could be trouble for Luke, and even worse trouble between them in their private life.

'On what basis?' he asked.

'An open line of investigation.' This sounded weak too. Altogether she wasn't doing well.

'Then if and when you have some evidence for concern, tell me,' he said reasonably, 'and we can talk to Molly about it.'

The stir-fry was pushed back on to the heat again. 'And', he added, 'if Marsh and Daughter decides to go ahead on the Fernbourne Five, give me an outline of the new proposal and I'll look at it at the same time.' Discussion ended.

The possibility of a clash between Luke the lover and Luke the publisher had always been there, she acknowledged bleakly. Now it would have to be faced. Luke was calm about it, but she was not. Meanwhile they would eat their stir-fry and postpone any more work discussion. And so to bed, where the problem might lie within her like an undigested pepper. The tempting thought of her own home popped into her mind. Thank heavens she had kept it. The bolt-hole it represented was a positive factor because although she would not use it, she knew she *could.*

She pushed the thought out again. Bolt-holes weren't positive, only temporary refuges. Only progress forward would be positive. If she didn't cope with this problem now, it could crop up again between herself and Luke, either over the Fernbourne Five or something else.

'Suppose I follow this up with Molly?' she suggested. 'You could come too, if you like.'

Luke considered this. 'No. We've different issues at stake. Have you got that table set yet?'

He was right, but the prospect of going alone to see Molly did not appeal. Too much like armed warfare. She'd sleep on it, she decided. Hours later, lying beside him in bed and listening to his rhythmical breathing – which, no doubt, she thought comfortably, would one day in their faraway future together become rhythmical snoring – she realized she was thinking of the poem on Alwyn Field's gravestone: 'I heard his music too.' She woke in the morning with fleeting snatches of dreams of Pied Pipers and rats and children all racing for some far-off blue-misted mountain. What Pied Piper had Alwyn been chasing? Elfie, the muse of poetry, happiness? And what would lie beyond it for Marsh & Daughter? Not a paradise, that was for sure.

When she reached the office the next morning, she had almost convinced herself that there would be no clash with Molly Sandford, only to discover that the news of a possible rival publication outraged Peter even more than it had her.

'That was very remiss of you, Georgia.'

'I couldn't have known that Molly was going to pounce on him,' she said in her defence. The good thing about Peter was that he always moved on quickly.

'Why go to Luke?' He frowned. 'No disparagement to Frost and Co, but why not a London publisher?'

'Perhaps they all turned this mysterious project down, or perhaps reprints of poetry and old-fashioned children's books are small beer for mass-market publishers.'

'Or maybe it's another step to block Marsh and Daughter from writing anything.'

'This,' Georgia pronounced gloomily, 'is promising to be a real humdinger of a stir-fry. All the ingredients mixed up with no dominant flavour.'

'There is,' Peter observed firmly. 'It's Damien Trent. He's been thrown back in the Fernbourne wok. Mike had a personal look at the laptop files and found a folder for the Five; that's the good news. The bad news is that the files in it only had straight biographical information on the Five. He thought we'd like to know that there was nothing giving any clue as to what Damien was doing in Fernbourne, and still doesn't believe the Five are necessarily connected with Damien's death, although he's prepared to consider it if more evidence turns up. Meanwhile he's working on a much simpler line – local yobs and dealers.'

'So where does that leave us? Back in yesterday's garden?' The woods at Shaw Cottage seemed frighteningly close, and for a moment the sound of that whistling haunted her again.

Peter looked at her scathingly. 'Never look on it as yesterday, Georgia. This is today's problem. It's not so much the Fernbourne Five who are the hurdle for us, but the Fernbourne Trust, and with Trent's death the cauldron is bubbling.'

'Because we two witches are stirring it? I suppose that's better than being in it.'

'For once we're innocent. The general heat is causing it. The arts centre is a big project, and there's a lot at stake. It's going to be Clemence's legacy, and Matthew Hunt's, but it's also Janie's future, Molly Sandford's reputation and part of her livelihood. Moreover, it's Birdie's big day, which means Christopher's too.'

'And for Ted Laycock?'

'Nothing obvious. More trade for the pub?'

'But resurrection of the plagiarism and Field's suicide could threaten the arts centre, although that's going to happen with or without us once the press gets stuck in.'

Peter frowned. 'I'm not so sure. The suicide has already been dealt with in Hunt's book, and the plagiarism is a dead issue, which, if need be, I'm sure the trust has plans to gently slide into the Five's story. Their *official* story, that is. What could be at stake is the basic story itself. If the suicide was murder, or the plagiarism accusation false, then they become very much today's problems for the trust. That's where the danger lies.'

'For them or for us?' she asked, but he did not reply.

As soon as Georgia reached Fernbourne that afternoon she felt a difference. For a start, there was no sign of any police presence now. It was nearly three weeks since Damien's death and the scene of crime cordon had long since been lifted. It seemed to have been replaced by a different kind of barrier, however, and this time it was invisible. As she parked the car, passers-by seemed to be hurrying their steps, faces set firmly looking in front of them. 'Nonsense,' she told herself uneasily, but when she went into the village shop she had the same reaction from another shopper. On the other hand Emma's mum was eyeing her aggressively, as though ready and waiting if she dared to say anything about the Fernbourne Five. And then Georgia saw why. It was Wednesday, when the weekly *Kent Sentinel* was published. Over the front page was a huge headline 'Fernbourne Murder' and underneath was a picture of the beautiful Emma and Adam, plus a caption in which they both declared how terrible it was that no arrests had yet been made. That Mrs Baker objected to this publicity was evident from the scowl Georgia received when she took a copy to the counter to buy.

'So you're still here,' said Sarah Baker grimly.

'Yes,' Georgia agreed, offering a smile as well as a pound coin.

A pause. 'What's it to you, if I might ask? You're not from round these parts.'

Georgia could answer that truthfully. 'I talked to Damien Trent; he was interested in the Fernbourne Five and so are my father and I.'

'Troublemakers,' Sarah muttered. 'Like them newspaper people. Some folks like stirring up trouble. Why can't you let things be?'

'Unfinished business has to be settled sooner or later.'

'Then we can do it for ourselves.' The till shut with a clang.

'With rough music?' Georgia asked, perhaps foolishly. She wanted the Bakers' cooperation and this was hardly the way to achieve it.

Sarah glared at her, then turned away. The conversation was over, and so, cursing herself for mishandling the situation, Georgia retreated to the pub to collect what remained of her common sense. She ordered a coffee from Bob, but to her surprise it was brought to her by Emma Baker five minutes later.

Even wearing a white hat and enveloping overalls Emma looked both stunning and yet unaware of it. To have her working in the King's Head must be a feather in Adam's cap in the battle for her favours with Sean, and Georgia wondered whether Sean knew of this cosy arrangement.

'Do you usually work here,' she asked, 'or are you just helping out today?'

The lovely face looked genuinely pleased at her interest. 'It's my gap year. I'm filling in here before uni. I'm saving up to go on my travels after Christmas.'

'I saw your picture in the newspaper. It must be hard to have had the police hanging around so much. Unsettling for the village.'

Emma looked troubled. 'Damien was nice. It was awful the way he died.'

Georgia seized her opening. 'Did he talk to you about why he was here?'

Emma looked at her sharply and giggled. 'Mum says you're all nose.'

'Nothing wrong in that,' Georgia rejoined cheerfully. 'If people aren't curious about what's going on around them, all sorts of ghastly things happen unnoticed. Journalism was a good job for Damien.' She held her breath and sure enough there came a prompt reply. Thank heavens the pub was not crowded and no curious eyes were on them.

'He wasn't a journalist. He said he might be some kind of relation of mine. I asked Dad, and he said Damien asked about a Joe Baker, but the only Joe he knew didn't have any children, and he was long gone anyway.' A frown clouded her brow, as though this hadn't quite satisfied her. Nor did it Georgia. She felt there might be more to be learned from the Bakers. The difficulty would be in wheedling it out of them.

'Did Damien mention Alwyn Field?'

'The poet?' Emma asked with unexpected interest. 'No. Field killed himself over his love for Elfie Lane. I'm going to read English Lit,' she explained proudly. 'Romantic, isn't it? Him and Elfie and Gavin Hunt. A cosy threesome.'

'Like you, Adam and Sean,' Georgia pointed out, amused.

Emma blushed. 'Mum says let them fight it out and don't get involved. Brother Nick doesn't like either of them, so he says the same.'

'But what do you say?'

She shrugged. 'Sean's good at the sex.'

Georgia blinked. There were probably only eighteen years between Emma and herself in age, but a lot seemed to have changed in attitude if not in emotions. She hoped this was just an attitude that Emma decided to strike, but she wouldn't put any money on it.

'Do the words "rough music" mean anything to you?' she asked idly.

Emma looked puzzled. 'Don't think so.' A pause, then too quickly, 'I'd better get back.'

Molly Sandford's office was in Clapham in a tall terraced house overlooking the Common, and it was also her home, judging by the bells on the door. Georgia discovered that Molly was one half of a partnership, Sandford & Petter, but today when she reached the first floor reception there was no sign of the Petter, only a receptionist and closed doors. Georgia had decided to follow up her suggestion that she tackle Molly as soon as she could, albeit with strict instructions from Luke not to trespass on his domain. She had not been amused, and told him so. She needed no such reminders.

One of the closed doors opened and Molly emerged from her office, all gracious smiles and smart black suit. To Georgia it was a reminder that she was playing the game on someone else's turf, but she could give as good as she got. Molly's black suit was matched by her own dark green one.

'Luke told me about your visit,' Georgia began, as she followed Molly into her office. Victorian spacious dimensions, with ultra-modern décor, she discovered. Not her own cup of tea at all. 'Sorry I wasn't there.'

Molly looked amused, the curls of her dark hair softening the basic toughness of her face. 'Ah, so I deduce that Marsh and Daughter is definitely thinking of a book. I assumed your fascination with the Five couldn't be entirely disinterested. What I can't understand,' she said, waving Georgia to a seat, 'is what you think merits investigation.'

'Alwyn Field's suicide and events pertaining to it,' Georgia said bluntly.

Molly sighed. 'By events, I presume you mean his plagiarism of Roy Sandford's work in *The Flight of the Soul*.'

'That's one issue.'

'I can't see what it has to do with me,' Molly said, frowning. 'Luke must have told you we're planning straight reprints, which, even if you did concoct some kind of story for a book, wouldn't be affected.'

Georgia swallowed back anger. Some day she'd get her own back for that word 'concoct', but not today. 'Are you including *The Flight of the Soul* under Roy's name?'

Molly's eyes narrowed. 'Yes, unless you have evidence to the contrary. If you don't, we're wasting time. Even if there is some kind of story about that, or anything else to do with the Five, the hard truth is that you would be second in the field with your publication. Fernbourne Arts Centre opens next summer, which is when we will publish the reprints. It doesn't leave you a lot of time to investigate, write a book on the results and get it published, does it? Whatever it said, you'd lose sales to us if you published later.'

'Not whatever,' Georgia retorted coolly. 'Not if it reveals and proves an entirely different story to yours.'

Molly flushed with annoyance. Nevertheless she sounded amused when she replied, 'I do believe you're threatening me. That would be premature, until you've found your so-called *story*. Which you won't, because there isn't one.'

This wasn't good. Georgia was puzzled as to why Molly was defending her wicket quite so vigorously. 'We're focussing on Alwyn Field,' she pointed out, 'and on whether there's any doubt about his suicide. Even if there is, it needn't necessarily affect your interests. We wouldn't be invalidating the work of the whole group.'

'With most principals dead, you could indulge in pure conjecture.'

'If you've read our books, you must know that we don't,' Georgia rejoined, struggling to keep her temper.

Unexpectedly, Molly laughed. 'Let's call a truce. Why don't we work together? We create a market for you, and you follow on with your little book in due course. We could sell it at the manor.'

A Greek bearing gifts? And 'little book'? 'I doubt if that would work.' Georgia tried to sound reasonable, although she was beginning to dislike Molly intensely. 'If we find evidence that the plagiarism accusation against Field was unfounded, it would throw a spanner in the works if you've just republished it under Roy's name. But it wouldn't in itself affect the question of whether Alwyn was murdered or committed suicide. The issue was settled by the time he killed himself.'

'Presumably the depression caused through the slur on his reputation would continue?' Molly whipped back. 'Besides, there's darling Elfie. That's reason enough for suicide.'

'I agree both dovetail with long-term depression,' Georgia said fairly. 'And Birdie doesn't seem to have queried the verdict at the time. Nevertheless the open verdict at the inquest suggests a query in itself.'

Molly seemed disconcerted by this objectivity. 'I suppose you're right. But Alwyn wasn't doing too well all round. I think his father was supporting both him and Birdie. My grandfather was Roy's brother, and I remember his talking about Alwyn as a wimp compared with Roy. Roy was the great white hope all round. His parents went through an awful time when he died. After the bombing at the Café de Paris, the bodies were naturally in a mess, and some couldn't be properly identified at first. Roy's was one of them. Biggin Hill had to testify, so did Roy's parents and chums, and they found scraps of uniform and so forth. Can you imagine the trauma his parents and siblings went through?'

Yes, Georgia could. Only too well; a tremor of sympathy ran through her.

'How well known was Roy at the time of his death?' Georgia asked.

'Better known than Alwyn. There were two collections of his poems, of which the second, *Verses to Dorinda*, was outstanding. Alwyn had had one published by a small press, *Of Loves and Landscapes,* and quite a few singly published in those literary magazines that used to come and go in the thirties.'

'Did they write in similar styles? I've only read Alwyn's.' Peter had managed to get hold of the disputed *Flight of the Soul* and *A Mourning in Spring* in which 'The Piper' appeared.

Molly considered this. 'I'm no literary critic, but I'd say not unalike. The subjects were much the same: love and war, frustrations and partings, the sense of a dying era, and nature's influence on man. The main difference was that Alwyn had a great love of the countryside, but Roy was a townie at heart, despite living at Shaw Cottage from about 1938 onwards. His parents lived in west London.'

Georgia hesitated, then decided to go for it. 'What's your personal take on the plagiarism? There seem to be varying opinions as to how far Alwyn was to blame.'

'Guilty as hell,' Molly said promptly, then grinned. 'But I would say that, wouldn't I? When *The Flight of the Soul* was published, Roy's family never saw it. Why should they? The book had Alwyn's name on it. As Clemence has probably told you, it was only after the war that Gavin found Roy's manu-script drafts. Alwyn said Roy must have copied them from his own poems for reference but Gavin couldn't believe that. It was far too weak, and Alwyn couldn't even produce his own manuscript. And –' Molly glanced at Georgia – 'before you say Gavin was prejudiced because Elfie loved Alwyn, forget it. I remember Gavin myself, and one thing that everyone agreed on, even Elfie, was that he could divorce his personal feelings from his professional judgement.

'It was only because of the tiny margin of doubt that it was a genuine mix-up because of the two minor poems already published under Alwyn's name,' Molly continued, 'that the Sandfords were persuaded not to go to court. But naturally it never was reprinted – but now it's going to be, with any luck.'

'And so Roy is to be the unsung hero of the Five?'

Molly shrugged. 'Yes. He deserves it. My private view is that Gavin was a stuffed shirt, Alwyn was a creep, Elfie a moonstruck goose, Clemence a solid pudding. Roy was the one who lit them up. Sorry if this shocks you,' she added iron-ically, 'but you could say the same of any group of artists,

I daresay. A case of the whole being mightier than the sum of the parts.'

'Yet you judge Roy as an individual.'

'Justified,' Molly retorted. 'If you look at his work, Roy had the touch of genius about him. The others followed in his wake.'

Georgia didn't agree, thinking of Clemence, but now was not the time to say so. 'Did the group have a mission like the Pre-Raphaelites, or was it just a group of artists drawn together by proximity?'

'Neither. My PR slant is that they believed in independent personal choice, hence Matthew's *The Freedom Seekers*. You remember the famous Oxford debate of 1933 that in no circumstances would the house fight for king and country? Roy voted for the motion, and it was carried as you know, but that didn't stop either him or many of the others joining up when war came. The Fernbourne Five didn't believe in being tied down by majority opinion. Gavin fought in the Spanish Civil War, and it was after that that they started the group, when his first novel was published. Clemence has always stalked through life in her own plodding way, and Elfie seemed determined to be different by wistfully floating surrealistically over everything. So that,' she concluded, 'is to be the mission message for the arts centre posters. Any comments?'

Georgia had quite a few, such as why, if she was so cynical about the Five, was she a trustee? Self-gain? Probably, and why not, since it was her livelihood?

'By the way,' Molly said as Georgia was leaving, 'did Luke tell you about my new project?'

'Naturally not. It would break boundaries.'

'How frustrating for you,' Molly murmured. 'There's fortunately no such embargo on my telling you.'

Georgia restrained herself from a tart reply. 'I'd be interested to know.'

'I'm sure you will. It's the first complete biography of Roy Sandford. I'm calling it *Bright Flame*.'

Instantly, Georgia was back at that tombstone in the churchyard. 'The bright flame of the Five, snuffed out . . .' She recalled Damien's words clearly.

'Did Damien Trent come to see you?' she asked so suddenly that she hit an unexpected bullseye.

Molly flushed. 'Who?' The wrong answer. Molly would surely know who Trent was. She recovered quickly, however. 'Of course, that man who was killed in Fernbourne,' she continued. 'Yes, he did come here. He wanted information about the Five, and Alwyn Field.'

'Why choose you, not Matthew?' Georgia knew she had her on the run now and there was a split-second pause before Molly replied.

'I agented the reprints of Gavin's novels. I think the publishers put Trent in touch with me.'

Nice one, Georgia thought. She tried one or two more questions, but it was obvious that Molly wasn't going to budge from the familiar Fernbourne Five story. Even if it wasn't the truth – let alone the whole truth. For all her protestations, Molly was keeping something back.

'I thought you might like to get a taste of Fernbourne,' Georgia said innocently, as she and Luke settled in at a corner table in the King's Head that evening. 'After all, you'll probably be dealing with the manor next year.'

Luke ignored this. 'How did you get on with Ms Sandford?'

'I can understand why she's a Ms.'

He laughed. 'So are you,' he pointed out, and she could have kicked herself for playing into his hands. But he let her off the hook. 'There was a short marriage, Molly told me, and now she prefers her maiden name. So answer my question.'

'I would sum it up as everything will be fine provided Peter and I toe the party line.'

'Is that difficult?'

'It could be, if the truth clashes with it. And what's this about a biography of Roy Sandford?' She was still mulling over the significance of Damien's visit to Molly. Her explanation was possible, but it didn't explain Molly's obvious confusion, and her not having mentioned it before. Did Mike Gilroy know, for instance?

'A biography is overdue, so Molly says,' Luke replied. 'He's the forgotten one of the five, so it would sell. I gather Molly's got a new slant on him. It could bring a lot of publicity if we play our cards right and Molly's well placed to do that.'

Georgia was puzzled. What new slant could that be? 'I've got it!' she exclaimed.

'I love it when your eyes light up like that.'

'Don't distract me. It's Birdie, isn't it? She was in love with Roy, and not much is made of that in Matthew's book.'

'And he loved her, according to Molly. Alwyn stood between them.'

'How could he?'

'He lived in the same house. He could have barricaded the bedroom doors, locked them in their rooms.'

'Very funny.' She returned to the fray. 'Is the plagiarism being fitted into this new story? For instance, Alwyn was so mad at Roy for making eyes at his sister, then threatening to deprive him of his housekeeper, that he pinched his poems.'

'Could be,' Luke said, looking more interested now. 'She didn't tell me much, just rambled on about PR. There's so much known about Gavin, Elfie and Alwyn that Roy and Birdie got overlooked. So Molly can do a great publicity job at the opening of the manor.'

'With Birdie's personal appearance,' Georgia said. 'Of course. Birdie's own story of her own love affair from her own lips released to the world courtesy of TV and the Fernbourne Trust at the wonderful new arts centre. Books on sale right now.'

'I like the sound of the last bit,' Luke said, looking hopefully for a waiter.

When one finally came, it wasn't Emma, and the pub was clearly under pressure. She could see that Luke was beginning to get itchy about this, and so now was not the time to ask him whether Marsh & Daughter's book might fit into this glorious sales bonanza.

Service continued to be slow, and it was past eleven o'clock before their dessert arrived, courtesy of a harassed Doreen Laycock.

'Where's Emma this evening?' Georgia asked sympathetically.

'You tell me,' was the grim answer.

Even as Doreen spoke, Georgia could hear a commotion outside their window with a crowd of youths, then a girl's scream. In a trice Bob Laycock was out from behind the bar and rushing outside with Luke and several other men following in his wake. Rather more cautiously Georgia did too, by which time the action had moved round to the side of the pub, and by the time she reached them the situation was getting ugly. She'd seen Doreen seize the phone so presumably police were on their way. Meanwhile Adam Laycock was pinned against the wall by a hoodie whom she recognized as Sean, and a group of youths was circling round, including one she thought she could identify as Emma's brother Nick. Emma was screeching at Sean to leave Adam alone.

Sean's response was to release Adam, turn round and seize hold of Emma. 'She's mine, you fucker,' he yelled over his shoulder at Adam. 'And I'll get you if you touch her again.'

He dragged her away from Adam, swinging her round as a shield as Bob and Luke tried to get her away. Nick Baker was struggling to hold Adam back from the attack.

'He's a murderer, Emma,' Adam was shouting frenziedly. 'Ask him whose gun it was.'

In a trice, Sean had flung Emma away, and pushed Adam back against the wall, and this time Georgia could see to her horror that he had a knife in his hand, and that Luke and Bob weren't going to reach him in time. Adam was using both hands to stave Sean off and blood was already running down his arm. No sooner did Bob or Luke pull him off than he'd break free and come back in again.

'Take that, you ruddy hooligans!'

A voice from above and the contents of a bucket of water landed on the heads of the fighting cocks, sufficient for them to part briefly, spluttering, and both of them were firmly seized. Alice, Georgia thought thankfully, had her own effective methods of dealing with situations.

Six

'I don't like this one little bit, Georgia,' Peter told her on her arrival at the office the next morning. She had telephoned him after her return from Fernbourne to tell him briefly of the fight outside the pub, but had kept back the rest until working hours. She knew the police had arrested Sean, but it was still too early to expect any more news.

'Sean and Emma have nothing to do with the Fernbourne case,' she pointed out.

'Haven't they? It seems to me that Fernbourne has been a village ill at ease with itself for many a long year, and the underlying causes are breaking out in the younger generation.'

'A lofty thesis,' she retorted, 'but can you really believe that rancour between the village and the manor decades ago is manifesting itself in a teenage pub fight now?'

'Yes, I can. Children pick up attitudes and standards from their parents, and only later choose whether to accept or reject them. That's how feuds keep running.'

She was forced to agree that was possible in Fernbourne.

Peter's frustration broke out in another direction: 'And what's more, look at *that*.'

It took her a minute or two to realize what 'that' was: a blank window on the computer screen. She began to laugh at the descent from serious to trivial.

'Nothing,' Peter continued bitterly, ignoring her mirth. 'Absolutely nothing. I've been fighting it since yesterday morning. Everything leads to the Great Wall of China. No outsiders wanted here.'

'But you still think there's something on the other side?'

'I don't know,' Peter said irritably, 'but doubtless the Barbarians, Huns and Tartars didn't either.'

'They did,' Georgia reminded him. 'There were trade routes

which brought back rumours and information on the fabled riches of the East.'

'We haven't even got rumours,' he grumbled. 'There's nothing to suggest the Five weren't as romantic, admirable and tragic as Matthew maintains in his book. It's not often,' he continued glumly, ignoring her attempt to interrupt, 'that I create a file for Suspects Anonymous and fail even to nail down the outlines of a case. Instead we're circling around getting nowhere.'

Suspects Anonymous alternately delighted and infuriated Peter. When it was good it was very, very good, pointing out inconsistencies or positive matches in a mass of hitherto unconnected facts. When it was bad, however, it sat there as dolefully as they did, waiting for its next gulp of information. As it was doing now.

'Usually we'd find a chink or weak link,' Peter continued, ignoring another effort to break into the conversation, 'but this is holding strong. Nothing but sweet cooperation from the Fernbourne Trust, and hostility from the village which thinks, perhaps quite rightly, that we're sticking our noses into something that doesn't need to be disturbed.'

'There's another problem.' Georgia managed at last to divert his attention from the screen. 'This mysterious project of Molly's is a biography of Great-Uncle Roy Sandford.'

'Damn.' Peter didn't waste time over spilt milk. 'The worst scenario.'

'It's timely.'

'Maybe, but it doesn't explain why she came to Luke as the prospective publisher. Of course –' he suddenly brightened up – 'it could be really good news.'

'How do you make that out?' she asked, astonished.

'Look at it this way. The manor opening is going to be a big deal. It could tie in with London exhibitions and so forth, celebs down here for the opening, press swarming around, Birdie's great day. Agreed?'

'Yes, but—'

'The reprints might be neither here nor there, but a biography? Luke doesn't have the distribution system and selling power of a mass-market publisher, so this could mean that the trust is determined to pre-empt any book of ours. Which – and here's the good news – must mean there's some substance to our case.'

'Could be,' Georgia replied. It was time to produce her rabbit from the hat. 'Damien Trent visited Molly.' That had convinced her that Damien was more deeply involved in the Five's story than she had initially thought, which made her feel both guilty and relieved at the same time. Now at least she felt she was getting somewhere.

Her father's eyes gleamed. 'Tell me all.'

'Not a lot to tell. Molly reluctantly told me he was asking about Alwyn Field and the Five. No great surprise, but I'm pretty sure she was holding back on me.'

'Hum,' was Peter's contribution to this. 'If Luke takes this biography on, he'd better beware of shifting sand. It could be an attempt to spike our guns, knowing he wouldn't take both books. Then she could do the dirty on him at the last moment.'

'How do we stop that?'

'By going full-tilt ourselves. Are you still game, Georgia?'

'Yes, but what do I tilt at?'

Peter growled in exasperation. 'You sound like a boring Greek chorus. *Do* something.'

Growl it might be, but it was also a plea, Georgia realized. 'Alice,' she said. 'I'll try her.'

She decided to drive straight to Fernbourne, making a point of calling in to tell Luke where she was going, as last night's events had shaken him. 'Not just a village with a yob problem,' he had remarked as they had driven home. 'Deeper than that. There's something bubbling up in Fernbourne. Georgia, take care, won't you? Don't get trapped in whatever's going on.'

He'd never said that before, and he wasn't normally one for seeing bears in bushes. Besides, it only echoed her own belief – and Peter's. Safety was always an issue with Marsh & Daughter, but only as a sideline that she felt able to cope with. This seemed different because the threat was not only silent but its direction uncertain.

The journey was beginning to seem familiar, but even so as she drove through Chartham and over to cross the A2, it still felt like alien territory. Who had stood in tears amid the alien corn? Ruth in Keats' 'Ode to a Nightingale'. Along this single-track road high up on the downs there was nothing to be seen but fields of alien corn that had once been golden. Now they were brownish stubble, with the corn bales vanished, and it was a desolate scene of winter to come. Normally she'd have seen it as a positive sign of the harvest, but not today. The nearer she got to Fernbourne, the more she wanted to turn round and drive hell for leather in the opposite direction.

'Balderdash,' she told herself briskly. All that could happen would be that she would be frozen out once again by the wall of silence. Nothing more. And yet for once she was conscious of her isolation out here, mindful that, despite every mobile, BlackBerry and iPod in the world, when crunch came to crunch it was just you against the world.

As she turned a corner, she could see the first green trees, which meant that Fernbourne was only a mile or so away, and very shortly the entrance drive to the farm shop came into view. Just past it was a lay-by, where she could see a young couple arguing. Arguing intensely, she realized with shock. He was shaking her – no, he had his hands on her neck. Everything seemed to be happening at once. She recognized Emma and the man – boy – who seemed to be half throttling her, half dragging her further away from the road. It was Sean Hunt. What the hell was he doing there? He was supposed to be in police custody.

She slammed on the brakes, turning sharply into the lay-by, and was parked and out of the car in a trice. Emma was half croaking and Sean was yelling abuse as Georgia grappled with him, trying in vain to make him let go of Emma. Thank goodness for self-defence lessons. As he turned his head towards his assailant she used a deft palm heel to jerk his head back and, as his grip loosened, a front kick to follow up. A howl, and to her relief he was on the ground. No time to be lost. She grabbed Emma's hand, pulling her towards the car, pushing her into the passenger seat, even as Sean came at them again. This time he was an easier target. She floored him, but the sight of his distorted crazed face terrified her as she leapt back into her car, and they were off, leaving Sean doubled up at the roadside.

Emma promptly burst into noisy tears. 'Thanks,' was all she could stutter hoarsely.

Georgia swallowed, trying to regain her equilibrium with deep breaths, but she was still shaking. 'I thought Sean was safely locked up. What on earth happened?'

'I was going to the farm shop,' Emma wept, 'and he jumped me. He blames me for what happened last night.'

'You?' Georgia asked incredulously, then saw how shaky Emma was. She was bent over in the seat, wrapping her arms round herself in shock. 'There's a sweater on the back seat. Put it on. I can stop if—'

'*No!*'

Point taken, irrational though it might be that Sean was chasing them.

'The boy's crazed out of his mind,' Georgia said gently.

'He's been charged for the attack on Adam, but he was given bail this morning,' Emma managed to say. 'Mr Hunt went to the police station.'

Georgia could hardly believe it. 'Sean ought to be apologizing to you, not throttling you. What about the gun, for heaven's sake? If Adam's right about that, Sean's even more dangerous, Emma.'

'He said he never had one. And he had an alibi for Damien's murder. He was in the Dirty Ducklings—'

'The what?'

'It's a club. He was there with Nick, but Nick said he wasn't, so Sean blamed me.'

Georgia was even more bewildered. What on earth was Mike Gilroy's team playing at? 'Why isn't he being questioned about the gun and Damien's murder, if the alibi didn't stand up?'

'The manager saw him, kept his eye on him all night, because Sean's known as a troublemaker. So he couldn't have killed Damien.'

Time to think that one out later. Her first concern was Emma. 'You'll be away from here soon and travelling the world,' Georgia said comfortingly.

'But I . . .' Emma broke off but it was clear what she'd been going to say: 'But I love him.' For all her offhand words earlier, sex was exerting a more powerful hold than perhaps Emma herself had realized. How could she convince Emma that distance and then new faces at university next autumn were going to help? That making mistakes was natural; it was what to do about them that was important. Georgia remembered again how she'd felt about Zac. She'd only been a year or two older than Emma. She remembered her own blindness to any suggestion that something was amiss, even though Zac hadn't used physical but mental bludgeoning.

All done with charm and lies. No, they weren't really lies because he had believed them. That's why he was a con man – albeit a bad one. The result had been the same as with Emma and Sean; a blanket had come between herself and the truth. Whatever she said to Emma now, she wouldn't be able to shift her blanket, so there was only one thing she could do.

'I'll take you to your mother, Emma.'

'She'll kill me. She hates Sean,' was the gloomy prediction.

'No she won't. She'll be worried about you, and anyway she'll be pleased that she's been proved right.'

'Yeah, but . . .' Emma shrugged. 'OK. Whatever.'

Georgia regarded her soup and baguette without enthusiasm. Not that they were bad – on the contrary, the soup tasted home-made and the baguette had an interesting filling of avocado and bacon – but she realized that the morning's encounter had shaken her to the point where her appetite had disappeared. At the moment everything about Fernbourne seemed sinister. Innocent men got murdered, there was a culture of violence amongst its youth, and its elders were probably caught up in some web she couldn't understand.

If she forced herself to eat, it was possible that some of this distinct lack of cheer would vanish. Instead it became worse, because just as she finished the baguette, with each mouthful becoming more of an effort, Matthew Hunt came sweeping imperiously through the door of the pub. He looked furious, a man with a mission, and instinctively she braced herself. Had Sean reached home and his grandfather been fed some cock and bull story? He only cast her a brief glance, however, before tackling Bob and demanding to see Adam.

'Why's that?' Bob continued to polish glasses. Not much sycophancy there.

'I'm told he's been slandering my grandson.'

'Your grandson, Mr Hunt,' Bob said, keeping his cool, 'attacked my son with a knife.'

'It was self-defence. I've witnesses to that.'

'I'm sure you have. Too frightened to say otherwise.' Another glass was set carefully in its place.

'I'll let that go for the moment. Are you going to let me see him?' The ice-cold fury in his voice was even more evident.

'Only if I'm present too.'

'As you wish.'

They retreated into the private quarters and Doreen came into the bar, glanced at Georgia, but didn't say a word. Georgia could still hear most of what was going on in the private quarters, as the conversation was being conducted at full pitch. Doreen did a good impression of not hearing a word, but finally gave up and was listening, as appalled as Georgia.

'What's this about a gun? No one else has ever seen one,' Matthew was shouting. 'Pure malice.'

'That's a lie,' Adam retaliated. 'He boasted about it. He kept it hidden in one of the manor sheds. We all knew about it.'

'If this story has any truth in it, it's clear any of you could have access to it then. My grandson is being slandered. He was stitched up for a drugs offence he didn't commit by you thugs. He served his sentence and now you're intent on doing it again. I'll see you don't succeed. You're studying at Canterbury, aren't you, Adam? First year. Right, I'll be informing the university that you've a bad record. My son has had his house turned upside down as a result of you. There's no trace of a gun and that's not because it was the one left lying beside Trent's body but because it didn't exist. There's no registration of one at his or my address, and the police are satisfied with that.'

Of course not, Georgia fumed, when unregistered ones were freely available to those with money – and Sean would have that.

'He's being victimized, and that won't go on.' The volume increased. 'You attacked him last night . . .'

That did it. Georgia could contain herself no longer. With a brief apology to Doreen she pushed behind the bar and through the door marked Private.

'Sean's hardly a victim, Mr Hunt. He's a vicious and dangerous young man.' She hurled the words at him and he spun round in shock at this unexpected attack.

'This has nothing to do with you, Miss Marsh. Would you kindly leave us alone?'

'Wrong. It has everything to do with me,' she declared.

'Did you know I found your victimized grandson physically assaulting Emma Baker this morning? He was throttling her and I only got her away by using physical force myself.'

'You?' Sheer astonishment halted his tirade for a brief moment. 'Nonsense. I drove him home from the police station, and set him down when he saw his girlfriend. He told me he was attacked by some rough types simply because he was kissing her. Were you involved too?'

'Not *too*, Mr Hunt. I was the only one. There was no kissing when I arrived. Emma was in serious danger. You'll find her with her parents and you can ask them whether they're calling in the police.' Georgia could see Adam was pale with shock at what he'd heard.

'Whatever you imagined you saw,' Matthew retorted coldly, 'you clearly misjudged the situation and if you maintain that you were the only one who attacked him then you are in a serious position. He was hobbling with pain when he returned home, and I shall be reporting the assault to the police.'

Doubt was written all over Bob Laycock's face. Georgia wasn't a small woman but she could see that the idea of a fit nineteen-year-old being laid low by her seemed unlikely to him.

'I don't think you'll find Sean anxious to do that, Mr Hunt,' Georgia said grimly. 'At the very least, it wouldn't help his macho image to be felled by a woman. Moreover he has me to thank for saving him from a far worse charge. I think you'd quickly have the Bakers putting the police right over the true situation. It's unusual for a kiss to leave bruises all round a girl's neck.'

'You'd have the Laycocks speaking out too,' Bob said sturdily. 'The boy's a menace, Mr Hunt. I'd be a witness to his attack on Adam last night. I reckon Adam will go into the witness box too now he knows what Sean did to Emma. Won't you, Adam?' A nod was all Adam could manage. Georgia could see he was near to tears.

Matthew's eyes narrowed. 'I don't think I should pursue that line, Bob. It might not be in your best interests.'

Bob flushed. 'Our lease is secure.'

'Is it?' Matthew said scornfully. 'If it wasn't for Ted, I'd see it terminated for this.'

So the King's Head was held under a lease from the manor. Was that why Ted was involved with the trust? Surely not. There must be more to it. She saw Matthew looking at the doorway, and when she turned round, she could see Ted Laycock standing there. He said nothing, and his set expression was impassive.

What, Georgia thought, shaken, was all that about? Matthew had walked out, leaving her to go back to her drink as though nothing had happened. She'd have loved a coffee but the Laycocks were in conference, and she didn't want to disturb them. She found it interesting that Hunt had pulled his punches to some extent with her, as if trying to cling to his urbane chairman of the trustees' role, but what was the relationship with the Laycocks? Just a question of the lease? Ted was a trustee, the village representative, so she and Peter had assumed, but in the battle this morning he had seemed almost to be on Matthew's side, if only by his silence. But why? Adam was his grandson, and Ted must know he was entirely innocent in the fight outside the pub that evening.

Georgia felt like crawling back home and washing her hands of the whole sorry business, but obstinacy prevailed. She asked herself whether, if she had been just a casual passer-by when Emma was being attacked, she would have walked away? No, she would have plunged right in and then lingered to ensure Emma was all right. And that's what she would do now, despite the chance that Emma was so besotted with Sean that, having recovered a little, she too might accuse Georgia of having attacked Sean unprovoked. Luckily she felt the chances of Emma's parents believing that were remote. Besides, she needed some shopping, and the Bakers stocked some rather good home-made frozen curries that Luke and she had both liked.

The minute she walked into the shop, she realized that something had changed. As soon as she saw her, Sarah's face lit up.

'Nick,' she yelled. '*Nick.* Look after the shop, will you? I've got to talk to this lady here. That's if you've a moment?' she asked Georgia. It was a rhetorical question as she was already leading the way, and a sulky-looking Nick passed them, with a curious look at Georgia. So the news had travelled.

'How's Emma?' Georgia asked, as she was shown into their living room, and ushered to the sofa.

'In bed. Doctor's coming to check her over.'

'She's not worse, is she?'

'Thanks to you, no, Mrs Marsh.'

'Georgia, please.' So Emma's mum knew her name – well, nearly. Village grapevines were highly efficient.

'Ken!' Sarah shouted, and her husband duly appeared through the door to the kitchen wiping his hands on the towel. She'd seen him before. Thinning hair, thin-featured and a pleasant face. 'Just seeing the dairy stuff stored,' he said to his wife, and then to Georgia, 'So many rules and regs. You daren't breathe on a tin of beans in case it takes a writ out.'

'Now,' Sarah said in determined fashion, 'we wanted a word with you, Georgia, didn't we, Ken?'

Ken nodded. 'We wanted to thank you for looking after Emma.'

'Thank my self-defence trainer,' Georgia said. 'It's just lucky I was passing.'

'I don't think he'd have really harmed her,' Ken said. 'Just wanted to scare her and get his own back on us Bakers.'

'Because of Nick and this alibi business?' Georgia asked. She was by no means as sure as Ken, but it wasn't politic to say so.

'Could be. We don't know. That's between Nick and Sean. Good thing that Emma's going away after Christmas. Sean doesn't know our Em. She won't forget this – she's not daft. Takes after you, Sarah.'

His wife smiled, altogether a different person than the one Georgia had been used to up until today.

'So that's one thing,' Ken continued. 'The next is this business up at the manor.'

'An important step forward for the village, isn't it?' Georgia said.

'Good for trade, no doubt of it. Bob's all for it and so are we. But trade isn't everything. Trent's been murdered, and we don't know why. He seemed to think he might be related to us, but that was news to me. I just told him Joe was dead.

Least said, soonest mended. Now you're here, and we choked you off too.'

'Don't worry. I'm not a long-lost relation,' Georgia assured him.

He looked at her seriously. 'No, but you're interested in that poet who hung himself at Shaw Cottage. It may not be connected, but you'd been good to our Emma and we don't want to see you go the same way as Damien Trent. We gave you the brush-off and we reckon the trust is doing so too. And it may be not a polite one.'

'Well put,' Georgia said wryly.

'We can't do much about Trent now, but we can look out for you, and the best way to do that is to help you – for what you did for Emma. I can see you're not the sort to give up.'

She smiled, uncomfortably aware that at times she was very tempted.

'So I've been asking around a bit,' Ken continued. 'My parents are gone now, and my grandparents, but there are still a few around who remember when Field hung himself. One titbit is that a chap came to the village in the mid-1970s. He was asking questions about the Five, and about that poet's suicide, *and* about where he could find Joe Baker. Trent wanted to talk to Joe about the poet too. Bit of a coincidence, yes? Not what you might call first-class evidence, but it might be of interest to you.'

'It is,' Georgia agreed. 'Great interest. Do you know any more about this man in the 1970s?'

'No one heard any more. It was generally reckoned at the time, so I was told, that he fell foul of Mr Hunt – Gavin Hunt, that is, Matthew's father. I remember him, nice chap, but I wouldn't want to rub him up the wrong way. Very . . .' Ken paused. 'Correct.'

'What about Joe Baker and Damien Trent?'

Ken looked awkward. 'I told him I didn't know anything about Joe except the name. We've always been touchy about Joe, so we don't talk about him. He was my granddad's brother. He was alive in the 1970s, of course, when that other chap came, but he never said anything about a visit from him to my grandparents or parents. Not that they passed on to me anyhow. Joe probably sent him off with a flea in his ear. He was a crotchety old so and so.'

Georgia saw another door slam in her face. 'Could you tell me who it was remembered his coming here?'

'Best not,' Ken said awkwardly. 'Might not like their name given to strangers – if you'll pardon the word.'

She would. She was getting used to it now. 'I understand. Is there nothing else you can tell me about Alwyn Field?'

'Oh, yes, quite a bit,' Ken replied grimly, to her amazement. 'I kept schtum to Trent about this, because the family isn't proud of it. Trent asked me about the rough music. Heard of it?'

She seized the opening with gratitude. 'Yes, I have. Was there rough music connected with Alwyn? Was he the victim or was it on his behalf, because he'd been unfairly treated?'

'No doubt about that. Against him, Georgia.'

'What for?' At last, at last, she rejoiced. 'Because of his love affair with Elfie?'

'No way. Look, I knew Joe as an ancient great-uncle in the background. He was the butcher here, and his brother, my granddad, ran the grocers, which is now this place. Joe was always going off the deep end. His wife, Auntie Min, she was different, the doormat type. Don't believe in being a doormat, do you, Sarah?' he joked.

Sarah looked complacent. 'Poor old Auntie Min missed women's lib. I didn't. It's only the time we're born into it, and, after all, we can't choose that.'

'Well,' Ken continued, 'my parents were the buttoned-up sort, no scandals in our family sort of folk. Joe and Min had a child, a daughter called Jenny, and that was what the rough music was about. She left the village during the war and never came back. Neither Joe nor Min ever spoke of her and my dad was only a kid when she left, so my generation didn't know much about Jenny. Anyway, I found out later that this Jenny was raped by Alwyn Field, who wouldn't stand by her when she fell pregnant. She left the village and there the trail goes blank. What that did to Min, I can't imagine. She died long before Joe.'

'*Rape?*' exclaimed Georgia. 'But Alwyn was in love with Elfie.' This was a corker to take on board, and one that left a far from pleasant taste.

'Doesn't stop some men, does it?' Ken observed. 'Maybe he was consoling himself when Elfie refused to leave Mr Hunt.'

'When was this?' Georgia asked.

'Not sure. Most say it was early in the war. People were coming and going all the time so no one really knew it had happened at the time, let alone about the baby.'

'But if there was rough music then they must have known,' she argued.

'No, the rough music was later, after the war. Not long before Alwyn's death.'

Now her head really was spinning. 'But that's so long after the event, particularly if Jenny wasn't in the village any longer. It doesn't make sense.'

'Perhaps not, but that's what happened. She could have come back for a visit and Joe found out about the baby then or she confessed later who the father was. Or maybe when this story about his pinching poor Mr Sandford's work came out, Joe remembered his grievances. Whatever, Joe was at the head of the crowd. He organized the rough music.'

'It's remembered that clearly in the village?'

'Yes and no. These things lie buried and gradually die out of public memory, but if something reawakens it – like Damien asking questions, or you – then you find it's still there. It was the last time that rough music took place, so perhaps that made it stick, but the bad feeling that it was the manor and their mates against us villagers lingered too, I guess. We aren't proud of what Joe did, so we don't boast about it. None of us do. But this old lady I spoke to had written an account of it in her diary. She wasn't much more than a kid at the time, and it made a big impression on her.'

'You don't have the diary, I suppose?' Too much to hope for.

Ken laughed. 'Afraid not. You sleuths can't have everything your own way. I was allowed to read it and then it was whisked away. This lady's parents went round collecting pails and pots and pans, and she was given a washing-board and a washing dolly to bang it with. This was late in 1948, and they went up there quite late one evening, carrying flares to light the way. Rough old lane it was then. Alwyn Field came to the door, but old Birdie was out there like a flash to protect him, swearing at them to get away because Alwyn was innocent, and a wonderful brother. They were all dolts, she said. Only it made things worse because Alwyn was then shouted down before he could speak. Birdie went back into the cottage with him and they kept it up for two hours or more.'

'Did the police come?'

'We had a village policeman then, and the lady wrote in her diary that he was banging away with the rest of them. Jenny Baker was his sweetheart.'

'Good day?' asked Peter idly as Georgia walked in late that afternoon.

'I've known better.' She sank into the chair, exhausted. She had felt honour-bound to let Peter know everything that had happened and a phone call seemed the wrong way to do it.

'How was Alice?' he added.

'Alice?' Georgia asked blankly.

'You were going to see her,' he reminded her gently.

She'd completely forgotten. 'I had to take a rain-check on her,' she said, and explained why.

Peter listened attentively and in silence, obviously distressed when she told him of the Emma and Sean episode. Finally he remarked, 'Ill winds bring silver linings, but I don't like this particular ill wind. Or last night's. You're getting too blown about by them.'

'At least today's could be a lever to blow open the case. Suppose the rape was what Damien came to see Molly about?'

'It wouldn't seem to be any kind of motive for murder now. In fact rather the contrary, since it gives another reason for Alwyn's suicide.'

'You're right,' she agreed glumly. 'We needed to explore reasons for murder, not more for suicide.'

'Unless you put Joe Baker in the frame.'

'Revenge best served cold? But why leave it so late? I suppose it's possible Jenny didn't tell him who the father was until after the war. We don't know they never met again, only that she didn't return here to live.'

'That could explain it.'

'Then Joe's so hopping mad that he murders Alwyn.'

'Having let the whole village know that he is the chief suspect by encouraging them into rough music.'

'People don't think clearly in those circumstances. Or,' Georgia thought this through with a seed of excitement growing, 'perhaps he did. The rough music provided the reason for Alwyn's suicide. All Joe has to do now is come along and murder him in a way that *looks* like suicide.'

Peter stared at her. 'Georgia, have I ever told you I have a remarkable daughter?'

Seven

Peter must have been even more worried than he had disclosed on Friday about her experiences in Fernbourne, as the intervening weekend had done little to calm him. On the Monday morning he greeted her without any preamble, echoing Luke's sentiments.

'It's good that the Bakers have come on board, but Fernbourne is beginning to show its teeth, and they're being gnashed at you. Do you think we should call this off?'

'Any community has hidden teeth.' Georgia tried to be fair. 'Troubles rumble along in the background until a tiny incident makes it explode. I was in the way, that's all.'

'It's an ominous sign. Have you told Luke what happened?'

'Not yet.' He had been hard at work on the accounts and autumn publications over the weekend. A chink of light had arisen over the bleak financial horizon, however, in the form of a large prompt payment from his wholesaler. 'Anyway,' she objected, 'we can't head him off from his joyride with Molly Sandford just because Alwyn turns out to be even more of a rotter than we thought him. Or because of a lovers' quarrel that has nothing to do with it.'

'Rather more at stake than that,' Peter replied grimly. 'I don't like the way Alwyn Field is shaping up as chief candidate for Rat of the Year award. Seducer of friend's wife, plagiarist and now rapist. Quite a fellow – if it's all true, of course. Does the victim of a soulful, idyllic romance take revenge by raping another woman? It seems unlikely.'

Georgia agreed. 'Whether he did it or not, Joe Baker certainly believed he was guilty.'

'Mike would still take some convincing that a suicide or murder in 1949 really is connected with Damien Trent. He's still only playing with the idea at present, even though I've filled him in on the latest developments. He's already checked Damien's family tree, but there was no trace of a Baker.'

'Could he have been adopted?'

'If you're thinking about his being Jenny Baker's child,' Peter said sweetly, 'forget it. Damien was born in 1978. Anyway, we should recheck . . .' He caught sight of her expression. 'All right. Mike's territory. I'll ask him to do it. Sometimes,' he added, 'I find his insistence on boundaries a little frustrating.'

Georgia imagined Mike's quizzical face if he'd overheard that little gem. 'Practical though,' she murmured. 'We admit ourselves it will be hard to find much evidence for Alwyn's murder, even though we now know about the rape.'

'Difficult but not impossible. There are lots of cases of suicide that at first looked like murder, including a poor chap in the 1930s who was convicted for the murder of his partner who was found strangled in her own bed, almost certainly by herself. Mike's told me that the Field inquest report confirms the lack of evidence of a struggle, and that the alcohol and sedatives were the only reason for the open verdict. Field would have needed a lot of manhandling if he was unconscious, though.'

'Joe Baker could have been a Tarzan. He was a butcher after all. But he'd have to know Birdie was away, if he was going to have a drinking session with Alwyn and then kill him.'

Peter ruminated. 'Too many unanswered questions.' He picked up Matthew Hunt's *The Freedom Seekers* and turned to a photo of Alwyn, in which he was pictured with one arm round his sister, the other round Elfie, and was smiling into the camera. 'This was taken in the spring of 1939. I know it means nothing, but he simply doesn't look like a rapist. He looks like a victim.'

Georgia took a closer look. Alwyn was dressed in flannels, pullover and shirt with rolled up sleeves and his relaxed body language suggested he was between his two great supporters. 'You're right.'

Peter sighed. 'No help for it. It's back to the Dragons' Lair about the rough music and rape. If you're sure about going on, is it Dragon Birdie or Dragon Clemence for you?'

'Clemence,' said Georgia at once.

'On second thoughts, let's both go to see Clemence. It will send a message to the trust.'

'Doubting my abilities?' Georgia asked amiably.

'Is that likely? I'm thinking of how best to get results. Has it occurred to you that Matthew Hunt isn't going to forgive you easily for his son's misfortunes, not once but twice? Georgia, I really am doubtful about this case. It's all very well walking into a minefield when one is convinced of a mission. To take an afternoon stroll into one is just plain stupid. We have no clear path yet, and it looks increasingly likely that we never will.'

Georgia pondered this. Quite a few of their potential cases landed up on the shelf and it was tempting to put Alwyn Field's right there next to them.

'I'd hate to give up,' she said at last. 'It would mean Matthew Hunt had won.'

'Is that a good reason for the decision?'

'No.'

'Do you still want to go ahead anyway?'

'Yes, with the next step at least.'

'Then we both need to be there.'

When Peter telephoned, however, it appeared Clemence was not available even to speak to them on the phone, let alone meet them. Janie anxiously explained that her mother had been overtaxing herself physically and her doctor had told her to concentrate on her work, not irrelevant matters. Into which category it seemed that Georgia and Peter fell. A second attempt the following day produced an even more anxious Janie and the news that Clemence was visiting a friend. At the third attempt later that day Peter called with the same result.

'I quite understand,' Peter told Janie gravely. 'Tell Mrs Hunt I can easily find out what I need to know from Mrs Atkin.'

Even Georgia could hear the alarm in the voice at the other end of the line. 'Birdie?'

'Don't worry,' Peter assured Janie. 'I won't tire her too much, and I'll check in with Christopher first.' He replaced the receiver, remarking with satisfaction, 'Something seems to have been stirred up.'

'Let's hope it's not a mare's nest.'

That evening Peter rang Georgia at Medlars in the middle of their dinner.

'Are you OK?' she asked anxiously. Peter seldom rang in the evenings save in emergency, if he felt one of his 'turns' coming on, or had a minor accident. Even then it was usually Margaret whom he summoned.

'Of course,' he announced blithely. 'About tomorrow. I've a date with Birdie, provided their lift is working. But it appears Christopher has taken a fancy to you, and insisted on your presence too. I'll drive and drop you off so that you can trot along with Christopher alone.'

'Why on earth does he want to see me?'

'Your charm, darling.'

So what was all this about, Georgia wondered? It was more likely that Christopher rather than Birdie had suggested her presence. Birdie didn't strike her as the sort of person to be overawed by male company. But why? Was this something to do with her row with Matthew Hunt? Was Christopher going to deliver words of warning? That seemed unlikely as Matthew was fully able to do that himself. And in any case what would Sean have to do with Alwyn Field? Georgia gave up the attempt to puzzle out any sense in this.

'Drop me in the village,' she asked Peter the next day. A large box of chocolates from the village shop would be a passport to Birdie's approval and at the same time she could ask after Emma, not to mention have a brief word with Alice. The latter hope was dashed, as Alice was out. She was luckier with Emma, who proved to be fully recovered although Georgia noticed there was still a silk scarf elegantly arranged over her shoulders and neck. She assured her that there had been no repercussions from Sean – or Matthew.

That in itself was odd, Georgia thought, as she walked to Christopher's cottage. An apology might have been expected, if only because Sean wouldn't want to hand Emma over to Adam without a battle. Silence from Matthew or Sean did not bode well.

Christopher looked pleased to see her, which was a relief, and without more ado he led the way to the footpath at the rear of his garden. It had been raining and so she had hoped to avoid this, but it was clearly his set route. Rain or shine he would plod along here with his hold-all of Birdie's current needs.

'They seem no nearer to finding Damien Trent's murderer,' she said conversationally, when he remained silent. She still half expected a message from the chair of the trust to be delivered through his henchman, but nothing so far.

'Won't find him,' Christopher assured her.

'You seem very certain,' Georgia said. 'Do you know who murdered him?'

'Yes,' he said simply. 'I do.'

That made her very uneasy. 'Have you told the police?'

'No.'

'But who—'

'Can't say.'

'But you should.' If his lips were sealed, did that imply the trust was implicated?

Try as she would, Christopher refused to elaborate. All he would say in response to questions about Damien's murder was, 'Matthew said not to talk about it. Not to you.'

So the word had gone out to his henchman. She suppressed her annoyance. It wasn't Christopher's fault. 'I met him,' she explained.

He looked puzzled. 'You weren't here then, were you?'

They were at cross-purposes – not difficult where Christopher was concerned.

'Do you mean Alwyn Field's death?' she asked hopefully. Was she getting somewhere at last?

'Matthew said he hung himself.'

'Alwyn Field? I thought you implied he was murdered.' Her head was beginning to spin now, with the effort of keeping up with Christopher both mentally and physically, as he strode ahead leaving her stumbling over the rough ground behind him.

'No, never did that,' he threw over his shoulder at her.

'Damien then,' she tried once again desperately. 'Does the whole village know who killed him? Is it keeping silent for a reason?'

She had to get to the bottom of this, but Christopher must have remembered Matthew's orders, for he merely said, 'I don't know.'

For all his simplicity, Christopher was not lacking in intelligence, Georgia realized. He was the kind of person who remained dedicated to one course in life at a time. At present that was his mother. By extension, however, it was also the Fernbourne Five and Matthew Hunt.

'My father's hoping to ask your mother more about Shaw Cottage,' she said, trying to sound casual. 'It's a shame you didn't like Elfie Lane and had to move out.' Christopher made no comment, and so she persevered. 'When she died, didn't you consider moving back there?'

'I like my cottage better. Mum said it was good for me to be independent.'

Her brief glimpses of the interior of his cottage revealed nothing that suggested he was a fan of the Five, and plenty to suggest his parental upbringing. The hunting scene paintings on the walls and the off-putting cases of stuffed birds were down to his father and the watercolours and drawings of local scenes were all Birdie's. No sign of independence there.

'Even so, she must have been upset when you left.'

'Mrs Elfie was there.'

I'm making a pig's dinner of this, Georgia thought. Detectives were supposed to take control and here she was very much in her witness's wake. She was relieved when they reached the home, still not sure why he had demanded her presence in view of Matthew's edict. Peter was already installed with his chair next to Birdie – to Christopher's displeasure, Georgia noted. Birdie seemed even more frail than she had on her first visit. Perhaps frail wasn't the word. She looked brittle and autocratic. The beak nose was turned firmly towards her.

'I wanted to see you,' she announced, thus settling one puzzle. 'Do put that bag on the bed, darling,' she ordered Christopher and he hurried to obey. Birdie accepted the chocolates graciously, and the long elegant fingers closed around the box. Then it too was handed to Christopher for disposal.

'You were asking about Alwyn, weren't you?' Birdie took command of the situation, her quick eyes dancing everywhere. 'It seems everyone wants to know about him now. I won't have it.' She stabbed her finger impatiently at Peter. 'I've had Matthew here, Janie, even Madam Clemence arrived. Quite an honour. But that's enough. I've been told to say nothing and I shall not. My brother's dead, and he shall rest in peace. Is that understood?' She sank back against her cushion as though to indicate the interview was over.

'It might be hard to avoid talking about him,' Peter said

rationally. 'You're speaking at the opening of the manor next year. Alwyn was one of the Five, and so his name is bound to come up. A lot of people will be interested in him. That's the point of the ceremony.'

Brave words, Peter, Georgia thought.

Birdie seemed to cede the point. 'If it does, it does,' she said dismissively, with her quick glance and sly sideways smile, as though she were in a delightful conspiracy with her audience. 'But I don't have to talk about it now.'

'Not if you don't want to,' Peter agreed. 'There is a biography being written about Roy Sandford, however. You know about that?'

Birdie looked pleased with herself. 'She's been here too. Molly understands.'

'About your love for Roy?' Georgia put in.

The gaunt face was turned to her. 'Certainly. That's new and important. All you want to do is rake around the old pigsties.'

'If there's nothing in them, it should be no problem,' Peter said lightly. 'We hoped you might like to talk about the old days, even though you went through a bad time with your brother and—'

'What bad time?' she rasped indignantly.

'The rough music, when the villagers came to your home banging their pots and pans. Is that what Damien Trent wanted to ask you about?'

Her expression registered nothing. Her hands tightened on the arm of her chair, but all she replied was a flat, 'Yes.'

'Did you know Joe Baker?' Georgia tried.

'What does he have to do with anything?' she asked sharply.

'He led the rough music and probably incited it.'

Another pause. 'He was the butcher,' she said loftily. 'I do remember him.'

'Did you like him?'

'*Like* him? He was the butcher. Not my lover.' An amused tinkle of a laugh. Then, as if she realized this might give a bad impression, the charm was back. 'Joe was all right when you got to know him, and he had a lot to put up with from that dreadful daughter of his.'

'Jenny?'

A cool look. 'A minx, that girl.'

'She was the reason for the rough music.'

'She claimed Alwyn attacked her.'

'And did he?'

'Very probably.'

'But Alwyn loved Elfie.'

A scornful laugh this time. 'Elfie had a husband. Not that one would have known it. She was a strange one. She and her love-in-a-mist. Couldn't help liking her – until you saw the way the men fell at her feet in worship.'

Including Roy? Georgia suddenly wondered. Was that a reason for disharmony at Shaw Cottage? 'Clemence told us Elfie's parting from Gavin was amicable,' she asked, 'but that doesn't seem to fit with his idolizing her.'

'My dear girl, there was nothing amicable about the way Gavin used to barge up to the cottage demanding to know where they were copulating.' Another quick grin that dared them to rebuke her for her naughtiness. 'He wouldn't take no for an answer. He would storm into our house, search the gardens, search the bedrooms, until he found her and Alwyn together. Sometimes he did, sometimes he didn't. Ten to one they'd just be sitting hand in hand, or she'd be drawing him or he her.'

'You mean they didn't consummate their relationship?' Georgia asked incredulously.

'Goodness me.' A delicate hand was held up. 'Consummate indeed. Yes, they consummated it. They consummated it every opportunity they got, and there were many of those.'

'How do you know?' Peter asked with interest.

A laugh. 'You can't catch me, Mr Detective. You mean, did I see it with my own eyes? No, but I heard. And I lived with that woman for years, so I was told every detail, saw every photo of them.'

'Making love?' Georgia was taken aback.

'As good as. You look at some of her drawings of elves and pixies and you'll see Alwyn, all desire and lust. Look at the drawings of Alwyn himself – no, you can't. Or any of his drawings of Elfie. Master Matthew took everything to do with the Five away, as soon as they'd succeeded in putting me behind bars and her ladyship had died.'

'Why would he do that?'

Birdie looked tired but she rallied at this. 'He didn't want anyone to see his mama in the altogether, particularly with a pixie of her own at her side. Alwyn mooned over her like a lovelorn sheep.'

Georgia couldn't stand this. 'Yet he raped Jenny Baker.'

She thought she'd gone too far, but Birdie answered dispassionately. 'She asked for it. I told him she'd be trouble.'

'Did the rough music affect him?'

'Of course it did. What do you think?'

How did Birdie constantly manage to put her in the wrong? Georgia wondered. 'Why was the rough music so long after the event?'

'Don't ask me,' Birdie said. Then she frowned. 'I reckon Joe had only just found out. The girl wouldn't tell him straight off.'

'Elfie must have been upset by it. Even though she wasn't living with you then, she must have heard about it.'

'She didn't believe it.'

'But she chose to stay with Gavin,' Peter pointed out. 'Perhaps that was the reason.'

'Gavin was richer,' Birdie snorted.

Georgia tried another tack. 'Do you remember when the rape happened?'

Birdie looked at her as though she were out of her mind. 'How could I? She was at it all the time. The girl used to come to the house or garden all doe eyed and swaying hips. She was like the wicked witch of the east, unlike Madame Elfie who was . . . I can't remember.' She snapped her fingers in frustration. 'Billie Burke played her.'

'In *The Wizard of Oz*?' Georgia suggested.

'That's right. A GI bride she was . . .'

'I don't think so,' Georgia said gently, but Birdie was asleep. Or pretending to be. The audience was over.

'Vicars' wives seem to have changed from the stereotype I recall,' Peter remarked as they drove home, leaving Christopher still with his mother.

'Old age, perhaps,' Georgia said charitably.

'I'm inclined to think it's role-playing.'

'Why should it be?'

'Getting ready for next year perhaps. Hindsight can turn fantasies into reality. Perhaps she believes what's she saying, but I doubt if Matthew would encourage her to put over that view of Elfie in her big speech.'

'So we're still hovering in square one. Whatever that stream at Shaw Cottage had to tell us, we haven't yet discovered it. We need one more throw of the dice – Clemence.'

'Unfortunately the dice seem to have been confiscated by Matthew Hunt,' Peter said wryly. 'I still can't get to speak to her.'

The doorbell was ringing, but deep in the middle of Suspects Anonymous with Peter the next morning, Georgia left it to Margaret to answer. Suspects Anonymous was more accommodating now that they had put additional data in, although attempts to get hold of Alice were as futile as trying to track Clemence down. Georgia heard Margaret's cry of surprise, then a familiar voice, and rushed out herself.

'Luke, what on earth are you doing here?' Luke *never* took time off work to come to the Marsh & Daughter office, save for the occasional pub lunch, but at ten thirty in the morning, lunch was hardly on the agenda.

'You tell me.' Luke was torn between humour and barely suppressed frustration. 'It seems we're off to Canterbury. I've got Mrs Hunt, aka Clemence Gale, in the car.'

'How on earth did you manage that?' She thought at first he was joking.

'I didn't. She did. A taxi dropped her at Medlars. Apparently we're both needed at an art gallery in Canterbury.'

'But I can't—'

'Mrs Hunt says you can – and that I can too.' If Luke was going to abandon work then she obviously had to seize the opportunity fate had presented.

'Give me a moment to explain to Peter.' She rushed back into the office to grab her coat and shoulder bag, and returned, with Peter's full approval, plus a grumble about wheelchairs.

'I'm sorry,' Clemence said at once as Georgia climbed into the back of Luke's car. 'I believe you've been trying to get hold of me, so I want to make it clear that I can make my own decisions about what I do or don't do. All right?'

'By me, yes,' Georgia said, wondering why Clemence was forced to go to these lengths to escape her daughter's jurisdiction. There was no doubt about Clemence being in her right mind.

'On the other hand, I don't believe in going out of my way

to upset Janie or Matthew. I understand he's been warning Janie that I'm being pestered by you against my will, and issued instructions that I am to be gagged. I have therefore organized this entirely legitimate excursion. I have to visit Canterbury over some of my current work, so we can conduct our business over lunch.'

So that was it. Fortunately the business was fairly quickly dealt with, and at midday Georgia was relieved to see Clemence's short determined figure stomping back to the car park as arranged.

'And now,' Clemence proclaimed with satisfaction, 'for lunch. Janie has clear ideas about what I should eat and where, but luckily for you I have quite different ones. She favours healthy fare, I favour good food. There's a pub I've heard of about five miles away, if you'd be so good as to take me there. I have reserved a table.'

Clemence elected to eat on the terrace, to Georgia's pleasure, and even Luke seemed to have resigned himself to abandoning work for ever and a day.

'We won't see the sun much more this year,' Clemence said. 'So I honour it where I can.' Outside, with the glow on her face, she looked a lot younger than her age, and much more relaxed than at the manor.

'I heard you were both mixed up with the kerfuffle outside the King's Head the other night,' she continued. 'Matthew told me. I gather Sean was involved, and the police arrested him.'

'Yes,' Luke said grimly, 'and then released him on bail.'

'I doubt if he was as blameless as I've been led to believe.'

'No.'

'He was a nice lad once,' Clemence said reflectively, 'and before you tell me that so was Adolf Hitler, I don't think Sean is quite in that class. There was a little problem with drugs at one time, and now he needs another lesson. Being sent off to an IT training course doesn't seem to have achieved it.'

'He has an odd way of wooing the village maidens,' Luke said firmly. 'I take it you know Georgia had to save Emma from being throttled after the police released him.'

'No.' Clemence looked startled. 'Matthew didn't tell me that.'

'Luke . . .' Georgia began, intending to tell him to go easy on this, but it was too late. Luke was still fuming over the affair.

'Georgia had to intervene physically,' Luke told her flatly. 'Matthew no doubt would tell you it was an unprovoked attack.'

'The Hunts always protect their own, I'm afraid,' Clemence said wryly. 'I admit I don't see Georgia in the role of yob-cum-prize-fighter. Was Emma hurt?'

'Yes, but she seems to have recovered now though,' Georgia told her.

'I'll speak to the Bakers.'

Georgia seized the opportunity. 'It's not the first time that the Bakers have been linked to the Fernbourne Five, is it?'

Clemence's face sagged. 'Ah. I suspected from something Christopher said that that's what you wanted to see me about.'

'I'm afraid so.'

'Don't be afraid. You've every right to ask. I never thought you'd rootle the story out. It's been long buried. I take it we are talking about Jenny Baker?'

'You didn't think to tell us?'

'No,' Clemence replied. 'It might have been relevant to the reason that Alwyn committed suicide, but you were seeking reasons for murder.'

She wasn't getting away with that. 'This *does* provide a reason for murder,' Georgia said.

'How?' Clemence asked sharply. 'Jenny wasn't in the village when the rough music took place.'

'Her father was. Rough music might not have satisfied Joe Baker's desire for revenge.'

Clemence fell silent, and it was clear she was shaken. Eventually she said, 'It still seems to me like suicide. Poor Alwyn was so moody at that time. He was always the weak link of the group. Elfie was still with Gavin and after the plagiarism was revealed Alwyn hadn't much career to look forward to. On the other hand, I grant you Joe was a nasty piece of work. What about the physical evidence of murder?'

'Nothing to prove or disprove it. Were you in Fernbourne at the time?'

'I was. Birdie was in London; she'd gone to stay with her parents for the weekend, but Alwyn had fallen out with them over the plagiarism – not unnaturally – so he stayed behind. Birdie said he was in a strange mood and asked if I could go over and cheer him up. I couldn't. It was my mother's birthday and I was in Sevenoaks with my parents. So when Birdie rang me up in a state the next afternoon with the news, I assumed as we all did that it was suicide. I agree that theoretically Baker could have had a motive for killing him. Alwyn always looked so delicate but he had a strong will, and from hindsight I wouldn't have thought that went with suicide, but then I'm not a psychologist. Nor, again from hindsight, do I think those lines of verse he left for Birdie and Elfie would be his preferred farewell. He loved both of them, and it seems more likely he would have left letters.'

'Unless he assumed they would know his reasons all too well. Anyway, he'd been drinking—'

'Drinking?' she interrupted. 'Alwyn? Surely not. He almost never drank.'

'Perhaps in secret?'

'It's possible.' Clemence looked doubtful. 'Birdie still firmly believes it was suicide?'

'Yes.'

She thought for a moment. 'I should tell you about Jenny.'

'You knew her well?'

'We all did. She had great beauty plus a strange kind of fascination. She had magnetic eyes that seemed to draw you in and yet keep you at a distance at the same time. The perfect Mona Lisa type. That's why we used her as our model.'

So that was it. No wonder Clemence had been reticent on the subject. 'You said *our* model – not just yours then?'

'Very much not. We all used her – how terrible that word sounds in this context. I drew and painted her several times. Elfie used her a great deal and so did Roy. He was a poet first and foremost but he was a gifted book illustrator too. That was going out of fashion, but it still had a market.'

'What about Alwyn?'

'He did some illustration work too, and so did Birdie. In fact the only one of us whom she didn't model for was Gavin, although even he wrote the sultry village maiden into a novel once or twice.'

'Did she just visit you as a model or come to the meetings as well?'

'Sometimes the latter, if there was a discussion going on that concerned her pose or her use in a particular style of illustration or painting. She had a natural talent for posing and like Lizzie Siddal for the Pre-Raphaelites she became part of the Five's lives.'

'And yet no one mentioned her to us,' Georgia pointed out, 'even though we were taken round the manor.'

'There's a simple reason for that,' Clemence said immediately. 'She left the village late in 1940, very suddenly. Obviously, looking back, I realize she was pregnant, but Joe said she'd joined the women's forces and that was that. Life moved on fast and we were all moving in different directions because of the war, so we didn't notice – in a professional sense – that she was no longer there, until the war was over and we began our serious work again. We asked for her, and found out she hadn't returned to the village. We assumed she'd married and had no reason to connect her departure with the Fernbourne Five, until the whispers started going round. The better known we became for our post-war work, the less we thought back to those early days. The Jenny we knew belonged with those, so it was a shock when we heard about the rough music.'

'Didn't you think it strange that that took place so long after the event?'

'Yes,' Clemence replied. 'I talked to Joe and he said he'd only just learned the truth of it.'

So that confirmed Birdie's memory. 'And Alwyn? Did you talk to him?' Georgia asked.

'No. That was Gavin's business if anyone's.'

'Did *he* talk to Alwyn?'

'I don't know.' She looked at them almost in appeal. 'How could I? I was head over heels in love with Gavin and any meeting I sought with him alone would have Elfie hot on my trail.'

'But she no longer loved him.'

Clemence laughed. 'Georgia, Georgia . . . When did that ever stop jealousy? Come with me,' she continued briskly. 'I took a taxi to Medlars, but if you return me to my home after we've finished here, I'll show you Jenny's portrait. Now you know something about her, you need to understand more.'

Georgia didn't dare look at Luke, but she could sense his reaction: There goes the afternoon.

'And you, Luke, might spot a suitable jacket design for your reprints,' Clemence added.

'Thank you,' he managed to say with every appearance of truth.

Luckily, Georgia could see, once they were in the studio at the coach house, that he was genuinely interested on his own behalf. The attic space of the coach house formed a first floor, to which a solid staircase led. Part of it was converted into a studio, as in Shaw Cottage, and here canvases were stacked in piles against the walls. Clemence walked over to one of them, and selected the canvas she wanted, which Luke rushed to help her lift out and place on an easel.

It was an oil, about four feet by three, with a stylized elongated figure of a woman in a black dress on the left side of the picture, and in the background on the right behind her shoulder, an unidentifiable man in shadow.. His whole body language seemed to be straining to focus on the woman, who was posed sideways to the viewers, but whose head was turned with a sly smile towards them as though she shared some secret with them. Striking though the subject of the painting was, Georgia realized that it was in fact the man to whom the eye was drawn; it was he and not the woman who was disturbing. Was it he or she from whom the power stemmed?

'I called it "The Abdication",' Clemence remarked. 'After Mrs Simpson of course, and the late Edward VIII cum Duke of Windsor, although it was intended to have universal application. Gavin didn't like it, so I never sold it. Anyway, the moment had passed. George VI was on the throne and war was looming. Besides –' Clemence frowned – 'it never fully satisfied me.'

'It's hard to tell who the victim is and who the pursuer,' Georgia said. 'Did you mean that?'

Clemence looked at her. 'No,' she said, startled. 'And . . .' She looked at the painting again from a distance for a moment or two. 'I think that's it, Georgia. It's not the abdication at all, *or* the woman. It's a painting of a seducer.' A further pause. 'No, that's not it either. Stronger, stronger,' she said to herself. 'How odd. I didn't see . . .' Then she pulled herself together. 'Damien Trent wanted to know about Jenny Baker too. He was coming to see me. But he was murdered before he could do so.'

'Murdered, Clemence?'

The new voice took Georgia by surprise. Matthew Hunt had come up the stairs without their noticing, and Clemence, she could see, was not amused.

This seemed not to worry Matthew in the least. 'I heard you talking up here,' he said, his eyes on Georgia and Luke, 'and assumed it was Janie with you. Now I see it is Miss Marsh again. And did I hear Jenny Baker's name mentioned?'

'Probably,' Luke stepped in. 'Why not?'

Matthew looked uncertain. 'And you are?'

'The trust's prospective publisher, Luke Frost. I gather Jenny was the model for this painting?' Luke turned, rather ostentatiously, back to Clemence.

'Is that the painting my father so disliked?' Matthew asked, peering at it.

'It is,' Clemence said shortly.

'Then there's no way the trust could authorize its use.'

'Has that been put to the board?' Clemence asked crossly. 'Perhaps, Matthew, it's high time it was shown.' Her eyes were fixed on her stepson. 'Whatever its message.'

'Now, now, Clemence,' Matthew said jovially. 'You know you're only teasing.'

'I seldom tease where Gavin is concerned,' was her rejoinder.

'Nor I about the reputation of the Fernbourne Five.' Matthew's voice was becoming distinctly steely. 'Is that why Jenny Baker's name seems to have arisen again, courtesy of Miss Marsh?'

'Yes,' Georgia replied. There was a subtext here which she could not read – and that was obviously intentional. 'She provides one motive for Alwyn's murder.'

'Does Birdie agree? I'm sure you've wasted no time in acquainting her with your theory?'

'No. She believes Alwyn committed suicide.'

Matthew ignored her, concentrating on Clemence, who – reluctantly it seemed to Georgia – said, 'You appear not to have solid evidence to the contrary.'

'Nor ever will have,' Matthew declared easily. 'Just as well, as I'm sure Mr and Miss Marsh are certain that you, myself and Birdie are all in one vast conspiracy to keep them away from some ghastly secret that unfortunately has escaped us.'

'I'm sure that's right, Matthew,' Clemence said gently.

Another look passed between them, and Matthew said no more.

'I'm sure she was giving us a hint, Peter,' Georgia said, when she reported back to her father later.

'About what?'

'That there's more to this question of Jenny Baker and Alwyn than we thought.'

'Then why didn't she make it clearer?'

'Because she's loyal to the group.'

'That portrait you mentioned,' Peter said thoughtfully. 'Has it occurred to you that Clemence might be loyal not to the group, but to her late husband?'

Eight

'I don't buy it.' Georgia was adamant, even though Peter and she had argued on and off for most of the following day. 'Clemence wouldn't deliberately have dropped a hint that something was amiss if the clue led to Gavin. Your theory rests on the assumption that the anonymous man in the portrait of Jenny was Gavin. Clemence didn't say that. Only that he didn't like the picture. Ergo, it's no evidence against Gavin.'

'Not accepted,' Peter replied for the umpteenth time. 'Suspects Anonymous—'

'Is a computer program. Not a substitute for the human brain.'

'You're not usually so pretentious,' was the mild reply.

'I'm not usually so certain.'

Peter sighed. 'Don't give me the you-don't-understand-the-female-psyche line.'

'I won't, but I do think I understand the way Clemence works. If Gavin were involved in bringing about Alwyn's suicide or murder then she would say nothing likely to make us suspect he was.' Why on earth couldn't Peter admit that?

'Even if it meant someone else suffering?'

'Too general a supposition,' she retorted briskly.

'Very well. How about this for circumstantial evidence? Even you can't avoid acknowledging that Gavin was heavily involved in the events surrounding Alwyn's death. It was he who instigated the plagiarism accusation. It was his wife who was the subject of a tug of war between Alwyn and himself. And you said yourself that Clemence looked shaken at the suggestion that Alwyn's suicide really might have been murder.'

They were getting nowhere, Georgia thought in despair, and time was passing. Even though it was still warm enough for them to be sitting in the garden, the dying September sun

announced the onset of autumn. Spiders' webs shimmered in
the shrubbery, with their owners balefully sizing up their
chances of taking up residence in the house. The Michaelmas
daisies were drawing bees in their hordes. No sign of a
declining bee population here.

Decades ago the Fernbourne Five could have been sitting
in the manor grounds or Shaw Cottage in much the same
way as she and Peter today, and she wondered what stresses
and tensions would have been present amongst them that she
and Peter hadn't yet grasped. Perhaps there had been none.
Perhaps the hindsight of today's angst-driven lifestyle was
driving them to think there were. And yet poetry was born
out of emotion, and the creation of the Fernbourne Five had
led to tragedy one way or another for at least three of its
members.

'Suspects Anonymous,' Peter tried again, 'created by your
cousin, Georgia, and therefore not lightly to be dismissed,
puts Gavin in the next frame to Joe Baker's.'

'On what basis?' This threw her slightly. Much as she might
deride Suspects Anonymous, Peter was right. Anything that
Charlie produced had at least to be considered.

'Good old motive. We can't go back and do a crime scene
investigation, so we have to look at the most likely explanation first.'

'And that's still suicide,' Georgia muttered defiantly, whether
through mere rebellion or something more complicated. She
couldn't tell whether she might be drawing away from this
case for sound reasons or through her reluctance to face what
might be found. But if so, why?

She knew the answer was probably still Damien Trent. There
were passions now being reawakened, of which his murder
was likely to have been one manifestation. That made the path
ahead not only more dangerous, but at the same time inevitable
if she were ever to get rid of the guilt she felt for not having
probed further during her conversation with him. His face
seemed superimposed on every mental image she had about
the Fernbourne Five, but stepping into these dark woods of
the past now brought fear as well as challenge.

Peter disagreed. 'Murder. Assuming – as Mike now seems
to think – that Damien Trent was murdered possibly for his
family connection, but more likely for his investigations into

the Fernbourne Five, Alwyn Field's suicide or murder is highly relevant.'

'But Damien went to see Molly Sandford first. Which brings Roy into it.'

'Nevertheless, Birdie and Clemence were on his list and we have to start somewhere. I vote for Alwyn still. Let's assume his death was murder, with the proviso that the finger-prints on time could have been caused by the injustice of the allegations leading to suicide against him. I'd back murder all the way. There are *too many* oddities here. Dreamer poet turning rapist? Possible but unlikely. Idealist poet turning plagiarist? Same again. Romantic lover poet kills himself? Possible, but far more likely he would stay alive and write about how sad he felt. He wasn't rejected by Elfie as a person, remember. She still loved him despite the plagiarism, so we're told. We don't know her reaction to the rough music, but nevertheless while he was alive there was still some hope for the future.'

'I suppose so,' Georgia said reluctantly.

'So Gavin fits the frame for the murder. You said it was the man who dominated the painting, despite being in the background. If it was Gavin, he was most certainly a controller. Clemence wouldn't consciously have seen him that way, but that's not unusual for an artist, even if she were in love with him. Gavin had most to lose if Alwyn remained alive. Game, set and match?' Peter concluded complacently.

'Only,' she persisted, 'if Gavin still loved Elfie. But he loved Clemence.'

'Precisely,' he said triumphantly. 'Clemence said it was only later he loved her, but was it? Could I remind you that Elfie moved into Shaw Cottage *after* Alwyn's death? To mourn his memory? Possible, but another reason could just be, dear Georgia—'

'She'd discovered Gavin was in love with Clemence.'

Peter looked taken aback. 'Possibly, but even more prob-ably—'

Georgia saw immediately where this was justifiably leading and finished for him, 'Elfie had discovered Gavin had murdered Alwyn.'

'Any pleas for the defence?'

She was so shaken that for the moment she couldn't think

of any, but then she rallied. 'Yes. What motive would he have for murdering Alwyn in 1949? Elfie was living at home and looking after darling baby Matthew.'

'The affair could still have been going on,' he said reasonably. 'Anyway, do we know her reasons for staying with little Mattie?'

'Of course.'

'No. We only know the story as handed down and given in Matthew's book. Bearing in mind that Matthew was born – from memory, since the dratted book is in the house – in 1936, he would, assuming he followed his father's pattern of schooling, have been at boarding school by 1947, certainly by 1949.'

'You mean,' Georgia grappled with this theory, 'Gavin could have faked this plagiarism charge, hoping it would put Elfie off Alwyn, and when it didn't, and she then announced her intention of leaving him after all, he decided to spike her guns. Clemence's claim that he didn't care about Elfie was the party line.'

'Yes.'

'No.' Georgia immediately contradicted herself, determined to defend Clemence. 'There's the matter of the rape too. That might have put Elfie off, don't you think?'

'Suppose Gavin incited the rough music too? It was so long after the event that he could have stirred Joe Baker up by telling him who the father was, or of course lying to him.'

'I suppose so,' Georgia admitted.

'Shall we explore that thesis?'

'Yes, but I still don't think it's the right one.'

Peter slumped in his chair. 'Why on earth not?'

'Clemence,' Georgia said wearily. 'It all comes back to her. If she was giving us a hint, then I'm sure it couldn't have been pointing towards Gavin, but to something else.'

'Something in which Gavin could have been involved, even instigated?' Peter looked unconvinced.

'Yes.' Georgia watched a spider crawl back to the centre of its web. Who could have spun the Fernbourne Five's web better than Gavin? Peter had a point, and yet webs were intricate structures, intended to catch the unwary.

The manor looked solidly reassuring as Georgia and Luke drew up in front of it the next morning. The ground and grass were still wet from the dew as the sun hadn't yet reached them, but the shade was peaceful rather than threatening. The scene would make an imposing setting for next year's opening. She had seized the opportunity to come with Luke when he had told her he was meeting Janie in the library, so that he could look through the entire range of the Five's work. It was Saturday, and Molly was at a conference, but she had agreed that Georgia could come with him. 'After all, it's mostly published stuff, even though it's not yet out of copyright,' Luke had pointed out. He had been somewhat guarded over his enthusiasm for Georgia's company this morning, but had eventually given way.

Janie was positively friendly, perhaps because she saw Luke first, Georgia thought meanly. Or perhaps, it occurred to her, it was because Janie lived too much in Clemence's shadow, and a solo appearance allowed her space for her own identity. Who could blame her for that?

'You're lucky,' Janie told them. 'The library is one of the few rooms we've finished working on. It was my father's study, so already well equipped with bookshelves. We've kept his desk, and added a showcase. The room through there –' she pointed to an inner door – 'is to be a computer and study room, but that's still on the waiting list.'

'Do you have any unpublished material here?' Luke asked, as she showed them around.

'I doubt if there's anything you'd think worthy of printing, but you're welcome to have a look. Most of the manuscript stuff is still in the study room, waiting to be sorted. I'll be making a start soon. I'm already in overall daily charge of the centre,' Janie added, with modest pride. 'Whose work are you particularly interested in?' she asked Luke.

'I've made an offer for *A Mourning in Spring* and *Verses for Dorinda*. That takes care of representing both Alwyn and Roy. I really want *The Flight of the Soul*, of course, but Molly's talking that one over with the trust.'

A recipe for going nowhere, Georgia thought.

'I'd like to get to grips with Elfie's work today,' Luke continued. 'That's been rather overlooked.'

Georgia thought she could see why. Elfie somehow tended to float in and out of her general picture of the Five. Perhaps that was because there wasn't much in her work for today's readership. From the look of the shelves and showcase here, Elfie had been a prolific writer. The showcase displayed an open children's book of poems with charming line illustrations, like the ones she had seen on the Internet.

'I can guess how many that sold,' Luke commented wryly.

'Quite well, perhaps,' Georgia suggested. 'It would sell to adults buying for children, poor things.'

'The originals of the illustrations would fetch a good sum on the market today, but I wouldn't think a reprint would go far,' Luke said. 'They're way out of fashion now. Elfie was a hangover from Eleanor Farjeon and Walter de la Mare. Not exactly mass-market material for the computer game generation.'

'I think this is her weirdest,' Janie called from behind them, waving a slim volume which she handed to Luke. Georgia peered over his shoulder.

'*The Woods Beyond the Stream*,' Luke read out, which gave Georgia an instant foreboding. Which stream? Which woods?

'It was written in the fifties,' Janie explained, 'after Alwyn's death, and when Elfie was living at Shaw Cottage.'

The stream must surely be *that* stream, then. And the woods, *those* woods, where Georgia had sensed a silent watcher waiting for her. Sensed or imagined? Georgia couldn't be sure now, but now she suspected that those woods might have been as creepy to Elfie as they were to her. She took the book from Luke, while he went to another bookcase, and looked through the illustrations. It was all she could do to stop herself from handing the book straight back to him. It had skilled line drawings with firm black curves and shapes, binding the trees and the mischievous faces peering through them into one. Mischievous? Bordering on evil in some of them. It was difficult to tell whether human or supernatural eyes were watching in Elfie's woods, but neither boded well for those caught lingering. Were they the spirit of the wood or Elfie's own nightmares, perhaps about Alwyn's death? The thought was not a pleasant one. Poems for children though? Hardly. One caught her eye:

> The stream hurries by
> And so do I
> Lest those woods so dark

Reach out to seize me
It's best by far to hurry by . . .

'Not guaranteed to win prizes,' she said ruefully. She couldn't see Luke reprinting this one. Come to that, she thought idly, she couldn't see Luke himself. Where had he vanished to? 'I suppose the ideas and illustrations might have had a fascination for children in the same way as Disney villains.'

'Elfie would have agreed with you,' Janie said, obviously pleased at her judgement.

'Even so, it's a dated concept.' Where *was* Luke?

'There are other possibilities,' Janie said. 'Elfie wrote one or two children's novels in the late fifties rather like Mary Norton's or Norman Hunter's, once she was over Alwyn's death. They were working up towards Roald Dahl's style but not so sophisticated then, of course. And there's this one.' She picked a very thin volume off the shelf and handed it to Georgia. 'This one was a complete flop. *Flowers*, it's called.'

Georgia's stomach turned. Each illustration and poem was of a different flower, but the flowers held only ugliness. The rose petals curled round an ugly mocking face; the lupin held a black elf with frightening menacing eyes; the hollyhock carried a worm in every bloom. And . . . she turned the pages . . . of course. Love-in-a-mist concluded the small booklet – but the poem was called 'Black Seeds'.

> Love needs its gentle mist
> Lips only to be kissed
> For when the veil is drawn
> Black seeds spill upon the earth
> But give no second birth
> For love lies bleeding and forlorn
> Ah it needs its gentle mist.

'This must have been written after Alwyn's death.' Georgia was repelled, remembering Birdie quoting from it. Love is blind. She wondered if Elfie had believed the story about Jenny Baker.

'It was published in 1950. She was bitter about his suicide. She felt betrayed,' Janie said.

'Is that the trust's view or yours?' Georgia asked pointedly, but before Janie could answer, they were interrupted.

'Could I ask why, *once again*, you are present, Miss Marsh?'

Matthew Hunt's furious voice from behind made her jump, and she turned to see the guardian of the party line with a look as angry as his voice.

She bit back her first reply, aware that Luke was back with them now, holding one of the Elfie books that they had been looking at. Keep it cool, she told herself. 'Certainly you may, Mr Hunt. I'm looking at the library with Mr Frost, with Molly Sandford's permission.'

He pointedly ignored her. 'I was told a publisher was coming, Janie, not Miss Marsh.'

Janie proved to be of sterner stuff than Georgia had given her credit for. 'Why shouldn't she be here, Matthew? The manor and its collections will be open to the public next year.'

This was ignored too. 'If Molly gave you permission, she was wrong to do so, Miss Marsh. There are private family papers here and as you are intent on sabotaging the reputation of the Fernbourne Five, I'd be grateful if you would kindly leave.'

There was the snap of a book closing. 'We'll both leave, Mr Hunt,' Luke said smoothly. 'I like to know what and whom I'm dealing with before I issue contracts. A disunited board doesn't bode well.'

If Luke had expected Matthew to retreat from his position, he was obviously mistaken. The full force of Matthew Hunt's displeasure was turned on him, as he replied venomously: 'There are other publishers, Mr Frost.'

'Indeed there are,' Luke agreed. 'And you are most welcome to find them. The trust should consider my previous offers to Miss Sandford withdrawn.'

'Was it something I said?' asked Georgia weakly, once they were outside. 'I'm sorry I caused this. You don't really want to pull out, do you?'

'Half and half. The half of me that publishes good Kentish books would like to start a Kentish classics list, and with a ready-made outlet like this, it's very tempting.'

'And the other half?'

Luke put on a mock growl. 'No one speaks to my girl like that.'

'Nonsense,' Georgia said evenly. 'Now tell me the truth.'

'The trouble is that living with a person leads to their reading you too well,' he complained. 'I'll come clean. While you were peering into books with Janie, I wandered into the next room. If you think I have a problem with storage, have a look there. There were boxes everywhere, and I happened to peer into a trunk marked "Elfie". In the middle of a lot of very strange drawings I found a file marked *The Flight of the Soul*. I picked up one of the sheets inside to have a look and then found another batch of papers at the back of the file, with the top one visible.'

'So?'

'Both had verse written on them. The handwriting was different, but the poem was the same.'

Georgia thought about this. 'Alwyn would have copied Roy's work in manuscript, not just typed them, if he wanted to do a thorough job. Since Roy was dead, he could hardly have copied Alwyn's work. So where does that take you?'

'I don't know yet.'

'*Yet?*'

'I took them to compare, and pinched a couple more as well.'

'You *what*? Is this really Luke the let's-follow-every-letter-of-every-law man who stands by my side?' Georgia was astounded.

'Let's say Luke the very-cautious publisher. At that point I was still publisher-elect for these books, but any sniff of a copyright problem and I run a mile.'

'With the evidence in your pocket, it seems.' Georgia began to laugh.

'I always thought,' Peter said approvingly, having heard this story over Sunday lunch at Medlars, 'that you would make a superb son-in-law.'

'Peter!' Georgia said in warning.

'I agree,' Luke meekly contributed.

'Shall we look at these again?' Georgia wasn't going to get drawn on to personal territory, and Peter should know that by now. She refused to be bullied. 'Can we tell by ourselves which is the original, and which is the copy, or do we get them compared by a graphologist? Cousin Charlie knows one, I think.'

'We'll do both.'

'We can have a good try now.' Once lunch was out of the way, Georgia pored over the scripts that Luke had laid before them on the table.

'While you were nicking these, Luke,' she said ruefully, 'you might have pinched something else in Alwyn's or Roy's handwriting, so that we could compare them.'

'Funny you should say that,' Luke rejoined. 'I also pinched this book autographed by Roy. That should give us a clue.'

Peter was ignoring this exchange in favour of scrutinizing the four pieces of paper. 'I know I'm prejudiced in favour of unlocking some dastardly secret here,' he said finally, 'but look at this.' He pointed to one of the poems. 'The word perchance has been scrawled out and the word perhaps written in above it.'

'Your meaning, sir?' Georgia asked.

'Look at the correction. The "e" is heavier than the rest of the word in this copy, but the writing is even in the other copy. It's thicker in this one, as if not done the first time to the writer's satisfaction. And further down the same thing has happened with the letter "r". There are similar examples in the other two sheets.'

'You mean these alterations were faked? Flimsy evidence,' Georgia decided.

'Why? The four sheets of paper are in two different handwritings. Two of them have to be copies and two the originals. The question is, which – and why,' Luke said reasonably. 'Either we have Roy's originals and Alwyn's fakes, or vice versa. The heavier marking on the amendments would be the indication of which came second. They don't necessarily have to be Alwyn's set just because Roy died earlier.'

For a moment Georgia didn't follow his reasoning, but then she understood. 'You mean if it's Roy's handwriting that has been forged, then it was a deliberate plot against Alwyn.'

Peter chortled. 'All right, let's look at the autograph in Roy's book, Luke,' he said, and Luke brought *Verses to Dorinda* over to the table where they could all see it.

'These two,' Peter said, after studying the handwriting in the book, 'are Roy's – or rather the ones that *look* like his handwriting.' He was pointing to the ones with the heavier ink amendments.

'Oh, glory,' Georgia said softly. 'And Alwyn's – provided that *is* his handwriting, and it seems pretty certain – is this set. Two of the originals that he couldn't find when the accusations were made.'

'Which means the plagiarism charge was trumped up,' Peter said flatly. 'We need that graphologist, Georgia.'

Mike's arrival on the doorstep of Medlars early on a Monday morning was unexpected.

'Social visit?' Georgia asked in surprise. 'Either way, there's coffee on the go. Come in.'

'Work, but coffee helps.' Mike followed her into the kitchen.

'On what front?' she asked, doling out spoonfuls of coffee into the cafetière. She was no expert on coffee, but Mike was, unfortunately, and so she always tried her best.

'Damien Trent. Could you run me through that conversation one more time? I know I've got the words down but the intonation might help.' He listened carefully and then asked, 'And he was really interested in Alwyn Field, not just that he happened to be passing?'

'It could be,' she said fairly, 'but I'm reasonably sure not. He'd gone so far as to think it odd that Elfie didn't move in until after Alwyn died. And after all he visited Birdie Field and Molly Sandford, plus he had a visit booked in with Clemence Gale. Pretty conclusive. Why?'

'You might not like this. Trent seems to have had some family connection with the Bakers after all, so it could just have been a research visit to Fernbourne, with a passing interest in anything to do with the Five.'

'You mean he was adopted?'

'No, but his father was. Trent's mother has been spending time going through all her late husband's stuff at my request. Eager to help, she said. Well, she has helped. She came up with the fact that in 1976, the year before she married Philip Trent, he had discovered, thanks to the new laws giving him the right to investigate his parentage, that he had been adopted and his mother's name was indeed Baker. Jenny Baker.'

At last! Georgia felt a lurch of excitement. 'That's good news, a definite link at last.'

'What comes next, you'll find even better,' Mike said, 'although it doesn't fill me with rapture. She found notes he'd

been working on before his marriage. Something must have
led him to connect his blood mother with the Fernbourne Five,
and he paid a visit to Fernbourne, during which—'

'He saw Joe Baker.' Of course. Surely this must be the
mysterious 'chap' of the seventies whom Ken had mentioned.
Her excitement grew. 'Why didn't he tell his wife he was
adopted? Presumably Damien found out through him?'

'Maybe Joe Baker warned him off the story.'

'*Yes*. You know, Mike, you're not a bad policeman.'

'Thanks. And you make lousy coffee.'

'He warned him off because he murdered Alwyn,' Georgia
reasoned. 'He could even have told him that, or more likely
Philip guessed that he had done it. Who else, after all? Philip
didn't mention it to his new wife, because he didn't want to
confess that his grandpa was a murderer.'

'I take it Joe Baker is therefore still on your list of possible
suspects – *if* there was a murder.'

'A very short list of two, and he heads it.'

'It adds up, but as he's no longer alive, and there's no proof,
we can't even add a note to the file.'

'You can't write it off, Mike, not with Damien's death
unsolved,' she said in alarm.

'I knew you'd say that,' he said glumly.

'What about Sean Hunt?'

'Situation as it was. His alibi holds up, and he claims the
gun was stolen. Any one of the lads in the village could have
pinched it. The shed wasn't locked.'

'He admits to having one?'

'Had to. Several witnesses finally agreed he'd been larking
around with it. He says it disappeared around the time of the
murder. Very convenient.'

'Any doubt that was the murder weapon found on the scene?'

'Still some at present. There are indications of glove prints,
but there's a chance of latent fingerprints underneath. The
lab's still working on it. But you'd expect there to be Sean's
fingerprints on it, so we're no further forward.'

'Do you still want to go ahead with the poetry reprints if the
problems can be sorted?' Georgia asked Luke on the Monday
evening.

'If they come to me, I'll consider it, but since the main one

I'm interested in is *The Flight of the Soul*, this copyright issue will have to be well and truly sorted first. How long will it take?'

'I took the poem scripts to Charlie today, so we'll have to give it a week at least. I know time's running short. It's already October and with the opening in June you'll have to move quickly.'

'The advantage of being a small outfit is that I can do just that. Speaking of moving quickly, it's time for dinner.' Luke smiled at her. 'One thing though: I see no reason not to encourage Marsh and Daughter on this project.'

'Encourage as in contract?' she asked, surprised.

'Maybe next month. I'm still a bit pushed till I can repay the bank loan.'

This reminded her uncomfortably that she still had not decided about the house. Selling it wouldn't be a cure for Luke's problems, but it would provide a comfortable personal reassurance once the cash was banked. Perhaps he saw her hesitation, because he joked: 'Plenty of dark woods beyond my stream at present. Good job I'm well armoured.'

It didn't seem a joke to her. Elfie's dark woods could well have been the dark shadow hanging over Alwyn's death. If Peter was right and Gavin was in the frame for murder, as well as Joe Baker, it would explain why she fretted in silence and produced that book a year or two later.

'If *The Flight of the Soul* is ruled out, would you still want to publish the other books?' she asked.

'At the moment I wouldn't want to touch anything controlled by those trustees under Mr Hunt's leadership until I'm sure there are no submerged icebergs. Between them those trustees have a lot of axes to grind, but I'm not sure they're grinding the same way. I can't see how they can hold the copyright, but they're throwing their weight around, which translates into trouble.'

Luke decreed he would cook supper so Georgia fulfilled her table-setting duties, much relieved at his reply. Moving the usual small pile of books off the table she saw it included another of Elfie's books, which seemed earlier than *The Woods Beyond the Stream* although it predated the need for a copyright line with the year of publication. Certainly the style was lighter. In this one – *Princesses I Have Known* – stories were mixed with poems and charming colour illustrations. One in particular caught her attention, a scene of bluebells – no, it was love-in-a-mist, of course. Elfie's flower. With mixed feelings, she remembered the poem in that disastrous publication Janie had shown her. This book was different. Between the flower heads on the frontispiece was a beautiful princess, with a crown of tiny flowers, her loose hair glowing in sunshine, and her face intent on the goldcrest pecking at her side. There was something about the expression on the face and tilt of the head that she couldn't quite place, and she put the book aside. But then, as Luke brought the supper in, it came to her.

'It's Alice Laycock,' she exclaimed in surprise.

'Chicken risotto actually.'

'This drawing, stupid.' She snatched the book up and showed it to him.

'Could be,' he agreed, as he set the dish down. 'If so, she was a looker, wasn't she?'

Georgia was certain now. The elusive Alice had been a model for the Five too, perhaps replacing Jenny. Ted, her husband, was now a trustee. Was that coincidence, or just the endless circle of village life? But either way, did that bind Alice into the web of the Fernbourne Five story?

Nine

Georgia had still had no luck in speaking to Alice. She had hoped that by ringing reasonably early in the morning she might do better, but it appeared that Alice was 'off-colour' and couldn't be troubled with visitors today. Especially her, Georgia had ruefully realized. There were compensations, however. It was Wednesday and over a week had passed without news from Charlie Bone, but when she answered a ring at Peter's doorbell, she found Charlie waiting.

'Morning, Georgia. Uncle Pete up yet?'

'Uncle Pete most certainly is,' came a roar from within. 'Margaret,' he called through to the kitchen where she was busy preparing his lunch, 'our guest has arrived. Let wine and cakes be brought forth.'

'Green tea will do.' Charlie followed in Georgia's wake, as Margaret appeared from the kitchen bearing a tray of cups and biscuits, always ready to hand if Charlie was coming. She had a soft spot for him, deeming him an influence for the good in her constant battle to get Peter to eat healthily.

'About that Fernbourne lot again, is it?' Margaret enquired of Charlie. 'Funny folk there. Always happens to places out in the wilds.'

'You make it sound like the backwoods of the Rocky Mountains, Margaret.' Georgia took the tray from her, reflecting that maybe Margaret wasn't too far off the truth.

'Where Fernbourne's concerned,' she replied darkly, 'I reckon it is. I had an aunt lived there once. All twisted up they are, like bindweed.'

Georgia agreed. With Alice unexpectedly turning out to be part of the inner group, this case was proving one of ever-decreasing circles – although she hoped with a more positive outcome than its proverbial one.

'Ahem,' Charlie put in plaintively, 'I take it no one is particularly interested in my news?'

'I am,' Georgia declared promptly, handing him the plate of Margaret's home-made biscuits. (Snacks were apparently excluded from Charlie's rules for healthy eating, as were his mother's eclairs.)

'I've an unofficial report from Rob Lawley on those handwriting samples – unofficial because no one paid him to do it,' Charlie announced.

'I owe you, Charlie,' Peter said gratefully.

'Good.'

'Now can I see it?'

Charlie handed it over, and munched his way onwards while Peter read it, with Georgia peering over his shoulder. 'So,' Peter said, 'preliminary tests indicate that there's something here to get to grips with.' He breathed a sigh of satisfaction. 'Samples One and Two are copies of Samples Three and Four; and Samples One and Two –' he double-checked – 'are those that appear to be in Roy's handwriting and therefore are almost certainly forgeries. So all we need to do is check is that Samples Three and Four are indeed Alwyn's originals.'

'*Almost* certainly?' Georgia queried.

'It's not conclusive,' Peter said regretfully. 'Roy could have copied these two poems for some reason before he died.'

Charlie coughed ostentatiously. 'But *this* is conclusive, unless you've got the master forger of all time at work here.' Charlie dangled a second envelope before them. 'The lab report on the paper – you owe Rob for this too, incidentally. As you'll see, all samples are written on cheap flimsy paper, which seems consistent with wartime paper rationing, but the watermarks clearly date Samples One and Two to the later 1940s, and Samples Three and Four to the early forties.'

'So *prima facie* it looks as if the plagiarism issue was a trumped-up charge,' Peter said delightedly. 'Charlie, I shall make you an honorary member of Marsh and Daughter for this.'

'Seconded,' Georgia chimed in.

'No way,' Charlie said promptly. 'Too much like hard work. So if the charge was trumped-up, who's your trumper?'

'Only one candidate with reason to do it, although as yet unproven,' Peter said immediately. 'Gavin Hunt.'

'That novelist bloke?'

'It is indeed that novelist bloke. The head of the Fernbourne Five. Father of the present chair of the trustees for the Fernbourne Trust, whose grand opening of the arts centre is in eight months' time.'

'Another fine mess you've got yourselves into,' Charlie said cheerfully. 'How's Suspects Anonymous doing with it?'

'A lot better now that we can feed your news into it.' Peter looked gleeful. 'There are some other useful indications too.'

Were there? Grateful though she was to Charlie, Georgia could see quicksand ahead – especially where Clemence was concerned. How would she take it if it turned out to be true that Gavin had faked the evidence? And even worse, suppose Gavin had had an eager helper in Clemence? No, that she could not believe.

Nor could Luke believe it when Georgia told him of this new development that evening.

'Clemence won't incriminate Gavin, that's for sure,' he said, 'and I don't see her a party to it.'

'Nor do I.' Georgia sighed. 'Will you speak to Molly or shall we? She'll have to know.'

'I suppose I'll have to, even though I've served notice of withdrawal of my offer.' Luke frowned. 'It's odd I haven't heard from her.'

'Perhaps Matthew never passed on your ultimatum.'

'He did. I spoke to Molly after that fiasco.'

'You didn't tell me.'

'Compartments, Georgia. We have to have them. She said she'd smooth things over.'

'To which you replied . . .?'

'That I'd consider my position then. Since when, silence. So now is an excellent time to call about this,' he decided.

'Even though it's not cast-iron proof?'

'That's the best thing about it,' Luke said firmly. 'I'll call tomorrow.'

The pie for supper was no sooner ready than there was a call, however, and Georgia froze when she heard the familiar deep voice. What did Clemence want? Surely Charlie's news couldn't have reached her yet?

'I'm sorry Mr Frost had backed out of his desire to reprint

the Five's work, Georgia. I'm doing my best to make Matthew see sense,' was all Clemence appeared to have telephoned to say.

'He didn't back out. He was put in a position where he had no alternative.' Georgia was rewarded by seeing Luke's nod of approval. 'He's still in touch with Molly, however.'

She expected to hear Clemence's amused chuckle at her diplomatic reply, but it didn't come. Instead: 'One other matter. Janie tells me that someone has disturbed the scripts in the proposed study room. The cleaner perhaps.'

Another truthful answer, even if a specious one. 'Certainly not me, Clemence. I didn't get as far as the manuscripts before I was thrown out,' she replied. 'But as that is to be a study room, would there be a problem if I had?'

A silence, then a sigh. 'My dear Georgia, when dealing with the past, there is *always* a problem where the successors are concerned. I wish you well, but I'm afraid Davids don't automatically win against Goliaths.'

Phew. Georgia realized that her hand was trembling as she put down the receiver.

'Well done,' Luke said.

'Not so well done. Clemence is a sharp lady. She knows about your scavenging in the study room, although I doubt if Janie could tell that anything is actually missing. She's warning us that the trust has too much at stake to stop the steamroller now.'

'They are all going to know very shortly, and the steamroller will start anyway. Do you mind?'

Georgia considered this. 'That's a problem Dorothy Sayers once posed in one of her crime novels: does one follow the truth no matter what, or let it pass by for the best of emotional reasons?'

'You think you'll have a clash here?'

She nodded. 'A loud one.'

'Justice for Alwyn Field against your liking for Clemence?'

'More than that. Justice for Damien Trent,' she said soberly. 'Would you think it pretentious if I said that he's handed me the baton, and I can't drop it?'

Luke took her into his arms. 'No. I'd say you had no choice.'

Next morning she waited in Peter's office on tenterhooks, hoping to hear that Luke had spoken to Molly. She even manufactured an excuse to return to Medlars when she couldn't stand the waiting any longer. Luke saw through this ploy right away.

'She's out,' he said briefly.

Damn. All day? All week perhaps? A horrible thought. Was Molly at the Frankfurt Book Fair – that was usually about this time in October. She rushed back to the office and checked the Internet. No, that was last week. She could hardly return to Medlars again, so she forced herself to consider other paths to follow to keep her mind off Molly. Was Alice still 'off-colour'? Pursue the Damien Trent case? Not until Mike gave them permission. What then?

'Stop drumming your fingers on the desk,' Peter said crossly. 'You're disturbing me.'

'At what?' she retorted. 'Suspects Anonymous?'

'No problem with that. At last it's showing a healthy interest in this case. Two icons, Joe Baker's and Gavin Hunt's, have been slugging it out for top place for Field's murder, and now Gavin Hunt has won by a small margin.'

'And that's good news?' she asked ironically.

He looked at her in surprise. 'At least it's a tenable thesis.'

Normally she would be tackling him with the 'what ifs' and 'whys'. Now she couldn't. Everything seemed to stop still with Molly Sandford, and she told Peter so.

'I see why you're worried. It's Clemence. You're afraid she could have been involved.'

'Exactly,' she said gratefully.

'I'm inclined to think not, but all we can do until we hear is go back to Alwyn Field, still the centre of the puzzle. What do you suppose he made of all this, assuming he was the real author? He would have known he was being stitched up. He must have been fighting his corner very hard – especially when he discovered the original scripts had disappeared. The Five would have been in and out of each other's houses all the time, so they could have been pinched from the Shaw Cottage studio, or he could have taken them to Gavin Hunt when he first raised the charge of plagiarism. We only have hearsay evidence that he said the originals were lost. Then Hunt did the dirty on him.'

Yes.' She took a leap forward. 'And suppose the rape charge was also false.'

Peter looked interested. 'With Joe incited by Gavin to lay
on the rough music? Are you suggesting Gavin was the father?'

The man in the portrait, yes, but Georgia hadn't got as far
as thinking of Gavin as Jenny's rapist. Surely that wasn't
possible. She felt as if she were fighting her way through a
Kafka-type web in this case from which there was no escape.
The ring of her mobile made her jump and she answered it
shakily.

'I thought you might like to know,' Luke's voice informed
her, 'that I've just spoken to Molly.'

'Did all hell break loose?'

'In a brisk, clipped way, yes.'

'And?'

'She'll be in my office at ten tomorrow morning.'

'What about the trustees?'

'Subject to availability, they'll meet tomorrow afternoon.
Either way, if Molly agrees there's a case to answer, they'll
be there. If she doesn't, I can shut up and get lost, while they
meet to decide a different course of action over the reprints.'

'Sounds risky to me. Don't hand that evidence over, will
you? I can see the whole lot disappearing.'

'Strangely enough, I trust Molly, though I share your cynical
thoughts. She won't tell the trustees about the plagiarism
charge until the meeting.'

'I wouldn't put it past Matthew to dash off and destroy
everything if he sniffs something afoot. He can't have known
it was there.'

'He'd have to reckon with Janie and Clemence, who—'

'Are unknown factors,' Georgia finished for him, wondering
whether her head or her heart would win this particular battle.
She ended the call and told Peter the news. 'So where does
that leave us?'

'In a hole if the trustees stand firm over the poems being
Roy's,' he replied. 'The onus of proof would be on us if we
went ahead with our book claiming otherwise, and I doubt if
our publisher would like that.'

'And Molly Sandford? She has her biography at stake. Roy's
reputation centres on *The Flight of the Soul*. She won't abandon
that lightly. The best cards are in their hands.'

'Then we need an ace.'

*   *   *

'What do you want to see her for?' Ted Laycock's voice was mild, but there was no getting past his stalwart presence behind the King's Head bar, guarding the door to the private quarters. Perhaps that was reasonable, since Alice was distinctly eccentric, and he must see himself as her guardian. Unable to bear the tension of waiting to hear from Luke about the outcome of his meeting with Molly, she had decided to take the bull by the horns and present herself on the Laycock doorstep. Despite Adam's more sympathetic presence while he was cleaning up the previous night's detritus, it seemed her journey was once again in vain.

'I was looking at Elfie Lane's illustrations,' she answered truthfully, 'and wondered whether Alice had been her model. There's a similarity of features.'

His eyes grew hard. 'You think so? No, Miss Marsh. Whether she was or wasn't, I won't have you raking up those days for her.'

To Georgia's surprise Adam spoke up in her defence. 'Won't do any harm, Grandpa. She's always talking about her Elfie anyway.'

'And what do you know about it?' Ted turned on him angrily.

Adam was made of sterner stuff than Georgia had given him credit for. 'As much as you,' he rejoined. 'You were only a kid in those days.'

'I was sixteen or seventeen.'

Adam shrugged. 'There you are then. You're always telling me I'm a kid.'

'Shut up, lad,' Ted said, not unkindly. 'You don't know what you're talking about.'

'What *are* we talking about?' Georgia asked politely, and slightly puzzled. 'I only want to talk to your wife about Elfie Lane, and you'll both be doing a lot of that next year anyway. You can't have a grand opening in silence.'

'Alice is out,' Ted said quietly and with that the subject was closed.

Frustrated, Georgia finished her coffee and went across to the shop to buy some toothpaste. That was her ploy in the hope of seeing Emma, but that too failed. Someone she didn't recognize was behind the counter, and told her the family was in Canterbury. Feeling it was one of those days when the world was against her, she returned to the church car park where she had left her car.

'Cuckoo!' came a voice from behind the churchyard wall, as she unlocked the door. It startled her but when she turned there no sign of anyone – at first anyway. Then a woolly red hat emerged, followed by Alice's face. Alice then strolled down to the gate into the car park and walked up to Georgia, peering into her face. 'Adam said you wanted a chat.'

'Ted didn't think it would be a good idea,' Georgia said doubtfully. If Alice were really unhinged, then she would win no brownie points from Fernbourne for taking advantage in this way.

Alice snorted. 'Come on, let's go.'

'Go where?' Georgia felt she was definitely losing the plot.

'Where do you think? The cottage. Adam's taking us.' She cackled, obviously seeing Georgia's bewilderment. 'Passed his test last week, he did. Come on, we'll cut over to Long Lane.' Beckoning to Georgia, she marched back through the churchyard and across the road to the footpath along which Georgia had walked with Christopher.

After a hundred yards or so, however, Alice branched off to join the tarmacked road. Here, parked in the gateway to a field, Adam awaited them, sitting proudly in the driving seat of an ancient Peugeot.

'I bought it for him,' Alice told her matter-of-factly. 'His dad don't know he's got it yet.'

'I wouldn't like to be in your shoes when Bob does find out,' Georgia laughed.

'Dad's all right,' Adam told her. 'It's Granddad has funny ideas, doesn't he, Gran?'

'He does that all right,' Alice agreed. 'Not the only one in Fernbourne either.'

Georgia climbed into the back, Alice into the passenger seat, and Adam set off with the confident driving of one to whom all dangers of the road are for other drivers. Georgia calculated that thankfully the distance to Shaw Cottage must be relatively short, even though Adam was following the lane to Birdie's retirement home, which must join up further along with the route Georgia knew. Catching a glimpse of Clemence at the front door of the home as they shot past it, Georgia was amused that today at least Clemence seemed to have had no difficulty in escaping Janie's ministrations. Perhaps it was just Marsh & Daughter on Janie's list of forbidden visitors – and no prizes for who would have ordered that. Clemence wasn't looking their way, but even so Georgia found herself instinctively ducking. The last person she wanted a chat with before the question of the plagiarism had been resolved was Clemence.

Alice had also noticed Clemence. 'Sat for her too, I did, but I wasn't good enough for her. Only used me once, she did. Said I was too pretty. Blooming cheek.'

'Wasn't that a compliment?'

'That lady,' Alice said darkly, 'isn't into compliments. Rules the roost, she does. Even Mr Matthew's scared of her. Stop here, Ad,' she commanded. 'We'll walk the rest. I like the view,' she explained as she climbed out. 'Remember walking up this lane in the spring. Used to love it. Smothered in primroses, and lady's smock everywhere.'

Adam sauntered behind them, whistling. Unusual nowadays, Georgia thought, uneasily remembering that whistling in the wood.

'Why did you want to come here today?' Georgia asked Alice, receiving a sharp look for her pains.

'You asked about the old days,' she replied. 'Modelling and that. Here's where I did it.'

'Was that before Alwyn died or afterwards?' Georgia's hopes rose. This could be the lifeline to Elfie that she had needed.

'Both. Posed for him, posed for Birdie, but it was Mrs Elfie I loved, poor thing. "Come on, Alice," she'd say. "Who've you bin kissing today? Do tell." Or she'd say, "Pretend you're off to meet your Ted. I want your eyes all soft and dreamy." Sometimes she'd say, "I want you evil today, Alice. All woman." No problem about that, I can tell you.'

She stopped with satisfaction at the gate to Shaw Cottage and regarded the garden with as much pleasure as if it had been as carefully tended as those of Sissinghurst Castle. Compared with Georgia's first view of it six weeks ago, the garden was looking even sorrier for itself, although a couple of green bags of waste indicated someone had been working here.

'Would Christopher have done this tidying-up?' Georgia asked.

Alice shrugged. 'Don't know. But he's a lazy bugger. Worse

than Adam here.' She dug her elbow into Adam's ribs in friendly fashion, and he grinned. If she were Emma, Georgia thought, she'd snap Adam up quickly.

'That Christopher only does things he's told to. Finds life easier that way. Don't we all? He only gets up in the morning because Birdie wants her comforts brought up.'

'He holds down a job.'

'Has to. He understands what money means all right, and Birdie don't have enough to give him pocket money.'

'Why leave the house to the trust then instead of selling it to them or someone else?'

'Part of the heritage, ain't it?' Alice said dismissively. 'They'll do the place up one of these days when they get the money. After Madam Clemence pops her clogs. They keep the weeds down and the roof on, and that's about all.'

Shaw Cottage seemed small beer compared with the manor though, especially since Alwyn was disgraced, so why was it worth the trust paying Birdie's retirement home fees? Was it planning to turn it into a mini museum dedicated to Roy, Elfie and Alwyn? That seemed unlikely.

'Come on,' said Alice impatiently, marching up the drive.

'Are we going into the house?'

'The garden. That's what I want to see.'

Alice led the way, muttering to herself with the occasional glance at Georgia. Adam ambled behind them. The grass at the rear of the house had been scythed down for the winter, which was obviously where the waste bag contents had stemmed from.

'Here's her garden. Her love-in-a-mist.'

Georgia's heart sank. Straight towards the stream. 'Are we going across?'

Alice looked alarmed. 'No. Never. Love-in-a-mist doesn't grow that side. She never crossed it.'

'Why not?' Georgia asked, even if she was in complete agreement with Elfie on that score. This side was bad enough.

'More mysterious that way, she'd say. Never find out what's in the dark woods of people. You think it's light and pretty but if you cross the stream, the dark falls. We were out here once and the glow-worms were out. She liked it, started sketching them. He was dead by then, thought it funny I did, that she would be here by the stream where he did it.'

'Where Alwyn committed suicide?'

'"I'm near him here," she'd say. Close to him. She was a funny one, one of nature's innocents, as they say. You expected all the rabbits and hedgehogs and birds to come out and sit around singing like they did in that film *Bambi*.'

'There was darkness in that film too.' Even now Georgia couldn't think of the scene of the death of Bambi's mother without remembering her terror as a child, and looking now at those woods over there it was all too vivid a memory.

'You can't have one without the other,' Alice said matter-of-factly. 'Mrs Elfie said that's why she put a little bit of dark in every picture, to remind children that life isn't going to be all love-in-a-mist.' She ruminated. 'Death in a mist. Ever popped open a seed case from a love-in-a-mist, Georgia?'

'I don't think so.'

'Fairy rings,' Alice said abruptly. 'Remember them?'

'No.' Where was all this going – anywhere or nowhere?

'Mrs Elfie had one. I'll show you.' Alice made her way back to the lawn area, though it hardly deserved that name now, and over to the built-up rockery at the far side. At its foot was what had once been a stone statue, and Alice awkwardly got down on her knees and bent over, examining the earth.

'Here it is!' she cried in triumph.

'Mushrooms, Gran?' Adam asked, puzzled.

Alice looked at him scornfully. 'Always thinking of your stomach, young man. Ferns.'

And then Georgia remembered her own childhood. She'd been much closer to the earth then, both physically and figuratively, and more aware of its richness. She had spent hours picking at dark tiny ferns and mosses that formed mysterious fairy rings. How could she have forgotten?

'Here's a bit of it.' Alice's fingers plucked at the fern. The fairies haven't gone, have they?'

Georgia glanced at Adam, who made a face.

'As long as the ferns were here, the evil fairies would stay,' Alice explained. 'Then Mrs Elfie would laugh and laugh. Like a kid, she was.'

She sounded it, thought Georgia cynically.

'She'd try to plant those black seeds, but they wouldn't grow. Not here. No love-in-a-mist where the fairies live.'

That poem. Georgia suddenly remembered that weird verse at the end of Elfie's book, and even as she thought of it, Alice said, 'Lots of black seeds swarming inside the seed cases. Black. I can see her popping one open now, in her pretty summer dress, and her fair hair, staring down at those black seeds. You never know what's inside people, do you?'

'No,' Georgia agreed, wondering what, if anything to make of all this.

'"Out of these black things come the blue flowers, don't they, Alice?" she'd say. Yes, I'd answer, though I never knew what she was after. "Let's scatter them on the earth," she'd say, "so there'll be blue flowers." Then she'd cry for Alwyn. Only not when Birdie was around, because that would upset her too. Very fond of her brother, she was, and bitter when he died. Mrs Elfie too. Sad, very sad.'

'Was she very eccentric after Alwyn's death?'

'Always a bit odd,' Alice conceded. 'That's what Mr Roy said.'

'You remember Roy Sandford?' This was hopeful.

'I was a kid when he died. Maybe thirteen or fourteen. Old enough to know he was a looker. Saw him the day he died. Joe Baker brought him from the station in his butcher's van. Digging for victory they all were in the garden that day. Me too. Then Miss Birdie and Mr Alwyn had to go on duty so off poor Mr Roy went alone to London. Them bombs were nasty things. Now you're here, then you're not. Ah well. Broke all their hearts when they found out.'

Alice caressed the ferns with her hands. 'Now the fairy rings are broken. All gone.' Slowly she stood up, and without looking at Georgia began to make her way back to the stream. 'Poor Mr Alwyn, poor Mrs Elfie,' she murmured as she reached the stepping stones.

'Did she draw the illustrations for *The Woods Beyond The Stream* from this side?' Georgia asked.

'Yes. More mysterious.' Alice stared across the stream. 'I never went across.'

'I did,' Adam suddenly piped up. 'Went all the time as a kid. Want to see?' he asked Georgia.

'Not me,' Alice said firmly. 'You go.'

Torn between cowardice and curiosity, Georgia plucked up the courage to follow him across the stepping stones, trying not to look at the tree where Alwyn had probably died. The leaves were falling fast from the trees now, exposing the undergrowth. This was the wild wood of *The Wind in the Willows* where anything might lurk, she thought.

'There's a path of sorts through here,' Adam told her, forging his way ahead.

'Where to?'

'You'll see.'

It followed the stream as far as the oak tree, and then turned into the undergrowth and woods. Georgia was glad she was wearing an old anorak as she fought her way through. All around her was the wet steamy smell of autumn and she wondered where on earth she was being taken. 'Here,' he said, stopping in his tracks.

The bushes opened up into a glade, where only overgrown grass broken by the occasional patch of brambles greeted her. The golden-brown leaves of horse chestnut covered the ground. She was surprised to find it was a companionable place, an oasis in the midst of these repellent woods. No fingerprints in this glade, thank goodness.

'I used to collect conkers here, when I was a kid,' Adam said. 'The best conkers they were, so it was worth it.'

Georgia could see why. To Adam the place brought back childhood memories, but to her it was only a moment's respite in the midst of an otherwise alien atmosphere, and she was relieved when they crossed the stream to rejoin Alice. She was standing stock-still, staring at them, hands thrust into the pockets of her ancient jacket.

'Time we were getting back, Gran,' Adam said anxiously. For all his rebellion, he wasn't going to risk upsetting his grandfather too far, and even Alice turned to go immediately.

'Got what you wanted?' he asked Georgia shyly at the end of another nightmare ride back to Fernbourne.

'Thanks, Adam. Yes.'

It might be true. The problem was she didn't know what it was she'd got.

'We've a dinner guest tonight,' Luke warned her immediately she came through the front door. Georgia had already noted that the lights in the oast house were out suspiciously early. Her heart sank though. She was dying to hear all about Molly.

'Is it Peter?' she asked hopefully.

'If he wants to come. It's Molly though.'

'Good.' Even better. She might not like Molly but at least this represented progress.

'We can go out if you prefer.'

'Let's eat here. Looser tongues and no flapping ears.'

'I doubt if Molly's tongue is ever loose.'

Peter elected not to come on the principle that Molly might feel outnumbered which would lead to tighter tongues, not looser. In the cosy atmosphere of Medlars with whatever they could rustle up for dinner she might relax and mellow.

Even Luke hadn't yet heard the results of the trustees' meeting, and he was as on edge as she was until Molly arrived.

'Very nice.' Molly gave Medlars her seal of approval almost as soon as she came in. 'A Wealden house originally?'

'Yes, but changed and extended over the years,' Georgia replied.

'Well done for not tinkering too much. Now –' a cool look – 'let's get the business out of the way first and then we can relax.' Molly was taking command, but perhaps that was no bad thing.

'Good idea,' Luke said heartily and made haste to serve drinks and seat Molly comfortably in an armchair.

'You'll be hearing formally from Matthew,' she began.

Of course, Georgia thought. He wouldn't miss that chance.

'Nevertheless the trustees have decided that we should get our independent assessment on the handwriting issue, based on more samples than you were able to produce.' Molly kept a straight face. 'If only to . . . um . . .'

'Keep me quiet?' Luke enquired.

Molly nodded. 'That's reasonable, don't you think? After all the plagiarism was never made public so in fact it suits the board if Alwyn is the original writer after all.'

'Very reasonable,' Luke said, 'considering your biography is affected.'

'Not yet,' Molly said swiftly. 'If the verdict goes against Alwyn, there's no problem with my biography. If it goes against Roy, we do have a problem with it, and that's when we decide what to do.'

'A unanimous decision, was it?' Luke asked bluntly.

Molly didn't give an inch. 'Let's say the decision was passed.'

'How did Clemence take it?' Georgia asked anxiously. 'After all, Gavin might be a natural suspect since he brought the charge.'

'She didn't demur,' Molly said neutrally.

Or couldn't, Georgia thought, forcing herself to be logical. Fine workmanship would be necessary. If Gavin didn't have the ability to do it himself, either Elfie or Birdie or Clemence might have been drawn in. Since the first two had nothing to gain and indeed everything to lose by any such involvement, Clemence would seem the natural choice for Gavin to turn to. But it went against every instinct Georgia had.

'Who will do the official verdict on the whole collection?' Luke enquired.

Molly looked at him in some amusement. 'You need have no fear. The material won't disappear. It's already in my car. And if you're worried that my biography might unduly influence me, I should point out that my reputation as an agent is even more important to me.'

The rest of the evening passed reasonably amicably, and Georgia even felt more rapport with Molly. All the same she was glad when Molly left and she and Luke could collapse into bed. She couldn't sleep however, her mind whirling around.

'Luke,' she whispered. 'Roy, the bright flame.'

'Put it out,' he muttered sleepily.

She couldn't. Could Molly really be willing to see the whole concept of Roy the bright flame vanish and his laurels ceded to Alwyn Field, the wimp? It wasn't, she was sure, going to be as simple as that. Could they really trust Molly? There could be black seeds at the heart of the Fernbourne Trust, ready to sow themselves while the mist was busy blurring Marsh & Daughter's eyes.

Ten

Mornings weren't usually Georgia's best time, especially Monday ones, but then she hadn't usually woken up with so much certainty that she was right. The inspirations of the dark usually vanished all too quickly with the coming of daylight.

Not this one, and yet she couldn't see where to take it from here, except to try it out on Peter.

'Roy Sandford. The bright flame,' she began as soon as was decent after she arrived in the office and caught up with the post.

'Not again. What about him?' Peter grunted.

Not the ideal moment to start, but she had no option now. 'We've been given the impression that Roy was the centre of the fire of the Fernbourne Five. But how often have we seen it burning?'

'Poetic but . . .' Peter halted what was obviously going to be a very grumpy reply, and took time to think about it. 'Only in connection with *The Flight of the Soul.*'

'If that should turn out to be Alwyn's work after all, what are we left with?' Patience, Georgia, she schooled herself. Build up a case first.

'Brilliant career cut short, loss of Birdie's lover, his strong personality—'

'How brilliant?'

'Great Oxford reputation. Got a first in history. Two books of poems well received,' Peter rattled off. 'One detective story, highly rated, *Snake in the Grass.*'

'Compare that output with Gavin's trilogy about the Spanish Civil War, Clemence's huge output of oils and watercolours, even Elfie's work – does he measure up to, let alone excel them?'

'No,' Peter agreed.

'So why the bright flame?'

'He died comparatively young, at twenty-eight, and tragically. To Birdie he's her lost love, to the others a lost talent. They subconsciously felt guilty at surviving when he didn't.'

Georgia was only momentarily thrown. 'Accepted, but is there any reason that the next generation should still carry the flame forward? Molly perhaps, but why Matthew and Clemence?'

'If they believe that *The Flight of the Soul* is Roy's work, yes.'

'Nothing else?' Surely he could see there had to be.

'No, but I think you're about to tell me.'

She was. 'Birdie loved Roy, yes?'

'Agreed, and Elfie loved Alwyn.'

'Not agreed.'

Peter's eyebrow shot up. 'She filled that garden with flowers for someone she didn't love?'

'No. You're forgetting something. Roy Sandford lived there. Suppose it was him she loved?' She was certain she was getting somewhere.

He frowned. 'Give me time . . . If the love affair was between Elfie and Roy, why no mention of it in the party line?'

'Oh, come on! Birdie, of course.'

'But that isn't documented in Matthew Hunt's book. So in theory Birdie's love affair with Roy could be a recent invention.'

'But it explains so much . . .'

'Stop, Georgia, stop,' Peter said firmly. 'It's a thesis, I grant you. But there's not one indication that it's right, save for the fact that Roy was living at Shaw Cottage with Birdie and Alwyn for a few years. We can bear it in mind. But let's keep to tangible issues, and work up from there.'

Georgia was forced to admit he was probably right, but that didn't stop her mind from racing ahead. When after all did the Elfie/Alwyn story begin? Way back, she conceded. Peter had known about it before he read *The Freedom Seekers*, and the story seemed well entrenched in village memory.

Peter was watching her. 'Don't take it to heart, Georgia. There might be something in your hunch. Why not talk to Clemence about it?'

'Clemence?' Georgia yelped. 'How can I, with this plagiaristic sword of Damocles hanging over her head?'

'Quite easily,' Peter shot back. 'The playing field is level now she knows about the allegations. It's her choice whether she brings Gavin's name into any conversation with you. I take it you wouldn't plan to raise that subject yourself – especially with this new idea of yours.'

Seeing her still undecided, Peter added casually, 'I'll come with you. While you're cosying up to Clemence, I'll distract Janie if she's around. I'd like to see that Fernbourne Room again. Shall I ring?'

'Yes,' Georgia agreed. At least it was something to do while they were waiting to hear from Molly.

'Good morning, Georgia.' The greeting from Clemence seemed as friendly as ever, when they arrived at her suggested time three days later. Perhaps Georgia was only imagining that there was more distance between them than before. 'Shall we go to the studio?' Clemence suggested. 'I gather Janie is looking after your father in the manor.'

'Or the other way around,' Georgia returned light-heartedly, as she followed Clemence up to her studio. 'He has firm views on not being looked after.'

'So,' Clemence remarked, 'has Janie. She might appear to be in the background but that isn't always the case.'

Just as well, Georgia thought, interested in this different slant on Janie. Matthew would take some coping with, and his half-sister would need strength of mind to oppose his wishes. She began to see why Ted Laycock and Christopher Atkin were on the board. They could be ballast, or perhaps acting as no man's land would better describe their role.

Clemence had a kettle and emergency supplies in her studio, to avoid having to break off work, she explained, to go to the kitchen every time she needed a drink. As Georgia helped Clemence bring another chair forward to the coffee table nestling in one corner, she waited to see if she would plunge straight into the plagiarism issue, but fortunately she didn't.

'Peter said you wanted to talk about Roy Sandford,' Clemence gently prompted her, and Georgia suspected from the faint irony in her tone that Clemence knew perfectly well what was in her mind.

Clemence listened impassively, as Georgia talked about Roy and his role. Even as she spoke, part of her mind was busy wondering how far to go. She decided on a gamble to draw Clemence out, and concluded: 'And it's so important for us to discover whether *The Flight of the Soul* was his work or Alwyn's, even though that isn't the real reason I wanted to talk to you today.'

'I'm so glad that need not come into the discussion,' Clemence replied, straight-faced. 'Just as well, don't you think? You only want to know what made Roy special for us, or whether we merely treasure his memory?'

'In a nutshell, yes.' Partly at least.

'Then the nutshell is the former. He was a fascinating extrovert and charming person. I'll show you the first portrait of him that I painted. I was going to put it in the Fernbourne Room, but decided against it. You'll see why when I show it to you.'

She took Georgia over to a large chest with shallow drawers, the kind used for prints and maps, and slid them open one after the other until she found the one she wanted. 'Here,' she said, taking it out and handing it to Georgia. 'Prop it up on top of the chest.'

It was an unframed oil mounted on board. At first Georgia could make nothing of it, but as she studied it the design began to fall into place. Roy's face came at her from every angle, with at least half a dozen images, each showing hands, blurred in their definition, stretched out before him, as though about to grasp an object – or an idea? Closer examination showed that the faces came from mirrors, reflecting different angles and expressions. All of them, coupled with the thrusting hands, displayed eagerness and compulsive energy.

'I called it "Double Janus".' Clemence studied the painting – or was it Georgia she was studying? '1939, I think. Certainly before he was called up for the forces in late August. It's not a literal title since this Janus is looking not just in two directions, or four, but at least six. Perhaps I'll rename it. How about "The Bright Flame"?'

Georgia had a strong feeling that she was being outmanoeuvred in this game of wits, but aware that she might have an ace she could play, she decided to let Clemence get away with it for the moment. 'In what way?' she enquired. 'A flickering flame doesn't last long.'

'Good try,' Clemence said approvingly. 'I'm not being fair,' she added immediately. 'Let me have another go. Bright flames push upwards but also kindle others. That's what Roy did. He could never stop long enough to decide exactly what he wanted to do, or where he was going. Gavin tried to focus Roy's creativity, but it was useless. First Roy would want to write novels as good as Gavin's, and indeed he did a passable one, short because he wouldn't put the time into developing it properly, and consequently never published. Then it was poems. Out come *Young Man's Fancy* and *Verses to Dorinda*, then essays – which disappeared after being published in various abstruse literary magazines – then it was detective stories that were going to be his true calling. That was the golden age for detective fiction, when intellect predominated. All those tedious Oxford dons running around falling over dead bodies. Roy wanted to use the genre as a metaphor for human life, he told me once. He could extend the boundaries. Heaven knows what he meant. He wrote one, and then typically lost interest. He sent up bright flames in every direction but never settled.'

'What about kindling others?' Georgia asked, hoping this might bring Elfie in.

'His enthusiasm sent us cracking onwards. Poor Alwyn was always trying to follow in Roy's footsteps. He even wrote that detective story, *The End of Lionel Draper*, after the war to keep faith with Roy, so he said. To carry on where he had left off. It was good too. If he hadn't . . .' Her face clouded. 'If Alwyn hadn't killed himself he could have had quite a future there. Unlike Roy he was a sticker.'

'What about Roy's love affair with Birdie – did that last?' She was working her way round now.

Clemence took her time with this one, however. 'Roy was the same with women. Always seeking something new to be his inspiration, and there was always Birdie, of course. She was a stalwart.'

'Was she his Dorinda?'

Clemence laughed. 'She likes to think so. Dorinda was a lady only of Roy's imagination.'

'Not Elfie then?'

'*Elfie?*'

Georgia was horrified to see how much she had shaken Clemence. If she'd wanted a reaction, she'd got it.

Clemence pulled herself together quickly, however. 'Wherever did you get *that* idea?'

Georgia decided to answer whether it was a rhetorical question or not. 'I suppose from the image of Alwyn the wimp, which comes from you all. Despite the plagiarism, despite the rape of Jenny Baker, Elfie still appears to have loved this wimp. And Roy of course also lived at Shaw Cottage.'

'My dear Georgia, let me give you some advice.' Clemence looked worried to say the least. 'Damien Trent also wanted to talk about Roy, as well as about Alwyn. I can't answer your questions, any more than I could have answered his, because I don't know all the answers. But please, please, do not put this notion about Roy and Elfie to Birdie. She's too old to cope with it. Roy is *her* property. It's his memory that keeps her going.'

Damien Trent too? Now Georgia knew she had to continue, albeit on a gentler note. 'Would Roy have married her if he'd survived?'

Clemence gave her an odd look. 'Probably. It might have been the answer.'

'To what?' She tried not to sound too eager.

'To his restlessness over the failure of the ideal woman to settle long enough for him to catch his butterfly dream,' Clemence replied, adding a deprecating, 'Dear me, I am getting pretentious.'

Georgia was not fooled. Clemence knew exactly what she was saying and the effect she wanted to give. 'The butterfly dream': Elfie Lane.

Seeing that Peter's car had vanished from outside the manor, Georgia went straight to the King's Head as arranged. When she arrived, however, she was surprised to find Janie present as well – which was a little annoying since she had wanted to launch straight into the subject of Elfie and Roy.

'Has my mother been boring you?' Janie asked brightly, but meaning, Georgia guessed, have you been pestering her?

'Not at all. She's been filling in blanks about Roy Sandford for me.'

Georgia had hoped for some reaction to this, and she got it. Janie immediately looked panic-stricken. 'Not *The Flight of the Soul*?'

'Don't worry. No troubled waters were entered.' Not strictly true, but she had only dabbled a toe in them.

Janie sighed. 'It's too bad. I realize that Luke has to be sure of his ground, but why ever did he think there might be a problem in the first place? Sorry,' she added quickly. 'I realize you can't answer that.'

'But I can,' Georgia replied. 'I realize it must look to you as though between us we're determined to dig up some kind of question mark over the Fernbourne Five's reputation—'

'It does,' Janie agreed bluntly.

'But it had already been dug up,' Georgia pointed out.

'When?' Janie looked taken aback. Peter was watching carefully and not participating.

'Over the original accusation that Alwyn had pinched Roy's work,' Georgia said. 'All we're doing is investigating whether Alwyn was unjustly accused, and Luke needs to be legally sure of his ground, as you say. Besides, even though the original case never came to court, it's highly probable that the media would have picked up the story next year, especially if you republish *The Flight of the Soul* under Roy's name. Every computer from the British Library down would reveal a discrepancy.'

'I suppose so.' Janie frowned. 'But we would plan on having both names on it.'

She looked from Peter to Georgia and unexpectedly laughed. 'I suppose it would be one in the eye for Matthew if we have to put it out under Alwyn's name alone.'

Georgia agreed. Matthew would be all too eager to hide any dirt under the carpet, no matter what rights Birdie might have to Alwyn's estate. No wonder Birdie was getting her spot at the opening. He needed to keep her sweet.

'It's hard on Molly too,' Peter said casually.

'Good grief, you're right. I'd forgotten about her biography.' Janie looked aghast. It's a bugger, isn't it?'

Georgia was amused. 'You sound just like Clemence.'

'Years of living with her,' Janie said briefly. 'I had some hopes of following in her artistic footsteps when I came back to live here, but they soon vanished.'

'Back?' Georgia picked up.

'I was married for ten years or so. It broke up, so I returned at Mother's suggestion to help her plan the future. My own painting sort of disappeared of its own accord.'

'Didn't you mind that?'

'Curiously, no. And I don't blame her,' Janie added hastily. 'Now I rather fancy myself running the manor side by side with my writing.'

'Writing?' Georgia was beginning to feel completely at sea, although Peter didn't look puzzled.

Janie smiled. 'It's seldom mentioned, particularly by Mother and Matthew who think it a sad let-down after my father's great works, but hey, you do what you can do. Right? I bury myself in romantic novels under a pseudonym.'

Georgia began to warm to this unexpected Janie. One up to her and one down to Clemence for not being proud of her daughter. 'Is Molly your agent too?'

'No way. Molly keeps her cards close to her armour-plated chest. I bet she didn't tell you about Great-Aunt Betty.'

'Who on earth's that?'

'The great Roy's sister. Molly is the grandchild of Roy's brother William. Elizabeth was the youngest of the three. She's still alive and still very much kicking. She's Molly's biggest hurdle. Ask her.'

'A car's just drawn up outside. Expecting anyone?' Luke asked, peering out of the living room windows. The gravel at Medlars gave ample warning of visitors. 'It's no one I recognize. Can you go?' He was busy taking the coffee cups back into the kitchen.

Georgia obliged. Package? Someone lost? Gas or electricity canvassers? Someone for Luke's office? That was less likely on a Saturday. She opened the door and froze when she saw the elegant blonde woman walking towards the door.

'Darling,' said Elena anxiously. 'Don't say you don't recognize me? It hasn't been that long.'

Georgia swallowed, desperately trying to regain her senses. 'Of course I do,' she said numbly. 'Come in, Elena.' She felt torn inside out. What on earth could her mother want, and what was she doing here unannounced? So far as she knew, Elena hadn't been back to Kent since she left eleven years ago.

'Why . . .?' Georgia's words stumbled as she led Elena to the living room. She could hear Luke in the kitchen, and it was better to leave him there until she had got to grips with this horror. First, the most important question. 'Does Peter know you're here?' He would freak out, that was for sure.

'No, darling.' Elena looked curiously round, obviously appraising their living room. 'I thought you could tell him. So difficult, you see.' The well-remembered winning smile accompanied a slightly anxious look in case this wouldn't pass muster.

It didn't. 'What is?' Georgia asked woodenly. Be damned if she'd be civilized and start fussing around with coffee and biscuits until she knew what this was all about. In any case, her own stomach was churning far too much for her to react 'normally'. What was normal about this? She hadn't seen Elena for about six years now, and that had been in France. Before that it had been once or twice in London when the divorce was going through. And before that . . . when she walked so blithely out on Peter, leaving him to cope alone. Their communication was down to the occasional card or letter.

'There's some news, you see.' Elena's French chic seemed to give way, and her voice trembled.

'Not . . .' Georgia could hardly frame the word. 'Rick?' Her brother at last, after all this time? A corpse, a skeleton? The room swam round her and she thought she was going to faint.

'Not definite,' Elena assured her quickly. 'Just something.'

Georgia took hold of herself. She had to get out of here. Find Luke. 'I'll get some coffee. You can tell me then,' she rambled. The break would give her time to adjust. Elena followed her into the kitchen, however, where Luke was pretending to be intent on brewing more coffee. He looked from one to the other, obviously aware of the tension and perhaps seeing a similarity, although Georgia took after Peter rather than Elena.

'You must be Luke.' Elena's voice had the familiar coo it tended to gain at the sight of an attractive man. Georgia realized she was being bitchy, however. Elena couldn't help cooing, and it was hardly important compared with news of Rick.

Luke was chatting to Elena as though she were some casual visitor, and Georgia knew he was giving her time to calm down.

'. . . the Dordogne,' Elena was saying. 'Near Dôme. Do you know it?'

What the hell did it matter, Georgia thought feverishly, besides Rick? She broke abruptly into their conversation. 'Is he alive?'

Elena looked aghast. 'Oh, darling, I don't think so. How could he be?'

Georgia burst into tears. Of course Rick wasn't alive. He'd died years ago. Of course, *of course.*

'Georgia darling.' Elena pushed Luke out of the way, and enfolded her in her arms. It felt awkward, since she was much shorter than Georgia, but Georgia didn't care. For a brief moment she was a child again, and nothing mattered apart from the immediate present.

Georgia allowed Luke to lead them to the table, and then fiddle around with cups and saucers while she recovered. Both of them were regarding her anxiously.

'I'll leave you,' Luke said promptly.

'Stay, Luke, please,' Georgia begged. She watched while he sat down as though this were some ordinary Saturday morning.

'It's just a possible lead, Georgia,' Elena was saying. 'I've never been back to Brittany, you can imagine.'

Yes, Georgia could. She never doubted Elena's emotional response to Rick's disappearance, only her way of handling the results. Her way of vanishing when the situation had to be faced. It had been Georgia and Peter who travelled to Brittany to get the police involved in Rick's disappearance. Peter and Georgia who threw themselves into following up every lead, with Peter pulling in every favour he could in his capacity as a DI in the Kent police. And when he'd had his accident . . . No, Georgia didn't want to dwell on this. This was here, this was now.

'I have a friend in Brittany,' Elena explained. 'She's just retired and is trying to find things to do. She decided – oh, darling, I didn't ask her to – to go to that farm that you and Peter tracked down. Where Rick had been staying. Near Carnac. You remember?'

Of course she did. Georgia would never forget. She and Peter had thought they were getting somewhere at last. Rick had been staying there and helping with the harvesting. The couple at the farm had recognized the photo. The pain they'd felt when the trail then went cold again returned in full force.

Rick had left. He'd been travelling by train and hitch-hiking, but the farm couple didn't know where he was heading. He didn't know himself, he had told them. That was Rick. Of course he didn't. Not like Georgia, who would plan every exciting move so that she could look forward to it with pleasure.

'Yes,' was all she replied to Elena now.

Elena looked at her doubtfully. 'What they did remember was a girl visiting them some year or two afterwards, asking after him. She was English. She'd met him, then they had parted, and she didn't even know he had disappeared. She didn't know his name either, but she did tell them where she came from. By the Kent coast.'

Georgia remembered now that there had been talk of seeing Rick with a girl, but no one had come forward, and it was vague. It might not have been Rick, and the police had dismissed it. And so had they.

'What was her name?' she asked jerkily.

Elena stared at her dolefully. 'They didn't know or couldn't remember. They thought it was a saint's name.'

In a Roman Catholic country, that could be most names under the sun. Georgia felt desolation sweep over her.

'I thought,' Elena said tentatively, 'you and Peter might like to follow it up.'

Georgia could have wept again. More mystery. More lines that would be impossible to follow up but still no answers. It would lead nowhere at all, and merely add fuel to a grief that had already been dealt with. Had it though? If she was honest, it hadn't. Like Roy Sandford. Like Alwyn Field. The past might lie fallow, but it was still fertile. It could spring to life at any moment. A moment such as this.

'Are you going to tell Peter?' Elena asked doubtfully.

Georgia looked at Luke to see if he were thinking as she was. He nodded slightly.

'No,' she replied to Elena as gently as she could. 'You are.'

No way would she risk keeping Peter in ignorance that his former wife had been here. For once Elena could face him herself.

Being in the same room as Peter and Elena together seemed unreal to Georgia. Elena had refused to come unless Georgia came too, to which she agreed, having warned Peter first, and now she watched her mother telling the story with an odd fascination as though this were a play and she a spectator.

'I see,' was all Peter said gruffly, when Elena had finished. Then he turned to Georgia. 'Would you mind, Georgia? I'd like a few minutes alone with Elena.'

At first she thought Elena would refuse, but she nodded brightly enough at Georgia, who fled to the kitchen, where Margaret was waiting with Luke and with pursed lips. Margaret remembered Elena from the old days, when she'd been queen of the village and, as had the entire village, been fiercely on Peter's side when Elena departed.

'But then there's never just one side,' Luke had commented on one of the rare occasions when Georgia had mentioned Elena to him.

Georgia had disagreed, but now, with Elena actually here, it might be easier to see it that way.

She waited on tenterhooks, hearing the rise and fall of voices, but half an hour passed before the tap-tap of Elena's heels proclaimed that she was on her way to find them.

'Darlings,' she beamed, 'I'm leaving now.'

'Is Peter all right?' Georgia asked quickly.

Elena looked hurt. 'Of course, darling. What did you expect?'

'Can we take you to lunch, Elena?' Luke asked politely.

'Luke, how charming of you. But I don't believe I could take the emotional strain. After all, I did live here. One day perhaps – if . . .' Then her lips trembled. 'If there's ever anything more to discuss.'

'I said we'd try to follow it up,' Peter told Georgia flatly, as soon as Elena had left and Georgia had rushed in to see Peter, fearful of what she might find. To her surprise he looked cast down, but not devastated.

Luke stepped in. 'Why don't we go to the pub for lunch? Margaret won't mind. You can eat her lunch tonight.'

Peter brightened up. 'So I could.'

'How can we follow up on anything so vague?' Georgia decided to broach the subject once they were established at Haden Shaw's magnificent White Horse. 'A girl living in Kent who visited Brittany thirteen years ago, and once again thereafter. She met someone she didn't know, and we don't know whether she would have any information in any case.'

Luke began to laugh, which broke the gloomy silence that followed. 'It makes the affairs of Frost and Co look straight-forward in comparison.'

'There must be a way,' Peter said after Luke had thus broken the ice. Then he must have read Georgia's expression correctly. 'Don't worry. I won't get fixated.'

'Will you be all right on your own tonight?' she asked uneasily. 'Shall I stay over?'

'You think I'll have nightmares?'

'Highly possible,' she said practically.

'I'll take a pill.' He saw her look of worry. 'I'm all right, Georgia. I'm better alone, and in any case you have Great-Aunt Betty to think about,' he joked.

'We both do,' Luke said casually, putting his hand over Georgia's.

'The game's afoot, Watson.' Luke's voice greeted her as she picked up the mobile on Tuesday morning. 'I thought you'd like to know right away.'

'Which game?' Georgia asked. It sounded good news, which was a relief in itself after the weekend's traumas. Unanswered questions – they seemed to pound at her head incessantly. If only one or two tiny ones about Alwyn Field could get resolved, it might help. This sounded hopeful.

'Molly's telephoned. They've got their scientist's prelimi-nary findings.'

'Which are?' This *was* good news.

'She wouldn't tell me. She's asked if she can come over after yet another trustees' meeting this evening. She's coming for dinner at the White Horse. If, mind you, there's anything we should know. And the invitation is for you too, not just me. She takes it for granted we're joined at the hip now.'

'And if there isn't anything we should know?'

'We can whistle for our supper, I suppose. One step at a time though.'

Luke was cheeringly calm as she waited impatiently with him in the White Horse that evening. She began to despair when no Molly arrived, but just as both she and Luke had nearly given up hope, Molly came in.

'Tired but triumphant?' Luke joked, as he rose to greet her.

He looked imperturbable. Maybe that was a special expression that all publishers developed, Georgia thought.

'The first part's one hundred per cent on the nail,' Molly said wearily. 'Not easy-going, these trustee meetings. The second part is partly true – for you anyway.'

'Ah,' Luke commented. 'Drink?'

'Yes, please. I'm staying over here so you can pour it down my throat unceasingly so far as I'm concerned. The good news for you, bad for me, is that our expert says the same as yours. The paper is pretty well conclusive. Our phantom forger could in theory have got hold of wartime paper in 1948, but he sure as hell couldn't have got hold of 1948 paper in 1941 or earlier. He's also confirmed the originals are in Alwyn's handwriting, and the others are forgeries of Roy's. So unless one argues that Alwyn copied them from Roy's originals written in wartime and now vanished only for someone to copy them again in the late 1940s in Roy's handwriting for some mad reason, it looks certain it was indeed a trumped-up charge against Alwyn Field.'

'That's what I call good news for Marsh and Daughter,' Georgia said thankfully. One hurdle surmounted at least. 'How do you feel, Luke?'

'It depends on the trustees' co-operation, don't you think, Molly?' Luke was clearly remaining cautious.

'That's the bad news for you.' Molly pulled a face. 'The board won't let *The Flight of the Soul* be released again under Alwyn's name. If you're still interested, Luke, you can reprint Roy and Alwyn's other works, and Elfie's, but not that one.'

Sheer vindictiveness was Georgia's first reaction, though Luke's face remained impassive – of course.

'I'll sleep on it, and ring you tomorrow, Molly. One question: who owns the copyright for *The Flight of the Soul* – or rather who would have owned it if it had been Roy's work?'

'As with Roy's other work,' Molly fenced, 'I handle it.'

'But who owns it?' Luke persisted.

'His estate,' Molly said reluctantly, 'went to his parents, since he died intestate. Their estate was divided between their surviving children, which now means my father as Roy's elder brother William died some years back – and anyway,' she swept on, 'since I'm the agent and literary executor for the parents' estate, that's my problem.'

'Not quite,' Luke persevered. 'You said surviving children. The contracts would have to be signed by, and the money go to, either living survivors or their estates.'

Molly grimaced. 'It's a fair cop. I surrender. It means effectively that my father now owns half of it.'

'And the other half?'

'Great-Aunt Elizabeth, Scatty Betty, as she's known. My father's aunt.' The tone of her voice indicated that was the end of the conversation. No way, Georgia thought, but as she was about to tackle Molly, Luke got in first.

'And what about Alwyn Field's estate? Does Birdie own the copyright?'

'Sort of.' Even Molly blushed at her response.

'I take that as a yes. So how can the trustees stop the publication?' Luke pressed. 'You're on the board, but not your father or this Scatty Betty, and don't you have a duty to them? They have the final yea or nay. And then there's Birdie too.'

'Someone has to make decisions in the interests of the Fernbourne Five. They speak for Birdie. If you must know, she assigned copyright to the trust. But,' she added hastily, 'she gets a cut of any royalties earned and a say in what happens.'

'In that case, does she know about this development? Does she know that Alwyn has been vindicated?'

'Not my problem.'

'Isn't it?' said Georgia sweetly. 'Even though the board runs her affairs, and even though, as you told us, you are the literary agent and in control?'

Molly looked at them. She began to speak then changed her mind. And when she did say something, it was clear that she was no longer fighting the trustees' corner. 'Oh, hell,' she said, frowning. She was clearly thinking something through. 'You know, I'm not sorry there's a spanner in the works over this biography,' she said at last. 'Ever since I began the damn thing, I had a feeling there was something wrong.'

'About Roy?' Georgia asked sharply.

'No. About the Fernbourne Five. Something rotten in the state of Denmark, as Shakespeare would have put it.'

'Then or today?' Georgia asked. 'The Five or the trust?'

'I don't know,' Molly confessed. 'And that, believe it or not, is the truth. I could be completely wrong, but this plagiarism issue has clinched it. When Damien Trent came to me with a cock and bull story, I sent him off with a flea in his ear. I'm not proud of that now, and I owe him. So I'm throwing my weight, for what it's worth, in with the good guys. Seen any around?'

'Would we do?' Georgia asked, feeling a whole lot warmer towards Molly. 'Luke, Peter, me – we can't all be baddies.'

'You could,' Molly said ruefully. 'But that's my problem. It's that book of yours that worries me, not you personally. Call me neutral on that, which is why I can't go too fully into Damien Trent's story.'

'Until when?' There had to be a catch, Georgia thought.

'Until you've met Scatty Betty.'

Eleven

What, Georgia wondered, was the problem with Great-Aunt Elizabeth? Scatty Betty was clearly a thorn in the flesh for Molly and probably therefore the board, but did that necessarily make her public enemy No. 1? How scatty was scatty? She and Peter would soon find out. Her father had been greatly annoyed to find out that Suspects Anonymous had been deprived of a potentially important player. Unfortunately, it was the first day of November, and a very chilly one, which made the prospect of coping with scatty ladies even less appealing.

She had found out through the internet that Welling, where Great-Aunt Betty lived, had been a mere dot on the Dover Road from London to the coast until the railway had pushed its way through in the 1890s. In the same decade London's Metropolitan area had stretched out its greedy paw to push back the boundaries of the ancient county of Kent from Lewisham as far as Shooter's Hill, once a notorious highwaymen's haunt and only a mile or so from where she was.

In today's Welling there was little sign of the original hamlet. It was effectively a London suburb now, albeit thriving with shops, and there was only a faint suggestion that there might once have been market gardens and fields between it and the urban sprawl of the capital.

Great-Aunt Betty Sandford lived in a warren of seemingly identical streets and houses dating back to the 1920s or 1930s, and set back from the main Bellegrove Road, so Georgia discovered as she negotiated the car round several corners. Peter had decided to join her today at the last moment, now that he had the bit between his teeth over Roy Sandford at last. He at least gave him level pegging with Gavin, as the way forward for Marsh & Daughter.

'The best news since toasted cheese,' he had proclaimed

with unusual conviction, after he heard about Molly's attitude.

'You don't like toasted cheese,' she had pointed out.

Perhaps that had been some kind of omen, however, for the
knock on Great-Aunt Betty's the door produced an almost
instant result in the form of someone who could have been
Dickens' model for Betsy Trotwood. She was tall, with short,
straight grey hair, an angular figure, a two-piece long-skirted
grey suit, and a somewhat demented look in her eye as she
peered past them into the road.

'Where's your car?' she demanded, wasting no time on
inessentials. What she saw obviously satisfied their hostess.
'Good, you've got Mrs Parkwood's spot. That'll teach her.'

So Miss Sandford substituted cars for Betsy Trotwood's
donkeys, Georgia thought, highly amused.

Next came the wheelchair. 'How are you going to get that
thing in here?' Betty Sandford asked with her next breath,
eyeing it grimly.

'I was hoping you could tell me that,' Peter replied with
equanimity. The matter had been waved aside when Peter had
talked to her on the telephone to arrange the meeting.

'French windows,' came the verdict. Slamming the door
behind her, Betty bustled past them to indicate the way to the
rear garden. 'Moves by itself, does it?' she asked with interest.

'With a little help from me and electricity,' Peter told her
gravely, obviously beginning to enjoy this.

It took ten minutes or so to get the chair inside the house,
not because the French windows provided a problem, but
because Great-Aunt Betty had forgotten to unlock the windows
from the inside, and also forgotten to bring her house keys
with her to regain entrance. Fortunately she announced she
had a spare key, whose position changed every week. The
place she first pounced on proved to be last week's position
and the upturned terracotta pot was empty of all but an indignant toad. The next one was more fruitful.

Once established in her own domain again, she resumed
authority. Molly had told them that Betty had been a teacher
all her life, and Georgia could well believe it. Head teacher
was more probable, and in the days when children were children and did what they were told. Even in her mid-to-late
eighties, the aura remained.

Georgia found herself meekly perching on the edge of a chair at Peter's side, while cups were whipped on to a tray and then whipped off again as Betty changed her mind about which ones to use. Everything was clearly under constant reappraisal in her life.

'Now,' she said sharply, when the tray was settled to her satisfaction – although it still lacked coffee. 'What's this about Roy?'

'You know there's an arts centre being opened next year in Fernbourne?' Georgia began tentatively.

'Naturally. No thanks to Molly, though. Just like her grandfather. Birdie Field wrote to me. *They* don't want me there, but I shall be. I've booked the taxi.'

'I'm sure they must want you,' Georgia said.

'Oh, are you? You'll see. They think I'll cause trouble.'

Georgia was beginning to see why Molly had been reluctant to mention Betty Sandford earlier. It was going to be difficult to rein her in. 'Why should that be?'

A smirk. 'They're afraid I'll spoil the image of Saint Roy.'

'You didn't like your brother?' Peter asked matter-of-factly.

'Of course I did,' was the snappy reply. 'Everyone liked blasted Roy. Despite the fact that he was a selfish pig-headed monster.'

Well, they'd been warned that Betty Sandford was eccentric, but that didn't mean she wasn't right, Georgia thought. 'Is that a sister's view or a general one?'

'Have you got a brother?' Betty turned the tables with a vengeance.

Rick and Elena flitted like ghosts before her. 'No,' Georgia managed to answer, not daring to look at Peter. 'Molly described Roy as a bright flame, and—'

'Molly would say that. He's going to warm her pockets very nicely. When you're brought up in the same family you get a different view, believe me, young lady. While bright flames are burning, humbler lumps of coal tend to get reduced to ash in the process. Birdie was a lump like that,' Betty snorted. 'He was always floating around with his arty friends, and all she got was a kiss and pat on the head most of the time. Still, she wants her moment of glory next year, and I've no doubt she'll get it.'

'Is that why Matthew Hunt didn't cover it in his biography?' Georgia asked.

A sharp look. 'I don't know. It surprised me too. I imagine Matthew, like all of us, had his doubts about Roy's allegiance to any one particular woman.'

'So as a brother and lover he had his drawbacks.'

'With knobs on.' With this observation, Betty sat back with the air of one who knew precisely the effect she wanted. 'I always used to tell my girls never to use that ugly phrase. It gives me great pleasure therefore to use it now.'

'What knobs?' Peter asked hopefully.

The gimlet eyes regarded him sternly. 'Would you expect me to pass on rumours?'

'Yes.'

That silenced her momentarily, and she, deliberately or otherwise, 'remembered' the coffee and went outside to fetch it. When she returned with it she was quoting: '"And you, Dorinda, what shall I bring to you? So much have I planned . . ." Read that poem, have you?' Betty asked.

'Yes,' Georgia replied. 'From *Verses to Dorinda*, although we've been told there was no Dorinda. Or rather there were lots of them.'

'Rubbish. Know how it goes on, that poem?' She didn't stop for an answer but continued: '"Myself I'd lay before you/ But for my heart which still lies lost." They all ran after him,' Betty added. 'Little blind mice who didn't see the carving knife. Fools. None of them found his heart.'

'Not even Elfie?' Georgia asked, still reluctant to abandon her theory completely. She received a black look from Peter for her pains.

'You mean Birdie,' was Betty's immediate reply. 'Anyway, how would I know? I was down there at lot, but I was his kid sister. Eighteen or nineteen. I wasn't interested in his love life; it was mine I was concerned with. He'd have an arm round this one, the other round another, and keeping his eye open for the next. A teaser was Roy. Poor Birdie. So jealous, he liked telling her she had rivals. He thought that was fun. What do you want to know all this for?' she suddenly shot at Peter.

'Alwyn Field,' he answered, 'and *The Flight of the Soul*.'

'Yes,' she said with satisfaction, 'Madam Molly told me about that. All sorted now, is it? Alwyn was a twerp, I never liked him. He was a bad influence on Roy.'

'But has Molly told you that Alwyn didn't fake those poems after all?' Peter queried.

She grinned at them. 'She didn't need to, did she?'

'Need to what?' Peter asked.

'Tell me. I knew all the time Roy couldn't have written them.'

'*What?*' he asked faintly. Georgia was just as flabbergasted as Peter looked.

Betty Sandford looked pleased. 'Surprised, eh?'

'Astounded would be more accurate. What on earth has all this been about then?'

'You should have come here earlier, if that's what you were interested in. I remember all the fuss about the poems after the war, when my parents were living. William – that's Mr Elder Brother – was hopping around as if he'd written the stuff himself, the pompous prig. I was working in Suffolk at the time, so couldn't give much time to it. I kept saying it wasn't Roy's style, and I'd have known if he'd written them before he died, because he'd have told me about them on my visits to Fernbourne. He told me about all his work. Wanted to impress me, and his lady friends weren't enough.

'Then Mr Gavin Hunt arrived at my parents' house after the war, strutting like the Lord High Executioner over his great discovery. He said he was there to discuss *The Flight of the Soul* with them, only he didn't discuss. He just told them, that was his way. Showed us the evidence and that was that. It was lawyers and courts and this that and the other. No one listened to me. I told Gavin I was on Alwyn's side in this, twerp or not. He wouldn't listen. Nevertheless, I got brother William and my parents to see it would be better not to go to court, because I swore I'd get up and say my piece. So it was all settled.'

'And Alwyn just accepted it?'

'There was nothing he could do. He was shell-shocked at first, but Birdie and Elfie believed him, and so did I, and that was enough for him. After all, he got the kudos during the war on first publication, and provided it wasn't published again that was OK. Gavin considered it wasn't Alwyn's style, but he was wrong. It was stronger, but his all right, if you look carefully. Roy was usually all for the passions of life, and Alwyn the dreamy one. "I will build me a home on some sweet Kentish hill / Screened by ancestral oaks from winter's chill." I always liked that poem. I'm a Kentish woman, you know. Not that Welling's got much in the way of ancestral oaks. A few in Danson Park maybe, but not in this part. *The Flight of the Soul* was another matter in style. Alwyn's dreaminess had a wider range – that comes of the war, I suppose. It changed us all in one way or another. It certainly did poor Roy. The evening it all ended. We didn't even know he had leave that weekend.'

'He didn't spend leaves with you?'

'Sometimes he gave us the privilege of his presence for a few hours, but mostly it was straight off to Fernbourne. He lived there after all. He went there from Biggin Hill – expecting everyone to fall over him as usual, but, typical Roy, he hadn't checked and Birdie and Alwyn were on duty that night, Birdie at a hospital somewhere, and Alwyn on air-raid warden duty. Gavin and Elfie were around, but that wasn't enough. We found out later he rang some chums, or they rang him, and off he went to have a good night out at the Café de Paris. And that was that. It broke my heart when I got the news. A waste,' Betty said. 'No more poems, no more women, no more *life*. That's what he had. *Joie de vivre*. Alwyn was the opposite.'

'But you agree Alwyn wrote all the poems in *The Flight of the Soul*, and you'd have no objection if it came out again under Alwyn's name?'

'No. Madam Molly will though, and Birdie wouldn't like it. She wants her Roy to get a big hand.'

'But Alwyn's her brother,' Georgia said. 'Surely there'd be conflict there.'

Betty chuckled. 'So if you were on that board, what would you do? Just what it has done. Not authorize it to be reprinted. They'll have some problems over Roy anyway, in that arts centre. Can't brush them all under the carpet.'

'Such as?' Peter asked.

'What are they doing about Jenny Baker?' She looked smugly from one to the other. 'Hasn't Miss Molly talked about her?'

'Not much,' Georgia said. Could this be what Molly had been holding back? 'We know something about Jenny from

Clemence, and we know that the rough music Joe Baker organized was probably one of the reasons for Alwyn's death.'

'You need to look behind the varnish, young woman. Have you seen pictures of Jenny Baker, and of Roy and Alwyn?'

'Yes.'

'Which of the two would you go for if you were a looker like Jenny?'

'No doubt about it,' Georgia said. 'Roy. Is that why Alwyn raped her, because she was chasing Roy?'

'Sometimes I think you youngsters don't know what life's about,' said Miss Sandford severely. 'Young Jenny didn't mean to chase Roy; it was Alwyn she got on with so well. She was a beauty, but a village girl, and she didn't know her own power. She was there sometimes, posing, when I visited. She was flaunting her charms at every man in sight, but not seriously. She was courting the village policeman, but liked to flirt. She felt safe with Alwyn. He wouldn't have hurt a fly.'

Georgia had a terrible feeling she knew what was coming next. 'But Roy would.'

'My dear brother took her at face value. I found her howling her eyes out one day. And she had been preening her feathers in front of brother Roy, so I guessed what had happened. I had it out with him, and he was pretty ashamed of himself, I can tell you. He denied anything serious had taken place though. He claimed it was just a pass that upset her. He would. When I heard later about the rough music and Alwyn, I thought I'd been right to believe Roy, but I've had time to think since then.' She made a face. 'Think they'll be telling that story at the arts centre opening? Somehow I doubt it.'

'Nor the story that Alwyn Field was probably murdered,' Peter said.

Betty Sandford looked startled. '*Alwyn?*'

'Now that we know he didn't steal Roy's poems and that he probably wasn't responsible for the rape of Jenny, the two planks for suicide have been considerably weakened.'

'Only if Alwyn was a fighter,' Betty shot back. 'But he wasn't.'

Georgia didn't have to wait long to hear from Molly, who rang almost as soon as she walked in the door at Medlars.

'How did you get on with Scatty Betty?' she asked.

'Fairly mind-boggling,' Georgia said. 'It upset a few apple carts.'

A silence, while the airwaves crackled with displeasure. 'She told you her views about *The Flight of the Soul*.'

'She did. I haven't told Luke yet.'

'And what else?'

'I think you can guess. Roy and Jenny Baker.'

No silence this time. 'Good. So you know now. That's what Damien Trent came to see me about. You can imagine I was pretty well knocked sideways.'

'Not sufficiently to tell us,' Georgia pointed out drily.

'Let's not fight,' Molly pleaded. 'I had to work it out.'

'I suppose so. Did you tell the trustees?'

'No.'

'For heaven's sake, why not?'

'Birdie.'

Georgia had forgotten. 'You're right. I'm sorry.'

'Damien's father had told him shortly before he died that he had tracked down Jenny Baker, his real mother, and that she had told him that Roy was his father, not Alwyn. But when Damien's father Phil had visited Fernbourne in the mid-seventies, Joe Baker had been adamant that it was Alwyn. Damien wanted to try the conundrum out on me. I gave him short shrift, I'm afraid. I wish I hadn't.'

If wishes were horses then beggars would ride. The old proverb ran through Georgia's mind as she put the telephone down. Luke would be encouraged when she told him the position over *The Flight of the Soul*, but what of Marsh & Daughter? Where did they go next, especially with a hostile board to reckon with? The hostility wouldn't matter, if only the path were clear. But instead it seemed to be getting murkier. She and Peter had talked little in the car on the way back home, agreeing that to sleep on it might help. It served its purpose, and by the time the morning came, she felt more able to face the problem.

Peter too was surprisingly upbeat about the visit to Great-Aunt Betty. 'Mad or sane, do you think?' he asked her cheerfully enough. 'Betty seems quite clear-headed even if she does like playing skittles with our assumptions.'

'I'd like to put her in a room with Clemence and see who wins,' Georgia said with feeling. 'My view is that Clemence would – with the reservation that she who shouts loudest often gets heard first.'

'Clemence shouts in her own way.' He paused. 'What has survived the night about that meeting yesterday – not your notes, your impressions?'

Easy one. 'The point when we mentioned that Alwyn had probably been murdered.'

He looked relieved. 'Right. I think we're on the same lines.'

'Betty was surprised that anyone would want to murder him.'

'No. We've parted lines. It was her emphasis that intrigued me. She said "*Alwyn,*" as though if it had been someone else she could have understood it better.'

Georgia thought back. 'That could have been a quite innocent reaction.'

'But was it? We'd just been talking about Roy.'

'I don't follow.'

'Far-fetched, I suppose,' he muttered.

'Roy died in a well-recorded Luftwaffe raid.'

'There were unidentified bodies,' he reminded her. 'They identified him by bits of uniform, and the fact that he was known to be there by witnesses. Clothing and possessions had mostly been destroyed. That month there was a new law going through with the result that if death was caused by enemy action there was less red tape to go through, so the process was much quicker. If you think about it, what proof is there that he ever went to the Café de Paris that evening? It's worth considering.'

'Why?' Georgia was thrown, somewhat annoyed at yet another central brick of the case being queried. 'No one has ever mentioned the possibility that he wasn't there.'

'To recall the famous line: they wouldn't, would they?'

'Are you implying that Roy was *murdered*?' Even as she asked the question, it became painfully clear that there could be motives for it. Nevertheless, surely Peter was sticking his neck out. 'We need some guidelines here,' she tried to reason with him. 'Our remit was to prove that *Alwyn* was murdered. And now you're talking about switching to someone else being the victim.'

'We have to, Georgia.' Peter was getting annoyed. 'Whatever the true story of Alwyn Field, it can't be told independently of the Fernbourne Five. There's too much baggage and the answer to the murder lies deeper than *The Flight of the Soul.*'

'Jenny Baker—' she began.

'For whose rape Roy is in the frame.'

'It's still a far cry to whether Roy was murdered. It's just daft, Peter. What do you think? That Joe murdered him? That Jenny came back to Fernbourne and arranged it all? That Alwyn was in love with Jenny and not Elfie, and murdered Roy in revenge for her rape? And how and where did this supposed murder take place?'

'I haven't said it did yet,' Peter said firmly. 'But we did agree Betty gave an odd reaction.'

'Coincidence. We were looking for anything to pick up on.'

'Well, I've picked on this.'

Georgia bit her lip. 'We're getting childish.'

'Children,' said Peter reflectively, 'don't see through glass darkly. And, by the way, Clemence wants to see us on Monday. She left a message on the machine. Luke's summoned too.'

'Quite a deputation,' Peter said when Clemence opened the coach house door. Luke had been undecided as to whether to come, but had given way. He wanted to get ahead with books he *could* publish, he had told Georgia sourly, not those he couldn't.

Clemence seemed in no mood for irrelevant pleasantries. 'I thought we'd sit in here,' she said briefly, leading them to her living room, which was pleasant but less intimate than the studio. Not so much of Clemence was evident despite the family photos and paintings on the wall. There was no sign of Janie, and this time no mention of her.

'I gather you saw Betty last week,' Clemence began.

'Did Molly tell you?'

'Of course. Both she and Birdie via Christopher imparted the news. I would like to know what your plans are now.' This wasn't the diplomatic, considerate Clemence that Georgia was used to and it worried her. Clemence was tense and anxious about something. 'The board, as you know, is standing firm on *The Flight of the Soul*,' she continued. 'Are you happy with that situation?'

'I can't say yet,' Luke answered – truthfully, as Georgia knew.

A sigh of exasperation from Clemence. 'And you?' She turned to Peter and Georgia. 'Are you going ahead with a book on Alwyn in view of this apparent clearance over plagiarism and . . .' She hesitated. 'Over the Jenny Baker rape?'

So Clemence had already heard about that from Molly. The trust was working quickly. Or had Clemence known all along? Georgia suspected, and hoped, not.

'Our answer has to be the same as Luke's,' Georgia replied. 'We can't give a definite answer until we've looked into this new situation.'

'And how do you propose to do that?' Clemence persevered. 'Through Betty? Not, I hope, through Birdie, as I warned you before.'

'Is your concern for Gavin's reputation?' Georgia tried to calm the situation down to get to the truth, and that, she suspected, was what was worrying Clemence. Clemence looked relieved.

'It's a major factor,' Clemence admitted. 'You must see that with Gavin having backed the plagiarism charge he's left in the firing line. Someone, after all, did the actual faking. Does your thesis accuse Gavin of this? Or . . .' She must have noticed Georgia's hesitation. 'No. Of course it's me, isn't it? You think I could have helped him.' There was disdain in her voice, and she did not wait for Georgia to reply. 'You think I was so in love with him and under his sway as not to think independently. It could be a viable thesis, I agree. It's incorrect, however. There were several people Gavin could have called upon for such assistance. He was no forger himself, but such skills were not uncommon in student circles in the late 1940s.'

'Is this what you wanted to talk about?' Peter asked gently.

'No,' Clemence replied quickly. 'I want to talk about Gavin himself. It seems to me he's getting a raw deal over this, the only member of the group not to have been defended. You defend Alwyn, everyone defends Elfie, Molly and Birdie defend Roy. Now it's my turn and I shall protect my husband. Gavin was an honest man, a writer of integrity. He was put in an impossible position over Alwyn and Elfie. He was bewildered by it, he couldn't cope. In his novels he wrote of complex relationships, but in real life he could never see the wood for the trees.'

'Or the woods beyond the stream,' Georgia murmured.

Clemence looked startled. 'Ah. Elfie of course. Gavin assumed that everyone around him was as honest as he was. He protected those he loved. And he loved Elfie. You're right that I was in love with him right from the time I joined the group in 1938, but it was love from afar. He was totally wrapped up in that woman and it was only much later that he turned to me for comfort and then love.'

'After she had left him, following Alwyn's death?' And Roy, Georgia wondered? Was he going to come into this?

'Yes.' Clemence paused. 'It was clear that she no longer loved Gavin. But Gavin would never, *never* have faked that material, no matter if it was Alwyn, or as your latest theory seems to go, Roy, whom Elfie loved. He wouldn't betray *himself* and nor would he hire anyone to do the dirty work for him.'

Luke broke in. 'But it was he who brought the charge. Is that correct?'

'Yes, there's no doubt over that. I recall it well.'

'Then who brought the forged material to his attention, or at least put it somewhere where Gavin would find it?'

'Elfie and Birdie had the skills, but not the motive. But I did wonder . . .'

'*Please* go on,' Georgia pleaded when Clemence stopped.

'Mere rumour.' Clemence dismissed her impatiently.

'It's too late for holding back,' Peter said bluntly.

Clemence surrendered. 'You're right. I thought Betty might have done it,' she said reluctantly. 'That's why I mentioned her to you. Did she tell you that she hated Alwyn?'

'No,' Georgia said, startled. 'She said she thought him a twerp. But she believed the poems were his, not Roy's.'

'Precisely,' Clemence said drily. 'She was convinced Alwyn had written *The Flight of the Soul*, which was more than I was. I believed Gavin. But Betty's feelings were stronger than merely thinking Alwyn a twerp, I'm afraid. She blamed him, and Birdie too, for luring Roy away from the family nest. You know what attachments little sisters can have to big brothers. She would have been a teenager when Roy was living here.'

'I can't believe that,' Peter said flatly. 'She was hardly flattering about Roy.'

'Now perhaps,' Clemence rejoined. 'It was somewhat

different then. She hung around here whenever she could to
keep an eye on him. Roy thought it highly amusing.'

Peter was clearly turning this over in his mind. 'Nevertheless
it's a far cry to faking that whole charge against Alwyn.'

'What about Roy's death?' Georgia decided to plunge right
in. 'Was there any doubt that he died in the air raid?'

She'd gone too far. Clemence froze in obvious shock before
she robustly replied, 'Hardly. What on earth do you mean?'

Georgia couldn't go back now, but neither Luke nor Peter
was giving her any help on this one, either verbally or in their
expressions. 'The body was never identified in itself, was it?'

'There was hardly sufficient to do so after it was torn apart
by a bomb,' was the tart reply. 'He was identified by other
means.'

'Was there any doubt that he was going to the Café de Paris
that day?' Peter asked, to Georgia's relief. She was beginning
to think she was on her own, out of her mind.

There was ice in Clemence's voice. 'I'm afraid there were
no tracker dogs available that afternoon.'

'Did the Sandford family raise any doubts as to whether it
was Roy's body?' Georgia forced herself to ask, although the
image of Rick was supplanting Roy's now, and she felt sick.
Suppose . . .

'Georgia, Peter, leave this ridiculous idea alone, I beg of
you.' The ice had gone from Clemence's voice now, and had
been replaced with some different emotion that Georgia could
not identify. Was it fear? And if so, of what?

'Are we sure we want to go to this?' Georgia asked. She and
Peter were having an early meal at the King's Head at Janie's
suggestion. Janie had arrived as they were leaving. It turned
out that she had been at a writers' meeting in London, and so
again Clemence had carefully chosen her time to meet them.
Janie had mentioned that they could stay for the Bonfire Night
celebrations in the manor grounds.

'It's usually quite fun,' she assured them. 'Hot chestnuts,
mulled wine, fireworks and the Fernbourne Monster as well.'

'What on earth's that?' Peter had asked, intrigued.

'A former owner of the manor, who managed to murder
not one but several wives. Seventeenth century, I think. Caught
when he tried to burn the house down with the last one in it.

Not long before that, Guy Fawkes had tried the same trick with parliament, and the two became rather confused in Fernbourne minds.'

'What happened to the lord of the manor?' Georgia had asked.

'He met his fate,' Janie replied. 'The village reckoned he'd brought disgrace on it and pre-empted a court hearing with a lynching. Hardly surprisingly his heir sold the manor after that.'

'Let's go,' Peter had suggested. 'It sounds good.'

Now Georgia watched through the King's Head window as small groups of people made their way in the darkness to the manor. She wasn't so sure as Peter that this was something not to be missed, even though she had telephoned to ask Luke to join them. He had arranged to meet them outside the coach house, at Janie's suggestion, and she and Peter decided to take their car up there too.

When they reached the manor drive after meeting Luke, she could see lanterns illuminating a huge bonfire, which wasn't yet lit. Nearer the manor, a bar had been set up under a canvas awning and tended by Bob Laycock. As she, Luke and Peter reached the assembled crowd by the bonfire, Ted and Adam walked past them, both whistling – it was obvious now where Adam had learned his skills. She could see a large guy on top of the fire, clad in breeches, jacket and wig, ready to meet his comeuppance for wife-murder. Ted and Adam were black silhouettes in the lantern light as they prepared it for lighting.

'Nice pile of wood,' she called out to them stoutly.

'Old tricks,' Ted answered, friendly enough. 'My dad taught them to me. Knew every tree in the greenwood, he did, and Bonfire Night was the highlight of the year.'

So even this was a job that was apportioned out. Ted was in charge now, and doubtless Adam was being trained for his turn. Janie had told them that Christopher Atkin was in charge of the firework display, and Georgia spotted him in a roped-off area beyond the fire, talking to someone whom she identified as Sean Hunt. He seemed to be strutting around self-importantly too. She wondered whether the Bakers ever played a role in this village affair, or whether it was solely manor-led.

The appointed hour for the festivities to begin was seven o'clock, and by fifteen minutes to the hour the crowd looked fully assembled.

'Shall we get closer?' Georgia suggested uneasily. They had all three purposely remained on the edge of the crowd so that Peter would have a better chance of seeing in his wheelchair, but something about this felt wrong to Georgia. Furthermore they were nowhere near the chestnuts or drink – though plenty of other people were keeping that revenue up.

'If you're sure we're not to be the guys,' Peter joked mildly. 'I have an uneasy feeling that a lot of Fernbourne sees us in just that role.'

A joke, but, as with all jokes, there was some truth to it. It might have been her imagination, but the groups making up the total crowd looked very tight-knit, and the three of them were excluded either by design or chance.

'It's well organized,' Luke remarked casually. 'Not even a sparkler in a child's hand.'

Instead of making the ritual seem more civilized, however, for Georgia this seemed to increase the air of spookiness. The woods surrounding them were very dark, and the flickering lanterns only pierced the gloom rather than lighting it, throwing the occasional light across the watchers' faces, all intent now on the bonfire.

Perhaps it was better to remain here on the edge, Georgia decided, even if with the gathering crowds they were being pressed further back towards the woods. At least here the wheelchair could not be turned over by a sudden surge forward, and the back route to the coach house was easily accessible. Why on earth should that be necessary, she asked herself, but no answer came. As the magic hour of seven approached there was a noticeable increase in the volume of noise, and all faces turned to focus on the pyre. The funeral pyre of an effigy of someone who had displeased the village, she recalled.

That rang plenty of bells. She shivered slightly and saw Luke frown. Perhaps it was getting to him too. She stared at the straw effigy of the villainous lord of the manor. What would it have been like to have been married to that monster? It put her own relationship with Luke into reassuring perspective. She put her hand in his and felt it close around her own.

How stupid to be feeling so unsafe just because it was dark, she told herself, but she didn't move her hand.

Promptly at seven Matthew appeared – of course, it would be his duty as heir to the manor – to light the fire. Sean was thrusting out the lighting tool towards him and his grandfather put it to the fire. Immediately flames began to curl round the smaller pieces of wood, insidiously making their way upwards. From the snatches she caught, Matthew appeared to be making a traditional speech about the Fernbourne Monster.

'. . . see the law's respected. We'll have no murderers here, nor no lawmen either. No house-burners, no wife-killers . . . to bring shame on the house of Fernbourne. What say you?'

'Burn him, burn him,' came the chant from the waiting crowd.

Burn . . . burn . . . burn . . . The flames had caught the effigy now, to a chorus of approving cheers. The crowd was surging forward, pressing all round her, and she was caught up in its movement. As she looked round at Peter someone barged between herself and Luke, and her hand was torn away from his by the assault. All she could hear were shouts and cheers, not what Luke was yelling at her.

Then she lost sight of him. The eyes of the villagers were glued to the fire, and the chants were of one voice. No one cared what was happening in this mass of people. Ancient grudges were not yet over, and could be fuelled again by the flick of a match.

'Luke!' she shouted, but there was no reply. She and Peter had been cut off and in the group of young men that surrounded them the only one she recognized was Sean Hunt, a flaming brand in his hand, and his minions around him.

Her immediate thought was for Peter, and she sprang across to shield the wheelchair as the group closed in on them menacingly. Immediately she was shoved to one side by two of the yobs, with the remainder pushing the chair over and toppling Peter out. She heard his shout for help, but then his voice was swamped by the general noise and she herself was being pulled away. She thought she glimpsed Luke being held back by a large group of other youths, but then Sean pushed in front of her.

'Your turn, Georgia darling,' Sean sneered, so close to her face that she felt his heat, while other hands were groping under her coat, her sweater and between her trouser legs. Her clothes were being tugged, and she pushed down, drowning in a sea of black and aware only of foreign hands and noise and unidentifiable moisture.

Then suddenly it stopped. More space, more light. No hands, thank God. She struggled unsteadily to her feet, aware that she was sobbing, and saw that the youths were fighting amongst themselves – no, it was obviously a new gang arriving. One had got Sean in his grip – and it was someone she recognized. Nick Baker was shaking Sean like a puppy by the scruff of his collar. Behind him she caught a glimpse of Ken and realized that the Bakers had come to their rescue.

'Dad,' she heard herself croak, as Luke materialized out of the darkness and began to heave Peter upright with Adam's help. So Adam too had come to their aid, and the sound of police sirens was comfortingly close.

'I think Peter's all right.' Luke seized hold of her anxiously, supporting her in his arms, and his face close to hers. 'Are you?'

'Now I am,' she said, and must have fainted, because the next time she opened her eyes, she was in the Bakers' home with Sarah and Luke at her side.

Twelve

'Time's running out,' Peter said quietly the next morning.
'For what? Do you mean the end of the investigation
or –' Georgia made a feeble attempt at a joke – 'for us?'

There was no laugh in response. Apart from bruises and
cuts none of them had suffered physically in the Bonfire Night
attack, but despite the fact that the Bakers had weighed in
splendidly on their behalf, neither she nor Peter was under
any illusion that Fernbourne would now be united on their
side.

Peter regarded her sombrely. 'The former, but don't rule
out the latter. We've been given our marching orders.'

'Was it our focus on Roy that sparked this off?' Georgia
frowned. 'If so, Clemence must be involved unless Molly's
playing a double game.'

'Surely that's still the problem. Why is the village so caught
up in this affair? Fernbourne doesn't strike me as another
Friday Street, with its boots in the muddy waters of the past.
This seems to be a living issue, which implies personal involvement. Would you agree?'

'Yes, especially now the Bakers have declared themselves
in our favour.' Not like their earlier case, as Friday Street had
remained suspicious to the end.

'They're beginning to see this affair goes deeper than the
rape. It stems back to murder.'

'Alwyn's?'

'I think further back than that. To Roy's.'

Now that the issue was out on the table for discussion, she
was reluctant to accept it. 'Everyone liked Roy.' The words
sounded lacklustre even to herself. 'Everyone', so Peter often
pointed out, was rarely used as a scientific term.

'He was a selfish monster to his sister. I think what surprised
Betty was that we were talking of Alwyn's murder when it

was Roy's she thought more likely. Perhaps she even thought that Alwyn had murdered Roy, and that was why she hated him so much. Look at Suspects Anonymous,' Peter continued. He clicked on the software, and selected Roy's icon. 'OTC at Oxford. Came down in 1935. A blank year. Then moves into Shaw Cottage in 1937. Reservist, flying planes at weekends from West Malling. Called up into the RAF September 1939. In early 1941 he was based at Biggin Hill with 609 Squadron. Forty-eight-hour pass. Failed to report back on the Monday – which set off a panic at Shaw Cottage. Went by train to Shaw Cottage on the Saturday, found Alwyn and Birdie setting off on night duty. Not proven of course. Nothing certain thereafter either.' Peter paused. 'We've heard no watertight evidence that he went to the Café de Paris, despite a presumption of death, or that he ever left Shaw Cottage. Thank you, ladies and gents,' he added wryly, 'I'll take your questions now.'

'Plenty of them. How did he get to London? Train? Someone would have driven him back to the station, unless there was a bus. Who? Were the chums he went with to the Café de Paris also killed? And where was Clemence? Where were Gavin and Elfie? Alice said they were *all* digging – does that include Clemence?'

'Is that the lot?' Peter asked mildly as she stopped to draw breath.

'For the moment.'

'Then I'll start. Can we rely on Alice's evidence that he did come to Fernbourne and that Joe Baker brought him to the cottage?'

'Almost certainly. Do you recall if Matthew Hunt covered it in his book?'

'He didn't. Only that Roy died in London. So, as you say, who gave him a lift to the train? As it stands, we have been told that Roy later had a phone call from a friend or friends and went to join them in London. That probably checks out by the way. A group of doctors and nurses who had just come down from Liverpool after escorting a Canadian convoy were at the Café de Paris that night. Biggin Hill reported his absence on the Monday and meanwhile Gavin had heard an account of the evening from a friend who had been there, and knew that there were uniformed officers present. The family identified the body but there must have been some doubt, to say the least. On the other hand, Roy might never have left the cottage.'

Silence. 'Pure fantasy as yet,' Georgia said uneasily.

'So it comes back to Clemence. Was she there digging for victory? If so, she must be able to tell us one way or the other whether Roy left, unless of course . . .'

'No,' Georgia said firmly. 'Not Clemence. I won't believe she was involved in murder – *if* there was one. I'll check with Alice first, since Clemence has warned us off the subject.'

'Why did she do that? Matthew's orders? Fear of upsetting Birdie? Is there any love lost between the two of them?'

'Maybe not, but the milk of human kindness might still exist.'

'Fear for Gavin is more likely – unless of course the warning was out of concern for us. It's possible, as Damien Trent was most certainly murdered.'

Georgia agreed. 'But why would any of them want to murder Roy?'

'Or all of them . . .'

She clutched her head. 'One at a time,' she pleaded. 'Let's take Birdie first. Not possible.'

'Why not? Suppose Roy had rejected her?'

Georgia sighed. 'What would she do with the body? She's a slight little thing.'

'Helped by Joe Baker, who drove him from the station. Suppose Birdie knew that Roy had raped Jenny and told him so?'

'But seven years later he was punishing Alwyn for the same reason,' Georgia pointed out scathingly. 'Suspects Anonymous won't like that. Next?'

'Alwyn. Motive?'

Georgia cast round in desperation. 'Suppose – oh, I don't know – suppose he found Roy planning to steal his poems?'

'Overruled. Roy was flying Spitfires in the RAF, and Alwyn was teaching by day and air-raid warden by night. Not much time to plan or spot plagiarism. Next?' Peter fixed her with a stern eye.

'Elfie,' Georgia said firmly. 'Suppose she did fall in love with Roy, the bright flame.'

'Why should she kill him – and what did *she* do with the body?' Peter asked. 'Did she have Joe Baker's help too?'

'There's no need for mockery,' she said crossly. 'It's a viable idea.'

'On paper, my dear Watson. But nothing to support it. After all, there are many drawings of Alwyn by Elfie. Have you seen any of Roy?'

'One or two,' she muttered.

'As there were of the other Fernbourne Five members. No, I think you should admit defeat on this one.'

She was forced to see his point. 'Then who?'

'We end as we began. Gavin.'

'Motive?' she asked dispiritedly.

'Not known unless you consider that blotting the Fernbourne Five's copybook by rape is sufficient reason?'

'I don't.' She hesitated. 'And there's Clemence herself. No motive known.'

'Agreed.'

'So if they were all there together, as Alice says, it hardly seems likely that Roy was murdered there.'

'Unless,' Peter said gently, 'he was murdered by Alice's "all".'

The manor looked perfectly normal in the daylight. Georgia had not been here since Bonfire Night a week earlier, and she had half expected it would retain the creepiness and menace that they had encountered that night. It didn't, of course. Their footsteps crunched over wet gravel, and the grounds were grey due only to the rain and cloud. Nevertheless they were both on edge. She, Luke and Peter had talked to the police, who were still considering charging Sean Hunt for assault, and this time Matthew had remained remarkably quiet. Peter had been eager to come at first, as there was something he wanted to ask Janie, but she couldn't be here, and he had decided to leave the field clear for Georgia.

It had been Molly's suggestion that they meet here, rather than at Luke's office, perhaps because this would be her home ground. She ushered them into the living room with the large sofas.

'Are you serious? Roy, murdered?' Molly looked genuinely taken aback.

'Very serious,' Georgia replied. 'We wanted your input on it.' She and Peter were at stalemate again. Alice, when asked on the telephone about the day of Roy's death, had been remarkably clear. Clemence had not been at Shaw Cottage that afternoon and even though Alice herself had left at six p.m. there was no way Clemence could have arrived there, with or without murder in her mind. She was suffering from chicken pox and was staying with her parents until she was over it.

So if, Georgia reasoned to her relief, they had 'all' been involved in his death, as Peter's way-out suggestion had it, at least Clemence was off the hook.

'It sounds unbelievable that Roy could have been murdered,' Molly said frankly. 'And you admit yourselves there's no evidence.'

'You could talk to Betty about it.'

'No, thanks,' Molly said promptly. 'It's true she occasionally burbles about brother William having persuaded their parents that the remains were Roy's rather too easily, but I don't think she ever thought as far as his being bumped off here. Have you talked to Clemence?'

'She warned us off this line.'

Molly looked troubled, and echoed Georgia's own thinking. 'She's afraid Gavin will get drawn in. You do realize that Matthew is not only a client and chair of the board but a friend of mine?' she asked. 'And that you're telling me his father is a likely candidate for *murdering* Roy? Sorry, way out of my jurisdiction.'

'Can you prove he isn't?' Georgia asked.

'Why should I?' Her tone wasn't challenging, merely enquiring. 'Now let's get this straight. I thought I was here to talk about books and contracts with Luke.'

It had been Luke who had initiated this meeting at the manor. Georgia had at first been undecided how far to confide in him over Roy, but had then realized that it was too late to separate their interests now.

'I've two courses,' Luke had decided. 'Either I publish nothing by this lot of jokers and steer clear of trouble, or I want the lot. I'm not playing by their rules any longer. I'll tell Molly so, and to hell with the trustees. I'm a publisher not a private eye. She can stop pussyfooting around.'

'I love you when you get this way,' Georgia had said admiringly. 'Where does that leave Marsh and Daughter?'

'Marsh and Daughter, my darling, doesn't yet have a story to sell me.'

She had fallen into that one with a loud clang. Now, in the cold light of day, she was hoping that her presence with Luke might provide just the thorn in Molly's side that could help them both.

'Suits me,' Luke replied to what was virtually an ultimatum from Molly. 'It's mid-November, you're opening in June. I'm prepared to make you another offer for reprinting *Verses to Dorinda*, *A Mourning in Spring*, *The Woods Beyond the Stream* and *The Flight of the Soul*. Provided, naturally, they are free of copyright problems. With time passing, I need yea or nay from you by the weekend.'

'There are plenty of other publishers . . .' Molly began.

Luke laughed. 'Don't give me that, Molly. I've been in the game too long. There aren't and you know it. Not to do all of them.'

'What about my biography?' Molly countered.

'That depends on its contents.'

'All right,' Molly accepted wearily. 'I get the picture. We'll negotiate everything else and either keep the biography on ice or . . .'

When she stopped, Georgia was appalled. 'You're unlikely to find another publisher.'

'Ah,' Molly shrugged, 'but there is such a thing as self-publishing. And if – and it's a very big if indeed – your cock-eyed theory has any truth in it, the board could rush out a biography in advance of you, Luke, assuming you publish the Marsh and Daughter book.'

'A threat?' Luke looked taken aback.

'Once it would have been. Now,' Molly said frankly, 'I'm not so sure. I'm a trustee but I'm also a Sandford and independently minded. Not quite so many vested interests as my co-trustees. Tell me again how this murder theory goes.'

Georgia hesitated. Was she just providing fodder to be shot down? She decided to take the risk and recounted it carefully.

'So, if your information is right, Alwyn and Birdie were on duty in the evening. Gavin and Elfie were around either at the cottage or at the manor and might have given Roy a lift to the station. Alice was around some of the time. But do we *know* Alwyn and Birdie were on duty, or are you saying they bumped Roy off before they left? From what you say,' Molly continued, 'no one had any known motive except . . .'

Georgia saw where this was heading.

'Joe Baker,' Molly finished as Georgia had predicted, 'who drove Roy from the station to the cottage. You know what I'd do? Clemence isn't going to squawk so go to see Birdie.'

'In what capacity?' Georgia asked her. 'As Alwyn's sister, as the woman who loved Roy, or with regard to Alwyn's estate, which she's handed over to the trustees? You weren't too clear about that, but I take it that's the case?'

Molly reddened. 'I didn't see why the board wanted it. Apparently Elfie maintained it was only fair as the trust were offering to pay Birdie's fees at the home. She went into the home a year or two before Elfie died.'

It was interesting, but Georgia let it pass. 'What did Elfie get under Alwyn's will?'

'Everything went to Birdie, I think, not that there was much.'

'Despite the great love affair?'

A frown, as if this were the first time Molly had thought this odd. 'They'd parted by then.'

Weak, Georgia thought.

How many of the answers they were looking for were locked up inside Birdie's mind, Georgia wondered? Even if that mind was still razor sharp, nevertheless her body was frail, and Georgia realized she must take care with any questions they put to her – especially about Roy.

'By the pricking of my thumbs/Something wicked this way comes,' Peter had declared last night. Far from abandoning his belief that Roy had been murdered, it had been strengthened after Georgia had told him the outcome of the meeting with Molly. She had found him in his room half-asleep, watching television when she called in to see him, but he had immediately jerked awake again, demanding to be told all.

'You know, Georgia,' he had said when she had finished, 'that sense of personal involvement is getting stronger. Now Molly's bound into it too, and she's two generations down from Roy.'

'Sean Hunt thinks it's personal enough, especially as regards me,' Georgia said ruefully. 'And so for different reasons do Emma, Nick and Adam.'

'The power isn't coming from them. It's coming from Matthew Hunt, from Ted Laycock, and Christopher Atkin, first generation down.'

'And Janie and Clemence?'

'The former a bystander, and Clemence – well, let's hope she is too.'

'You do believe she is?' Georgia had a sudden fear.

'I want to,' Peter answered. 'Very much.'

Georgia had decided to visit Birdie alone, without telling Christopher first, but either by coincidence or design he was once again there when she arrived. The home had probably notified him when Georgia rang them as a courtesy to tell Birdie she was coming. Fortunately he seemed happy to stay in the background as usual, but it was a sign that Matthew's hand was ever present.

'I wanted to talk to you about Roy, your love for him, and his death,' she began carefully. 'Do you mind, because I can leave it for another day, if you don't feel up to it?'

Birdie reacted quickly. 'Death? What about it?'

'Can I talk about it?' Georgia asked Christopher.

'It pleases Mother to talk,' he replied stolidly, sitting back with folded arms as though adjudicating on the proceedings. He and Janie made excellent aides in their different ways, Janie fluttering around solicitously while Christopher worked in the background, oiling the wheels of his mother's life.

'It was a tragic death for Roy to die in that air raid,' Georgia began tentatively. 'Especially since he was only there by chance. Could you tell me a little about him?'

If she'd hoped this would open the floodgates she was wrong.

Birdie nestled under her soft blanket. 'Handsome, good looking,' she began in a monotone.

'Did you go out together, dancing, or to the cinema, or concerts? Would you have gone to the Café de Paris with him if you'd not been on duty?'

'Of course I would.'

Georgia could hardly ask whether they slept together. 'Was *Verses for Dorinda* written for you?'

She looked highly offended. 'Yes,' she almost spat. 'Who else do you think?'

Wrong foot, but it was interesting that Birdie was so defensive. 'Would Roy have taken Elfie instead of you to the Café de Paris, if Gavin didn't mind?'

Birdie looked at her vengefully, but then to Georgia's surprise began to laugh. As her face filled out, Georgia began to see the lovely girl she must have been in the past, and yet she was doomed always to be the sixth unsung member of the Five.

'What's funny?' she asked, smiling.

'Alwyn wouldn't have liked that,' Birdie chuckled.

'Did Elfie love Roy too?'

A strange look this time. 'Oh, yes, she did that all right.'

How to take that, Georgia wondered? With caution, she decided. 'Did Elfie ever draw any pictures of Roy as she did of Alwyn?'

'Don't know.' The mouth set firm. 'I told you that Matthew took the lot.'

'When Elfie died?'

'He's her son. Cleaned out the studio, and I couldn't do anything about it. Nor could Christopher, could you, lad?'

The lad shook his head. 'No, I tried to have a look, but he wouldn't let me.'

What was going on here? Matthew couldn't have been worried about what might be in Elfie's papers, or he would have found the forgeries. Had he been worried that Elfie might have been in love with Roy, not Alwyn? Or that there might be explicit letters from Alwyn or Elfie there?

'Would it be painful to talk of the day Roy died?'

Birdie looked drained of colour as if the fit of laughing had exhausted her, but she stirred herself to answer without apparent difficulty. As Georgia listened, a picture began to come to life. Roy arrived with Joe late on the Saturday morning. Alwyn was teaching in a nearby school and so was living at home, but his air-raid warden duties meant he had to be out that night. That annoyed Roy, because he wanted to go up to London for some fun. She was heartbroken at having to leave with Alwyn, because if Roy went to London she would miss his visit, as he wouldn't bother to return on the Sunday. She never saw him again. The lawns at Shaw Cottage were dug up for vegetables in the Dig for Victory campaign, and she, Gavin, and Elfie worked hard during the afternoon. And yes, Alice was there too helping. Only Roy was allowed to relax. Then Alwyn and Birdie left. Gavin said he had enough petrol to get Roy to the station when they left to return to the manor.'

'Did Elfie get on well with Roy?'

Birdie cast a shrewd glance at her. 'Roy had friends everywhere,' she said unhelpfully. 'Gavin said someone rang him to invite him up to London.' More helpful.

'You're sure Roy actually went and didn't have –' Georgia hesitated – 'an accident here. There were air raids over Kent that evening.'

Christopher was the first to react at this sudden turn, but Birdie got in first. 'Who would have wanted to hurt my Roy?' she cried. 'He loved me. Gavin, Elfie, Alwyn, Clemence, we all loved him. Didn't we?' she hurled at Christopher.

If Peter's theory had needed support, here it was, Georgia realized, chilled. Accident? Birdie herself had immediately understood what Georgia was getting at.

The tears were running down Birdie's cheeks as she looked into a past that Georgia only wished she could share. Birdie pulled herself together with remarkable speed however. 'Next year,' she said briskly, 'I'll tell them. Everyone. All those television people about my Roy, and how he loved *me*.'

It didn't take long for the repercussions to strike home. Georgia's mobile rang the next morning. It was Luke.

'I have a visitor here, Georgia. Matthew Hunt would be obliged if you and Peter would join us in the oast house.'

'Why should I jump at the ringmaster's whip?' Georgia grumbled. 'Do you want to go, Peter?'

'No,' he said promptly. 'If it's for an apology over Bonfire Night it would mean nothing, so why give him the satisfaction?'

Luke met her at the oast house door. 'I'm afraid Sean's here too. Can you stand it?'

'In handcuffs?' she asked furiously. 'Or to apologize? But, yes, I can stand it.'

Some hopes of an apology. Sean obviously felt secure in his grandfather's presence. He merely gave her a considered look up and down, which made her flesh creep, as she felt those clutching hands once again.

'I've come here, Mr Hunt,' Georgia said directly to him, ignoring Sean, 'but I've nothing to discuss with you without some kind of explanation as to Sean's behaviour.'

'Sean wishes to apologize for any misunderstanding the other evening. Youthful high spirits got out of hand.'

'Can he speak for himself?'

'Yeah, OK.' Sean sounded bored and Georgia tensed in fury. 'Sorry and all that.'

'And now you can wait outside,' Luke told him firmly, white-faced with anger. For once Matthew did not argue. Sean's presence had obviously been at his bidding and for once Matthew must have realized his mistake. He made an effort at normality after Luke's return, but it was forced.

'I genuinely want to thank you for joining us, Miss Marsh. I suggested it as I'm sure you have had a hand in Mr Frost's decision over the Five's reprints. I'm afraid I have to tell you that there is no way the board would sanction publication of *The Flight of the Soul.*'

Luke sighed. 'Here we go again. Does the board own the outright copyright in Alwyn Field's work?'

'It's assigned to us as part of the agreement for our paying Miss Field's fees in the home. Did Molly not tell you that?'

'Yes, but I understood Miss Field has a say in what is done with Alwyn's work.'

'That need not trouble you. We hold the publishing rights.'

'Obviously you are at least agreeing that Alwyn wrote the book,' Georgia pointed out with relish.

A split second while Matthew rallied. 'The case isn't yet proven.'

'You're wasting our time,' Luke said crossly. 'Molly accepted the evidence about the forgery, as does Miss Sandford.'

'She's a confused old lady.'

'Astute lady,' Georgia corrected.

'What's so important to you about this issue, Mr Hunt?' Luke asked curiously. 'Don't you like being wrong?'

Matthew looked taken aback. 'The reputation of the Five,

naturally. Apart from the unpleasantness of this plagiarism issue, you are claiming that Alwyn was murdered, Miss Marsh. I gather from Clemence that you now think Roy's death mysterious and you're pestering Birdie. To cap it all, you're doing your best to manufacture lies about my mother.'

'Why should you be any more upset about Elfie having an affair with Roy than with Alwyn?' Georgia asked curiously.

He reddened. 'I've spent too long on the project to be diverted by red herrings obviously aimed at attracting tabloid attention. This crazy idea that Roy was murdered is the last straw.'

'And what about Alwyn's reputation being ruined? That didn't seem to distress you and that's what I don't understand,' Georgia said.

'Then you don't understand very much,' Matthew rejoined. 'I'm not going to see a label of murderer hung round my father's neck.'

'It's fortunate that we haven't suggested it yet.' Interesting, she thought, that Matthew immediately assumed Gavin was guilty.

'I've made my point,' he snapped.

'You have,' Luke agreed. 'And so shall I. My offer for the books is again withdrawn and this meeting is over.' He promptly rose to show Matthew to the door.

'Phew. Talk about a scrap,' Georgia said to Luke on his return. 'Where did he get the idea that Gavin was Suspect Number One for Roy's murder?'

'Clemence?' Luke suggested.

'Yes. Does that suggest it might have substance?' She broke off as her mobile rang. What now?

'Has Hunt gone, Georgia?' Peter asked.

'Yes.'

'You both need to get here right away.'

The tone of his voice told her this was urgent and she rushed straight out to the car, with Luke at her side. To her alarm as she parked outside Peter's house, Mike Gilroy was coming out.

'By the look on your face this is official business,' she said, worried.

'It is.'

'Damien Trent?'

'No. A new case in Fernbourne.'

Alarm bells immediately rang. 'Who?'

'Clemence Gale. Found dead this morning. And she didn't strangle herself.'

Thirteen

'My car,' Peter said briefly, wheeling himself to the back door which was his main exit for the wheelchair. 'Mike wants us over as soon as possible.' He was right, Georgia realized. They needed to feel a team here, in the faint hope that such professional unity could distance them from the horror that Mike's news had brought. Impossible to believe that this had happened: Clemence the artist, Clemence the wise counsellor, the solid rock of their investigation, and Clemence the warm-hearted woman. One day, after this case had been solved, she would have become a friend, but now someone had ruled that out for ever.

Peter's first thought had been for Janie, whom he'd rung immediately, while Georgia had talked to Luke. 'You go,' he had said. 'Too many feet are a mistake on a crime scene.' She knew he was right, but that it cost him dearly not to come. The important thing, he had said, was that they should find Clemence's murderer.

Peter drove almost in silence to Fernbourne. He told her he had only spoken very briefly to Mike, who had needed to hurry to the crime scene. Until they had been filled in on the whole picture, there was little point in their own speculation. There was only one question Georgia had to ask Peter.

'Was it our fault?' She knew he would answer truthfully. 'Didn't we ask the right questions, or did we get so near to the truth that we provoked this?' Clemence's warnings to her rang in her ears – warnings she hadn't heeded.

'It was her choice not to tell us everything she knew.'

This wasn't enough. 'If she knew something then the trustees would as well.'

'Not necessarily. Clemence could keep her own counsel.'

'Janie?' From his silence, she knew that was his fear.

'Even if she knew nothing, which is the likelihood,' Peter eventually said, 'Clemence's killer couldn't be sure of that.'

She thought of Janie in that vast empty house, with the woods closing in around it and the long, long nights. She would be wondering, as Georgia was herself: which of the people I've met could have done this?

'Our problem is,' Peter continued, 'that we know the melody, but that doesn't make the whole score.'

The now familiar fields flashed inexorably by as Georgia counted the minutes before they would see the trees of Fernbourne. As soon as they entered the village she braced herself for what they would find. Despite the brightness of the day, the drive up to the manor house now seemed alive with memories of what they had faced on Bonfire Night.

Two constables in the doorway of the manor came out to challenge them, but after Peter had spoken briefly to them, he received permission to drive on. He was stopped again when they reached the coach house and directed to an area set aside for mobile incident vans and cars. The rest was cordoned off. By the time they had negotiated entrance to the scene itself, Mike was there to meet them. He was known for his outward unflappability but today that seemed to have vanished.

'Where is she?' Georgia asked. 'In her bedroom?' She knew that was on the first floor beyond the studio.

'Yes. Window broken in the kitchen, and the daughter –' Mike consulted his notes – 'Janie Hunt, slept in the manor. The scene seems clear enough so far.' He hesitated. 'Want to see her, Georgia?'

Everything in her screamed out against it, but that was disloyal to Clemence. Peter wouldn't be able to get up the stairs, so it was down to her. 'Would it help?' she asked Mike.

'There's always a chance. You can't go in, but even so you need to be in whites.' Georgia was glad of that. Putting the scene suit on forced her into some kind of professionalism, and once so clad and following Mike upstairs, she managed a certain detachment. She was thankful that Clemence hadn't died in the studio, where they had chatted so recently, and she tried to fix her mind on that.

Detachment vanished, however, when she saw Clemence's body. It was useless telling herself this was the shell and

Clemence herself had gone. She felt herself beginning to choke, and sought words – any words, clichéd or not. That's what clichés were for. To establish some kind of basic communication when all else failed. 'Would she have suffered?'

'She looks as if she was a tough old lady, but that might have been more mental than physical, I guess.' To have Mike standing at her side was a support. 'Her fear would be the worst.'

Was that comforting or not? She could think only of the familiar face distorted by a strangler's hands.

'Take a careful look at the room, Georgia,' came Mike's steadying voice. 'Can you see anything odd about it?'

'I haven't seen this room before. Janie would be a better guide.'

'Sure. But you've a trained eye, and she's in shock.'

'Of course.' Georgia forced herself to concentrate on the room, not on the abused body on the bed.

'I don't expect you to note fag-ends and trace evidence,' Mike told her. 'But you not only knew her but knew her in connection with the Fernbourne Five, and there almost has to be a link. You might spot something.'

Paintings on the walls, dressing table, bookshelf, photographs . . . Then her eye fell on two canvases propped facing the dressing table. 'What are those?'

Mike signalled to a SOCO to turn them round, and Georgia's heart plummeted when she recognized them.

'I've seen them before,' she told Mike, 'but they were in the studio when I looked at them with . . .' She found herself unable to say Clemence's name. One was *Double Janus*, the other *The Abdication*. Jenny Baker's disturbing face looked out at them enigmatically, but beyond her the unrecognizable man still drew the eye. For some reason she brought them in here, I suppose to think about them.'

'What's to think about?' asked Mike pragmatically.

How to answer that? Georgia drew a deep breath. 'Perhaps it goes to the heart of the Fernbourne Five. The girl is Jenny Baker.'

'Damien Trent.' Mike immediately perked up with something concrete to go on. 'His grandmother.'

Georgia nodded. 'Grandfather uncertain, however. Alwyn Field or Roy Sandford.'

'Is the foggy chap in the picture either of them?'

'Could be, but that's not its point. It's the power of sexual control: who holds it, who wields it.'

Mike lost interest in the paintings. 'You said Damien Trent was coming to see Mrs Hunt, only he was murdered before he could do so. If, as you say, he'd sorted out this Roy Sandford as his grandfather, why come to see her?'

'I don't know,' Georgia admitted.

Mike had as usual put his finger on a weak point. Just what line had Damien been pursuing? He'd been no mere fan of literature or art, that was for sure. Mike must have noticed her mental – perhaps physical – slump, because he said, 'Let's join Peter. There were no signs of burglary that we could see, though we'll be asking the daughter to check. It doesn't look like casual crime; it's too far off the beaten track to be a maniac who likes killing old ladies for fun.'

Georgia didn't reply and Mike took her arm.

'Over to the big house for you. More comfortable there while you fill me in.'

She was relieved. That would put her back in working mode as doubtless Mike had intended. He took her to the room with the sofas, where she could see Peter and Janie, Janie at one end of a sofa, and Peter at her side, his arm round her shoulders. Peter didn't normally demonstrate sympathy with physical actions, and this reaction showed how much Clemence's death had meant to him too. A PC was doing her best to be unobtrusive by the window.

'I'll need you, Peter,' Mike said tactfully, 'and you too, Georgia, in a minute or two.' Reluctantly Peter followed him out of the room, as Georgia went across to hug Janie.

'It was my fault,' Janie blurted out. 'If only I'd been sleeping there this wouldn't have happened.'

'It might,' Georgia said gently. What she didn't add was that Janie too might then be dead.

After a few more words, she left the PC in charge, though Janie seemed oblivious anyway, and joined Mike and Peter in the Fernbourne Room across the passage.

'Right,' Mike said when they were settled. 'Tell me the lot, including every crazy notion you have or had. And I want a who's who in Fernbourne. We've done one from Damien Trent's viewpoint. Now I need your perspective.'

Peter managed a grin. 'Not often you ask for that, Mike.'

'Not often I've got nowhere in a case like Damien Trent's and not paid sufficient credence to the fact that you two were snooping around. The SOCOs have got glove prints for the coach house window and sent them off for comparison with Trent's killer's. If they match then what you tell me now is going to be vital. If they don't, I still need to know.'

It took a good thirty minutes to fill Mike in and even after that Georgia was by no means sure that they were on the same wavelength. It was easy to relate facts and theories, but how to convey even to Mike the atmosphere and all the hundred and one impressions that they brought? That, she supposed, was the point. Mike needed black and white and was an expert at dispersing any colour if he needed to.

'So where you are now,' Mike summed up, 'is that there's a strong suspicion not only that Alwyn Field was murdered, but that Roy Sandford was as well. Both seem doubtful to me. The police investigation at the time got nowhere on Field. On the other hand, if you're right, it could have led to the deaths of either Trent or Mrs Hunt, or both. I take it that the opening of the arts centre next year is at stake as well as this Fernbourne Five's reputation. Know what I think?'

'Tell us.' Peter was being unusually polite.

'Two murders in the last couple of months is using a sledge-hammer to crack a long dead nut.'

'One man's nut is another man's caviar, his most valued possession,' Peter shot back.

'Roy Sandford is the heart of the mystery, and particularly how he met his death,' Georgia maintained. 'Clemence warned us not to get involved.'

'That's not caviar. It's in the past,' Mike pointed out.

'The next generation can also be their protagonists in the present,' Peter fought back. 'Inherited legacies can be tied closely to the successors' egos. Take Matthew Hunt, Clemence's stepson. He's in the firing line. The new arts centre is his legacy to leave for the lucky future.'

'Why should he be concerned over Roy Sandford? What about Sandford's descendants?'

'I don't see Great-Aunt Betty marching down here.'

'She could have an emissary.'

If it hadn't been for the heavy lump that had substituted

itself for her stomach, Georgia would have been amused at
the idea of Betty Sandford as a hit man. Peter had different
ideas. 'There's Molly Sandford, but it's unlikely. She's a busi-
nesswoman in London.'

'Who else?' Mike demanded.

'Birdie Field is looking forward to the opening because of
the publicizing of her love affair with Roy Sandford. Her son's
on the board of trustees, but her reputation isn't at stake. And
if it's publicity she's after she'd get plenty whether the arts
centre goes ahead or not.'

'Janie Hunt?' Mike asked.

'No,' Peter replied very definitely. 'No motive.'

'What about the Laycocks? You said Ted was on the board.'

'His father was the manor gardener in the 1940s, and his
uncle ran the pub. Ted took over when the uncle died. The
pub is on lease from the manor.'

'Does he suffer from loyal retainers' syndrome? Years of
service sort of thing?'

'Probably, but not much of a motive. And it was his father,
not he, who worked directly for the manor.'

'Dig further. Anyone else? So far we've got several elderly
men and one old lady in her nineties. Oh, and a London busi-
nesswoman – I don't see any of them as stranglers. What
about the next generation? Plenty of drugs and gangs on the
Trent case files.'

'Shooting, yes, but strangling, Mike?' Peter said doubtfully. 'Matthew Hunt, Gavin's son, is head of the firing line.
A nasty piece of work, but a murderer? It's possible I suppose,
but I don't see him strangling an old lady with malice and
motive aforethought. His grandson Sean is a villain, as you
know.'

'I haven't forgotten him,' Mike replied grimly.

'Nor me,' Georgia said feelingly. She described Sean's attack
on Emma, and then their Bonfire Night experiences to Mike
and he frowned.

'That one didn't reach my desk from Uniform. Sabre
rattling?'

'More than that,' Georgia said. 'Much more. "Clear off our
turf, or we'll make you."' A picture of Emma began to merge
in her mind with Jenny Baker, and one of Sean and Adam
with Roy and Alwyn. And that took her back to Clemence's

painting: who was wielding the power there? Gavin the controller? Or Roy the seducer? Or Alwyn himself?

Peter dropped Georgia off at Medlars before driving on to Haden Shaw. Janie was under sedation and there was nothing more to be gained by either of them by remaining at the manor. Never before had Georgia been so glad to reach home. She couldn't even face calling in at the oast house and seeing the sympathetic faces of the staff.

And here was Luke, at home, by some miracle, and not in the office. He came to meet her in the hallway but for a moment she was too choked to speak. His arms were round her and that was all she wanted for the moment. 'Oh, I'm glad to be home,' she said at last. Another cliché, but a cliché that filled a need.

'Drink and then tell me,' Luke said, moving her with him and with one hand reaching out for the brandy already poured into a glass and waiting for her. He watched her as she sipped it.

'That's good,' she said gratefully.

'So now tell me.' He listened as she spilled out the story, occasionally putting in a comment or asking a question. When finally she came to a halt, he said, 'Molly's already down here. She's been to see Matthew. They're not telling Birdie the news yet. They're afraid of its effect. Now, if you can face eating, I've got lunch ready. It's going to be a long day. Molly's coming this afternoon.'

Georgia sank back in relief, feeling like a child coming home from school, with these comforting words. Only when she used to return home, Elena had never quite got anything organized. But Luke had. She realized without surprise that she'd begun to think of Medlars as home. Someday, if this terrible case was ever over, she'd put the Haden Shaw cottage on the market. Someday *soon*.

With lunch over, Molly had to be faced. Georgia wasn't sure she could summon up the strength, but when she arrived, Molly looked as in need of Luke's care as Georgia had been. She looked white, and lined for once.

'I've been to see Matthew,' she said abruptly. 'He's talking to the press. He's good at that. Better than me or Janie. She's not up to that, poor thing.'

'What line is he taking?'

'The truth. Appalling tragedy. Great achievements. Last member of the Fernbourne Five to die. The manor project will be a memorial to her work. Family devastated. All true, yet he said bloody nothing worthwhile about Clemence. Nothing. Might as well have been the dog that died.'

It was as if she'd ripped off her business mask, and with it went her usual articulate phrasing and logical thinking, Georgia thought.

'News hounds have to be fed, just like any other kind of hound, Molly,' Georgia comforted her. 'Don't judge Matthew harshly over that. We all live by words one way or another. Sometimes they mean something, sometimes they don't. We all knew Clemence. We all admired her, loved her.'

Molly didn't comment. Instead she said abstractedly, looking round the Medlars living room, 'I envy you this. It almost makes me want to pair off again. Almost but not quite. Then I remember the rows and know I'm fine as I am. Have dog, have cat, two in fact. That's enough.'

Georgia glanced at Luke, who shook his head slightly. Don't say anything, he was intimating. She'll say more. He was right.

'I've been giving some thought to what you suggested about Roy,' Molly continued after a pause.

It almost seemed unimportant now. 'That he was murdered? The police point out that we've no hard evidence.'

'I decided to talk to Great-Aunt Betty after all,' Molly replied. 'If her story about Jenny is right, it puts a different complexion on everything. Including whether Roy was murdered. She said she'd always harboured a suspicion that Alwyn might have killed Roy through jealousy. I can't see it, but that's the trouble with dead clients,' she complained, 'especially if you're writing a biography of one of them. In theory not knowing them gives you a more objective way in, but to my mind that's more of a handicap if you really want to get at *the* truth, not just your idea of it.'

'How are you depicting Roy?' Georgia asked. Anything to take her mind off Clemence and that last sight of her.

Molly grimaced. 'As a wooden lump at the moment. He refuses to come to life except as a cliché of a golden youth cut short in his prime. OK, but it doesn't satisfy me. I put that down to my lack of powers as a writer, and so it might be. But it might also be that I'm several pieces short in the jigsaw.'

'Join the club,' Georgia said with feeling.

'But with this news of Clemence, it seems wrong to be dwelling on Roy. I can't see that there would be any connection.'

'There must be,' Georgia replied. 'He's the key. I'm still sure of that. Alwyn followed, Roy led.'

'But key to what? His murder? And how on earth do you find out the truth about that now? And if someone killed him, they couldn't be alive today, and so it can't be a reason for killing Clemence.'

'There's a missing link. There has to be. And we'll find it.'

Molly did not look convinced. 'How did you first get the notion that Alwyn was murdered? Something must have kick-started you.'

Georgia longed to say the fingerprints of time, but drew back. Luke had not been told and therefore no one else should know. It was a Marsh & Daughter internal concern. 'Suicide seemed so unlikely,' she said instead. 'So long after the events that were supposed to have caused it. Elfie choosing Gavin not Alwyn. The plagiarism issue settled.' It sounded weak.

Molly gave her a long look. 'I'm not sure I believe you, but it will do for now.' She glanced at Luke. 'We'd better get on with the business talk, not that I feel much like it. I suppose it will get it out of the way, though.'

Georgia took her cue. She didn't mind, since she wanted to return to Peter as quickly as possible rather than leaving him at home alone. She needed to be part of Marsh & Daughter, not pacing the room alone at Medlars with Clemence's death so much in her mind – and heart.

Peter was delighted to see her. 'Good. To take my mind off Clemence, I've been playing with Suspects Anonymous till I'm blue in the face,' he said gloomily. 'The only thing it comes up with is throwing in Roy's icon in connection with Alwyn's suicide. Or,' he corrected himself, 'murder.'

'What do you mean by throwing him in?'

'As a factor. It keeps putting him in a suspect, even though it knows perfectly well he died in 1941. Do you think Roy Sandford is alive and well and living in Fernbourne all this while? Or – no, I've got it. He's Great-Aunt Betty in disguise.' Peter stopped. 'I suppose joking is a good idea?'

'Trying to is,' Georgia agreed, feeling her voice wobble.

'I've another titbit for you. Not much of a joke.'

'What is it?' She knew she wasn't going to like this.

'I've been advertising in as many local newspapers as I could find over the whole of Kent, not just the coast.'

Rick. Of course. She should have known he wouldn't leave it alone. 'Advertising for a girl who visited Brittany, on two occasions in the course of about twelve years, asking after a man called Rick. Not much chance, is there?'

'No, and there's nothing so far. But I suppose it takes time. The ads started appearing at the end of October. That's only a couple of weeks. Any other ideas?'

It was a needle in a haystack, no matter how frustrating it was that someone out there could have a mite of information for them. Even if they found this girl by some miracle, she had been looking for Rick herself when she called at the farm. She didn't know he had disappeared. The problem was how to answer Peter.

'Yes, I have. We *can't* solve Rick's disappearance, so let's make up for it by doing what we can to solve Clemence's murder, and that means, if we're on the right lines, solving Alwyn Field's and possibly Roy's too. A tall order, but somewhere is the master key that will open all the doors.'

Peter's eyes lit up. 'I agree. It's a way forward. Roy is the master key. There must be something that strikes us as odd somewhere. What's his link to Clemence?'

Peter's putting this into words had an immediate effect. Georgia saw a possible answer, and the link could have been there all the time. 'Clemence had brought her painting of Roy as a double Janus into her bedroom. It was in the studio when I last saw it. Is that something you would call odd?'

'Not in itself.' Peter concentrated. 'What's odd is the title. "Double Janus" – why?'

'It isn't a straight portrait. It's Picasso-like, almost cubist. Faces looking in all directions, six at least. The bright flame, Clemence said. Roy reached out in all directions.'

'If there are six directions, why call it "Double Janus"?'

'Janus was the Roman god who was custodian of the universe and had two faces.'

'I know that, but it was two, not six or more.'

'Near enough,' she said impatiently. 'She said it wasn't a literal title. He's merely looking in every direction he fancies.'

'Artistically?'

'Yes.'

'Is that what she said?'

'Yes – well, I presume so. At least that's what she then talked about.'

'She would. What about sexually?'

She stared at him. 'Sexually?' she repeated stupidly. 'He was always chasing different women.' But Peter didn't mean that, did he? A great fear started to take hold of her that they had been looking at this case the wrong way round from the beginning, sucked in by the legend of the Fernbourne Five.

'The melody, Georgia; we've been fed the melody together with the rest of the world,' Peter was saying. There was conviction in his voice now, not doubt. 'The great love affair between Elfie and Alwyn didn't exist. The bright flame of Roy. The great love story of Birdie and Roy. That didn't exist either. Or at least it was one-sided, if so.'

'Roy was *gay*?'

Of course, she thought. It had been there all along for those who had eyes to see and minds to think. Clemence had misled her. No, Georgia changed her mind. Clemence had given a hint to her, but she had not picked it up.

'*Alwyn* was gay,' Peter corrected her. 'Roy probably looked both ways. Bisexual. The Double Janus. Janus with two faces sexually and several artistically.'

She swallowed. 'Are we sure? Or is this another theory?'

'Look at the facts. They were at Oxford together. A year or so later Roy moves into Shaw Cottage, not the manor, when he joins the group. It could have been because of Birdie, but the mere fact that Matthew didn't even deem that love affair important enough to record in his book suggests the love was all on her side, and that was generally known to be the case.'

'But Birdie would surely have guessed about Alwyn and Roy? She was living in the same house, for heaven's sake. It would have been obvious.'

'Not necessarily. In all likelihood Roy and Alwyn wouldn't

have shared a room, especially if Roy was bisexual. You told me that there was one bedroom apart from the others, round a corner and thus separated from the main corridor rooms. If that was Birdie's, all manner of shenanigans could have gone on in the other rooms without her necessarily knowing.'

Georgia began to feel sick. The whole basis of their understanding of the Fernbourne Five, including her relationship with Clemence, was being knocked away beneath her. She felt as if she were being swept away by an unstoppable tide of comprehension.

'Look at the poetry,' Peter continued, hauling down volumes from the shelves behind his desk with the help of his long stick with the manoeuvrable claw. '*Verses to Dorinda*. Big joke. Dorinda did exist, but she was Alwyn. Look at these poems in that new light:

> "I seized Love in my arms
> To crush him to my will."

Or:

> "Myself I'd lay before you
> But for my heart which still lies lost."

'Typical Roy,' Peter added. 'He didn't know which way he preferred, AC or DC. He enjoyed the power, the control.

> "I told you I must leave, my love,
> That some day this time would come."

'And then there's Alwyn,' he continued in excitement. 'His *A Mourning in Spring* isn't a panegyric to his lost love, Elfie. It's a collection of his love poetry written over the years and presented as an elegiac whole in honour of Roy, killed five years earlier. Listen:

> "Only you
> Will mourn my passing soul;
> Only you
> Have loved the whole of me."

'See?' he concluded. 'Obvious, isn't it?'

'Yes.' Georgia steadied herself. 'And the tombstone and suicide messages from "The Piper".'

'Oh, yes. Roy had gone beyond the mountain into paradise. Roy was taken before his time, and he, Alwyn, was limping behind, as in Browning's poem. The boy who couldn't keep up. Alwyn had lost his whole world, Roy. His poems were said to be Roy's, not his, and to cap it all he's accused of raping . . .' He broke off. 'I'm supporting the suicide theory,' he said in amazement. 'But if Alwyn was murdered, that couldn't have been his own choice of epitaph.'

'Nor were they his suicide notes.' Georgia was up to speed now. 'The poems were originally written for Roy, not Elfie and Birdie. They were fakes too.' She stared at Peter, who was looking as flabbergasted as she felt. 'Let's stop,' she continued. 'Let's take the path you were on. Keep going with Roy and Alwyn being the key relationship. Where does that leave Elfie? Is her love for Alwyn completely fictitious?'

'My guess is not. But equally importantly, did the rest of the Five, including Elfie, *know* that Roy and Alwyn were an item?'

'Clemence did, or had guessed. I think they must all have known at some point or another – except perhaps for Birdie.'

'Could that be why Clemence died, because she refused to follow the party line any longer?'

'But she did follow it.'

A silence, broken only when Peter said heavily, 'Why does this damned jigsaw *never* fit?'

Fourteen

There were more ghosts than Clemence's at this funeral, Georgia thought. When she had arrived in Fernbourne today, the familiar intimacy of the church, manor and pub had felt claustrophobic. The Fernbourne Five seemed to be presiding here as a group, and the fact that this was a private funeral emphasized, rather than dispelled, this impression. Janie had decreed that the press and public could have their day at a memorial service later, and so Georgia had been surprised that she and Peter had been specially asked to attend. Janie had rung Peter to tell him that she would welcome their presence. Whether Matthew would be as eager was debatable, but today of all days, he seemed to be living up to the courteous urbane image he so carefully promoted, even though he looked strained and pale. Perhaps it was the presence both of Birdie, pushed by Christopher in a wheelchair, and of Great-Aunt Betty that made Georgia think that by some unspoken assent the ghosts of the Fernbourne Five, as well as their living descendants, were drawing together to present a completed jigsaw puzzle at last. Or, it occurred to her bleakly, to prevent its completion.

Even Alice had managed a degree of conformity in her dress, perhaps bludgeoned into it by Ted and her family. The younger generation was also present. Sean, looking scrubbed and for once angelic, stood next to Adam, and Emma sat with her brother and parents. Then Georgia forgot about the Five and about the village, and thought only of Clemence as the service began.

'You will come back to the manor, won't you?' Janie said once they were outside again. She was dry-eyed, and clearly intent on getting through the ordeal before collapsing.

Peter was doubtful. 'We're not popular here, Janie. We shouldn't come while feelings are so raw.'

'But so are mine,' said Janie quietly. 'Come, please. There has to be an end some time.'

At least the gathering wasn't in the coach house. In the more impersonal surroundings of the manor it was easier to keep emotion at bay in the interests of seeking Janie's 'end'. Georgia didn't have to wait long. As Luke chatted to Molly and Peter kept Janie company, Matthew headed straight for Georgia.

'This all has to stop,' he said almost apologetically, as though the form of funerals should not be abandoned in any circumstances. He was right, so why the need to raise this now?

'Yes, we reached that conclusion.'

'And what do you propose to do about it?'

'Discover whether our theories are fact or not. If we don't continue, your arts centre opening will have the cloud of two murders over it forever.'

'You hope to prove that Roy Sandford was murdered, when there's no body? Difficult at the best of times, let alone over sixty years later.' When she didn't reply, Matthew continued, 'I presume you think he was killed here in Fernbourne.'

'That would be our assumption.'

'So do you propose to dig up the manor grounds and Shaw Cottage too?' He still sounded tired rather than accusatory.

'Not without permission.'

'Ours or the police's? If it's ours, you won't have it. Not the board's anyway. Or mine, and after Clemence's death the manor *is* mine. The coach house goes to Janie. Ridiculous arrangement, but inevitable. I'll also refuse permission,' he added, almost too much as an afterthought, 'to dig at Shaw Cottage. Not because I fear you will dig something up, but because I won't tolerate your meddling any longer. It's undoubtedly led to one death, if not two.'

If he'd spoken in his usual hectoring tones, she could have taken this, but the flat normality of his voice sent a chill through her. This man meant what he said.

Before she could answer though, Peter did it for her. He and Janie had overheard Matthew's words, and both were clearly furious. 'So there *is* obviously something to discover, then?' Peter kept in control, but was rigid with anger.

'If there is,' Janie answered for him, 'for God's sake, Matthew, let's find it and get this over with.'

'Janie . . .' he began warningly.

'No,' she cut in. 'I'm sick of you speaking for the whole board, Matthew. You've got a bloody nerve. First, Birdie is still nominally on the board and has a say in what happens at Shaw Cottage, as does Christopher; secondly, I'm on the board and you're not speaking for me. Or, I imagine, for Molly.'

'That still leaves me with a majority if Birdie and Christopher see things my way. Ted certainly will.'

'Then call a meeting and put the issue on the table. Meanwhile,' she said shortly, 'sod off, big brother.'

Georgia blenched at the pressure Janie must be under. Surprisingly, however, Matthew looked strained and white, and almost pleaded with her. 'I can't, and you know it.'

Janie stared at him. 'I don't know it, whatever it might be. But whatever it is, it's time I did. And the whole world too, if this arts centre is to work.'

'Could part of this great secret,' Peter broke in, obviously trying to end the deadlock, 'be that Alwyn Field was gay?' Then, when there was no answer, he added, 'And Roy bisexual?'

Janie looked completely thrown, but Matthew still managed to keep control, Georgia noticed. So it was not news to him.

'There is no proof,' he said with a distinct edge. 'And why should the art of the Fernbourne Five be degraded because of their sexual leanings?'

'Because your book,' Georgia immediately replied, 'leaned heavily on the sexual affair between your mother and Alwyn Field.'

'I didn't know the situation,' Matthew almost snarled. 'My mother died while I was writing the book, and a lot of things became clearer then. Too late I realized that although my mother had told me the truth about her love for Alwyn, it was not returned, at least not sexually. That was in her mind. Does that make it less real? He didn't look at them, only deliberately at his empty glass, muttered something and strode away.

'I didn't know that,' Janie said wearily. 'I'd feel some sympathy for the poor old chump if he wasn't so pigheaded. He is my half-brother, after all. What's he still holding on to?'

'My guess is,' Peter replied, 'that he knows who murdered Roy, and where the body is hidden.'

'But there have been two murders since. Including my *mother's*. Doesn't he worry about that?' Janie's voice was almost a wail now, and Georgia put her arm round her.

'Peter and I shouldn't have come. This kind of spat was likely to recur.'

'I don't think my mother would have minded,' Janie said. 'It's me who minds. Clemence had so much bottled up from the past that she never talked about. That much was obvious. So much about what she said to me about the Five when I grew up didn't fit in with the official line – I don't mean major facts, just odd anecdotes and impressions of people and things that they did. You know, it was a *happy* group basically, from what she told me, although thinking back that could have been the pre-war days. It was the later times that she didn't talk about. And no wonder, if there was all that going on. Having bottled it up so long, I think she might have been amused that the cork flew out at her funeral.'

It was an age away from the summer's day when they first visited Shaw's cottage. No sign of flowers now, except an odd rose straying from summer into December. There was desolate and dying undergrowth, as far as Georgia's eye could see. She had had no intention of coming to the cottage after the funeral, but in a way it had been forced upon both Peter and herself. Peter had suggested it might be fitting, and in view of what was pasted to Peter's windscreen when they had returned to the car, it was obvious that if any answers were to be found at Shaw Cottage, today would be the time to find them. A crude message scribbled on a Post-it had been stuck on it: 'You're next'.

'Charming,' Georgia had muttered. Perhaps Sean wasn't feeling quite as angelic as he looked today. She had looked round to see if the perpetrator was hanging around. He wasn't, but Alice had been, and strolled over to join them as Luke gave them a wave and drove off. He obviously hadn't taken in what was happening, and was returning with Molly to Medlars.

'That Sean,' Alice had said with great satisfaction, 'ran like blazes when he saw me, in case I'd brought a bucket of water with me. What's he left you? An early Christmas present?'

'Not really. A get out of town warning.'

Alice snorted. 'Mrs Elfie wouldn't have liked that. To think he's her grandson. Didn't like nasty things, Mrs Elfie didn't.'

'She liked love-in-a-mist,' Georgia pointed out, 'and even that has black seeds.'

Alice's eyes hardened. 'Not her fault it happened,' she said darkly. 'You be careful, very careful.'

Georgia had been glad that Luke hadn't heard this. It would have confirmed his impression that everyone in Fernbourne was bonkers, and probably dangerously so. He had only reluctantly agreed to go straight back to talk to Molly about publications, rather than come with them to Shaw Cottage. That was, he agreed, a Marsh & Daughter affair. Nevertheless, she wished now that he had come with them. Alice's words had conjured up a question mark that was not pleasant to contemplate as she and Peter drove to the cottage.

'Where do you want to go first?' she asked Peter as they parked in the drive. There were padlocks on the gates now, and for the first time they had been forbiddingly closed. Janie had warned them of this and given them the keys both to the gate and the house. 'I don't care what the answer is, I just need it over,' she had told them vehemently.

'It's the garden rather than the house for us, more's the pity,' Peter answered her. 'The terrace first.' Once there he contemplated the bleak view in front of him. What was he looking for, Georgia wondered? What could emerge today that they hadn't seen before?

'Let's get this over with – and quickly,' Peter continued. 'If Roy didn't die in the Café de Paris, then he was probably murdered in Fernbourne before he could leave, rather than elsewhere. Agreed?'

'Yes. Which means here . . .' Georgia shivered. 'Possibly the manor, if he went there with Gavin and Elfie after everyone else had left.'

'Much more likely to be here. It would explain why the trust is so eager to keep the cottage within their control. We also know that Gavin and Elfie were here at least part of the time digging away for victory. If Roy was murdered, there are four suspects. Right?'

'Or any combination within them, plus the outside chance it was someone from the village.'

He frowned. 'I no longer see a group conspiracy. Do you?'

'No, but I do see a cover-up.'

'Even so, it's unlikely all the other three conspired at the time. Too many different interests. And where would the body be buried? It wouldn't be near the house. If Birdie and Alwyn were implicated in his death, they wouldn't tolerate it so near, and if they weren't implicated it would be too risky.' He looked out over the garden again.

'Let's picture it,' Georgia suggested. It was a cold day but she was shivering more from what she was imagining than from the cold. 'If the murder was planned it wouldn't have taken place in the house because of the mess, regardless of who killed him – unless he was strangled or poisoned.'

Peter shook his head. 'They'd still have to move the body. Outside would be safer.'

'During a walk in the woods?'

'Too uncertain. Roy could simply say, "I'm knackered. I'm going to bed for the afternoon." It's more likely to have been a spur of the moment murder.'

'What time of day? Afternoon, evening?'

'After Alice had gone. Early evening or night, which puts walks in the woods out of the picture. This was March.' He stopped abruptly, and Georgia waited hopefully. 'We know that as well as London, there was a German raid over the south-east that evening,' he continued, excited. 'What does that tell you?'

'If he was killed by a bomb, no need for—'

Peter shook his head impatiently. 'Air-raid shelters,' he interrupted. 'An outdoor Anderson shelter. They wouldn't have been having a midnight stroll round the terrace with the sirens warning of an imminent raid; they would have been in the shelter.'

That was the answer; Georgia was sure of it. Then she had doubts. 'Again, if he were strangled or poisoned there, perhaps,' she said. 'But other methods would still have been messy for such a confined place.'

Peter took little notice. 'Where was the Anderson? Nearly everyone had one.' He surveyed the grounds before him. 'I've struck gold,' he said triumphantly. 'Look.' He pointed to the far left side of the gardens.

'The rockery,' Georgia exclaimed. Of course. The huge mound, now earthed over, could still be hiding the roof of the Anderson shelter, and even the steps that led down to the small space below. And that was where Alice had hunted for fairy rings by the remains of the stone statue.

'Black seeds,' she continued. Had Alice known all the time what had happened? Had she been involved? The whole garden seemed to take on a more sinister aspect. 'Love-in-a-mist never grew there. Only ferns because of the damp. Do you think Roy could still be buried inside?' That was a frightening thought.

'No way,' he said reassuringly. 'The shelter would have to remain in use afterwards. It's much more probable that he was buried elsewhere.'

'Where?' But the answer was inevitable, and it hit her stomach hard. 'The woods beyond the stream.'

'Yes, but where?' Peter's practical approach helped her recover. 'We can't expect Mike's men to dig the whole wood up. I know they've got technology to indicate the likely places for a corpse, but we need to narrow it down. Besides, Matthew would be hopping up and down with fury at every false dig.'

Georgia swallowed, knowing there was only one answer. She'd have to find the possible sites herself. Come back another day with Luke? The temptation was strong. Then she thought of Janie's face, of the need to get this over quickly.

'I'll go now,' she said.

'No,' Peter said sharply.

It would soon be dark, and those woods were waiting for her with their silent threat. Suppose the watcher waited too? 'You're next', Sean's note had read. No one could be here today, however, with everyone concerned still at the funeral. Only ghosts from the past would be stirring.

'I'll take the torch,' she said matter-of-factly. 'You can track my progress.'

Go now, Georgia, she told herself, before Peter talked her out of it, which wouldn't be difficult. Go now before dark falls. In December dusk was short. She grabbed the torch, and began to walk towards the river, stumbling over the weeds and brambles. No love-in-a-mist now to mark the path that Alwyn had taken that day. Nothing but dead undergrowth and the smell of damp decaying leaves. No longer the pleasant ripeness of autumn but the stink of the detritus of the dying year.

As she reached the stream she hesitated, looking quickly back at Peter and waving the torch to reassure him. She could see the path that had led here from the rockery ended at the stepping stones she was about to cross, and images of a murderer dragging a body along it made her retch. Fantasies dreamed up in crime novels flashed through her head, wheel-barrows with grisly contents . . . *Stop*, she told herself. Stop this and go on.

What if she found a likely burial place? Mike Gilroy would have to be told and Matthew would then know too. He could continue to profess ignorance of Roy's murder, lying through his teeth. So could they all. Which path to the truth? Find it, Georgia. Find it *quickly*. Cross to the woods beyond the stream and find out where he lies. In that glade that Adam had showed her? Had Birdie known about her sweetheart's death? Had Elfie? Gavin? Alwyn? Had Roy betrayed Alwyn over Jenny Baker? Was Joe here all that day too, having brought Roy from the station in his delivery van? No proof, no proof. Go to the woods beyond the stream, she told herself again, and then hurry back to safety. Draw the curtains, light the fire, shut out the evil demons.

She steadied herself again. The first hurdle was to walk past the tree on which Alwyn had died. It still cried out for justice, but was Roy here too, joining his voice to Alwyn's? The fingerprints of time hit her again as she crossed the stones to the far side of the stream, where the woods lay dark and uncompromising. Somebody had written a poem about a trav-eller and a dark tower. Where lay hers, where to look?

And then a sound split the heavy silence, and she let out an involuntary cry.

Whistling. Casual, perhaps, not meant to alarm, just to warn. Someone was there, deep within the evergreen laurels and holly that masked the glade. Alwyn's ghost? Easy to imagine in the twilight here. No, something more human. Someone who watched over the grave. Someone who *knew*. Someone who had killed Clemence. *You're next* . . . Someone who knew she was out of sight of safety, as Peter waited on the terrace. Someone who had heard her stifled cry.

'I didn't mean to startle you.'

The soft voice. A man. Last time the whistling had been Adam's, but it wouldn't be Adam now. She listened to the rustling of bushes and the crunch of boots, frozen and powerless to move. Adam had learned his whistling from his *grandfather*.

It was Ted Laycock. He stopped a few feet from her, clad in gum boots and a long anorak over his funeral clothes. What lay in those deep pockets? A gun?

His expression was impassive, which made it all the worse. 'I followed you from the funeral. There's a short cut through the woods. You wouldn't know it, not being local.'

'My father . . .' she began.

'He can wait.' He cut her off dismissively. 'I'll tell you only. No witnesses that way.'

'You can't have killed Roy Sandford,' she burbled through trembling lips. 'But his grave is here, isn't it?'

He showed no surprise. Of course he wouldn't, she thought. They all knew about this. 'Yes. There.'

He indicated a spot further along the bank where the path disappeared into the woods by the oak tree and away from the stream. Beyond it the trees came almost to the water's edge, but before that point she could see a grassy patch. Ted's voice was so casual, he could have been pointing out a particularly fine rose.

'Not the glade then. Adam showed me that.' She managed to sound normal, as though she wasn't terrified of what the ending of this nightmare might be.

'He told me. I never knew he came here. The glade's where Mr Roy and Mr Alwyn worked.'

And probably loved, she thought desolately. 'Why are you here today?' she asked. 'As Matthew's watchdog?'

He looked surprised. 'No. It was my father. He told me to look after the grave. See no harm came to it. He told me about it when he was dying and said I'd have to do the same with Bob when I go. Twenty years I've been coming here. Every month or so, I check on it.'

'Why your father? He didn't kill Roy, did he?' And now? Was he going to kill her so that the grave remained untouched?

'Course not. He buried him though. He was gardener up at the manor. Adored Mrs Elfie, he did. She couldn't have moved and buried him alone, not even with Mr Gavin's help. He'd gone home to do some work, leaving Mrs Elfie here, and she called them over here after she'd done it. She was in a right state, Dad said, and no wonder. Someone had to get the body over here, so that was Dad with Mr Gavin helping when he could. Fair turned his stomach, Dad said.'

'So it was Elfie who murdered him.'

There was an inevitability about the truth. Of course Elfie had killed Roy. He was in her way and so she had to remove him. Once, Georgia remembered, she had thought Elfie was another Elena. Now she shuddered at the thought. Elena, confronted with such an obstacle, would simply turn and take another path in life, whereas Elfie had removed the obstacle.

'Didn't know what she was doing,' Ted told her. 'He was a no-good that Roy, so Dad said.'

'Did Elfie love Roy and he laughed at her for it?' Had she been right all along about Elfie and Roy?

'You've got it all wrong,' he said with disdain. 'And you a woman. She hated him and with good reason. She adored Mr Field and as she saw it Sandford took him away from her. He boasted to her about his sordid perverted practices. Told her Mr Field didn't love her, he loved him, Roy Sandford. She blurted it all out to Dad that night and Mr Gavin, he just stood there, not knowing what had hit him, poor chap. Sandford had mocked her and Mrs Elfie couldn't take it so she'd shot him. She knew Mr Alwyn's father had a gun he kept at the cottage. Then she rang Mr Gavin, who got hold of Dad, and they risked the raids and ran over here. They had a discussion what to do, but Mrs Elfie was howling so much they decided to bury him straightaway, once the all-clear had sounded. Dad did most of that. Mr Hunt was in a blue funk. Once it was done, he took over though. Knowing that Miss Birdie and Mr Alwyn would be back in the morning expecting to see Sandford, Mr Gavin left a note that he had decided to go up to London after a phone call from a mate and wouldn't be back that weekend. He was like that, Sandford, impulsive, so they didn't question it. Why should they? Then on the Sunday Mr Gavin had a call from a friend of his, a Lady someone, who'd been at the Café de Paris when it was bombed on Saturday night. Told him all about it, in graphic detail about the bodies etc, clothes torn off them, some of them being looted even while they lay dying – and how they had all been there enjoying an evening out. There was a group of people at the next table, she said, some of them in uniform.

When Sandford was missed because he didn't show up at Biggin Hill on the Monday, Mr Gavin had the story ready. He'd made a few enquiries and discovered they were having trouble identifying the casualties. As Sandford had gone to London to meet friends, he wondered if he could possibly have been at the Café de Paris that night, because that was one of his favourite haunts. It went on from there. It might not have worked, but it did. In the war you were losing people all the time. Mourning time was brief.'

'But what about Birdie and Alwyn?' Georgia asked, aware of goose pimples that had nothing to do with the chilly afternoon. 'They must have been grief-stricken. They both loved him.'

'Yes. Dreadful that was, Dad said. Both in love with the sick bastard and weeping their hearts out, not knowing what had really happened.'

'Did Birdie know Roy was bisexual, and that Alwyn was gay?'

'Didn't use those words then, and I reckon she didn't. We didn't think that way. If you ask me, she still doesn't know, so don't you go telling her,' he finished grimly, taking a step towards her. It was all she could do not to move backwards.

'And Alwyn?' she asked again. 'He loved Roy and couldn't even talk about it to anyone.'

Ted looked surprised, as though that was the first time it had occurred to him, but he only shrugged. 'Serve him right for upsetting Mrs Elfie.'

Georgia was repulsed, but she had to stand her ground. 'And Elfie?' she managed to say, since she was obviously all Ted could think about. Elfie had to be protected. Never mind that Elfie had killed a man in cold blood.

'It turned Mrs Elfie's head. Mr Hunt looked after her, told Mr Field she was going to stay at home with him and that was that. He'd lost her for good. Not that he cared.'

'Did Alwyn not love her at all, not even as a friend?'

'No idea.'

'But she moved in here after he died, at Birdie's invitation. That means Birdie never guessed about the murder.'

He hesitated. 'She was told after Mrs Elfie died. Mrs Clemence knew by then because of Mr Gavin. When he died, she had to tell Mr Matthew, and then later after Mrs Elfie went, he told Miss Birdie – Mrs Atkin I should say.'

'And presumably he had to tell her *why* Elfie killed Roy. That must have been a shock.'

'Maybe,' he said non-committally.

'If Elfie still loved Alwyn, wouldn't she be terrified he would find out she had killed his beloved Roy?' Georgia thought of the love-in-a-mist carefully planted all the way down to the stream. What mists there must have been at Shaw Cottage. And what black seeds.

'His own fault, weren't it?'

There was no arguing with him. Georgia needed to get out of here though, and quickly, and took her courage in both hands. 'And now?' she asked. 'You realize I'll have to tell the police?'

To her relief, he nodded. 'I suppose that's only right. Things have gone too far. First that journalist, now Mrs Clemence.'

'You'll be questioned.'

'Now Mrs Clemence has gone, I don't greatly care. She was a good one. She never knew about it at the time, but Mr Hunt told her when he knew he was dying. Told her he relied on her to protect Mrs Elfie.'

'And when Elfie died?'

'We talked it over and decided to let things be. We had to think of Miss Field's feelings. Besides, she might have wanted to sell the house. No harm done,' he added fiercely, perhaps seeing the reaction Georgia knew her expression must reveal.

'It might have saved two lives,' Georgia said.

'You're wrong about that,' he said quietly. 'And before you ask, there's the matter of my wife. Alice knows nothing, see?'

'But she was there that afternoon.'

'I said she *knows* nothing. She guessed a bit of it from what Mrs Elfie said about love-in-a-mist one day.'

'The black seeds,' Georgia said, understanding now.

'We told her she was out with the fairies herself on that one. She'd take it too hard otherwise. Much too hard. See?'

'I do.' Georgia meant it.

'So if you'll excuse me, I'll be going. You can tell your father what you like, tell the whole bloody world. They'll find the body, but you'll never prove the story behind it.'

She could hear Peter calling faintly in the distance, and turned to flash the torch, though she doubted if he could see it from here. When she looked back Ted had gone as quickly as he had appeared. Realizing how long she had been, she hurried back to Peter.

He looked relieved as he saw her approaching. 'You had me worried,' he called crossly. 'I couldn't see the torch any more.'

'I had myself worried,' she said wryly. 'I met Ted Laycock in the woods.'

An intake of breath. 'You're all right?'

'Yes. He showed me where the grave was.'

'And Elfie killed him?' he asked.

'Yes.' She hadn't the strength to ask how he had guessed that.

'I was watching you make your way down. Remember where that love-in-a-mist was growing?'

'Yes. Planted for Alwyn,' Georgia said. She was back to safety, though night had fallen. 'The legend was right all the time. Elfie adored Alwyn. What the legend did not report was that Alwyn loved only Roy. He must have been a gentle soul, unlike Roy Sandford, but he's still a mystery.'

'And that,' Peter said, as he turned the wheelchair to return to the car, 'is the point. He *is* still a mystery. We said Roy was the key, but we began with Alwyn, and that's where we must end.'

Fifteen

'We thought we should tell you ourselves, Janie,' Peter said, having explained what had happened after they had left the funeral. 'It could be the reason that your mother was killed.'

It had been his suggestion that both Georgia and he should visit her the next day. A low time, Peter had said. Georgia's immediate reaction was that they should wait, but Peter had merely replied once more, as had Janie herself, that the sooner this was over the better.

'Look at this place,' Janie said in despair. She was still living in the manor, and no wonder. 'It feels like a great empty barn now that my mother has gone. It had some purpose then, now it doesn't.'

'It does,' Georgia said, 'and you'll feel that again once you feel able to begin work again.'

'I suppose so, but it's hard to imagine it. What was going to be a great adventure now seems more like another wake ahead. Thanks for coming to tell me, though.'

'It does mean the end of the story is fast approaching,' Georgia said.

'The true story of the Fernbourne Five. That's good. I need to know how far my mother was involved.' She looked at them hopefully.

'In nothing that didn't meet her own standards of integrity,' Peter said firmly. 'And they were pretty high.'

Janie looked at him gratefully. 'Thank you,' she whispered. 'You know . . .' She was clearly struggling with tears. 'I didn't know any of this. She told Matthew, but not me. I suppose she would have done if . . . if . . . I must say,' she said quickly, 'I'm glad I drew Clemence and not Elfie in the lottery of life. Poor old Matthew. He'll take it badly.'

'Only if the police find and identify the body,' Peter said. 'I don't see him believing it otherwise.'

'Oh, I do. Come in here. I want to show you something.'

She took them into the study room, which was still as chaotic as it had been on their earlier visit – hardly surprising in the circumstances. 'This is all Elfie's stuff, and this is where Luke must have snaffled those letters.' She managed a grin. 'You wanted to know whether Elfie had ever drawn any pictures of Roy. The answer's yes. Have a look at these.'

She produced a folder and laid it on the study table for them to see. Georgia bit back a cry. What lay before her were black and white drawings of dark trees, nude bodies in overt sexual positions intertwined in the trees and branches, and stark corpses or ghosts. It was hard to see which in the latter case, and Georgia shuddered. These went far beyond those published in *The Woods Beyond the Stream*.

'The file's labelled "Dark Wood drawings". You can see why,' Janie said.

Georgia could. The file was dated 1941/2. 'These are her nightmares of Roy.'

'Yes,' Janie said. 'I felt sorry for Matthew. He took one look at these, and immediately said she had been ill. If he'd ever seen them, which I doubt, he must have blocked them from his mind. Like his mother, I guess, only she didn't succeed so well, judging by the nightmare quality of these.' She hesitated. 'Did my mother know about Roy's murder all the time?' she asked awkwardly.

'Only much later. When your father died.'

Janie nodded. 'Good. But perhaps she sensed what was going on at Shaw Cottage much earlier.'

'You mean the painting your father didn't like, "The Abdication"? We thought that was because he was the model.'

'No, Roy was. At least we know why my father didn't like it – he didn't want to be reminded of why Elfie had murdered Roy Sandford.'

'It might also have made him uncomfortable about the rough music against Alwyn,' Georgia pointed out.

'You could be right. He played no part in that. And he most certainly didn't like my mother's "Double Janus" either, and nor did Birdie. That's the painting that troubled my mother most, because when you think about it, it represents the passions of Shaw Cottage as much as Roy himself.' Janie paused. 'Should we hang them in the new arts centre?'

'Was Clemence proud of them?'

'As an artist, yes. It was the subjects that disturbed her. She found she was painting something she didn't fully understand herself.'

'Then do it,' Georgia urged her.

'Matthew won't like it,' Peter murmured.

Janie managed a smile. 'Matthew can go to hell.'

In daylight even in December these woods looked almost benign. Despite the scene suits, the diggers, the masks, the tents awaiting erection if the body were found – and despite Mike's formidable presence. Of course Mike had to be here, and Georgia was glad of it. He needed to see whether the body was really here before he called in the full team. If it was, then the usual grim procedures would take place. If it wasn't, he would consider whether to do a wider search. Laycock, Mike had pointed out, could well have been lying, or else deceived by the father as to where Roy Sandford's remains lay.

At first Matthew had declined the suggestion that he should join them, but then changed his mind – perhaps because Molly and Janie had been determined to attend. As, of course, had Ted. None of them spoke as they watched the diggers' progress. Peter had managed to get as far as the near side of the stream and Georgia had decided to stay with him. It was only ten feet or so away from the site, but even so it gave a measure of detachment.

As the time crept by, Georgia began to lose hope. There was nothing yet, although the diggers were several feet down. Another fifteen minutes crept by, and then: 'Here!' Mike suddenly called.

Torn between reluctance and duty, Georgia crossed quickly to the other side to join the main party. She stared down into the hole. There, lying against the dark soil, was a hand stretching out as it must have fallen when the body was lowered. Whatever Ted's father had wrapped the body in must have rotted away, for as the diggers carefully scraped a little more of the soil away, the whole skeletal arm appeared with scraps of what might have been a covering. Mike called a halt while he summoned the dedicated team.

'We don't want to go into overdrive and then find the bones are prehistoric,' he said, going over the stream to put Peter in the picture.

Small chance of that, Georgia thought. She was certain she was staring at the remains of Roy Sandford, which had been in the ground over sixty years. At her side Matthew was trembling, and ashen-faced.

'My God,' he murmured over and over again. 'Clemence told me about Roy's murder after my mother died. I didn't believe her, even though I felt I had to at least warn Birdie. I thought Clemence was prejudiced. My mother had caused a great deal of trouble between her and Gavin one way and another.'

'What the hell am I going to tell Betty?' Molly muttered.

'It will confirm her suspicions,' Georgia said, perhaps unwisely. 'Even if Alwyn wasn't his murderer, but his lover.'

'You're probably right. She never liked Elfie. She said she never trusted wistful ladies who wafted through life with a faint smile.'

'I'll talk to her,' Matthew said.

'You will not.' Molly turned angrily on him. 'Thanks a bunch, Matthew, but you've done enough. You set me up, all of you, as a patsy. I was the mug who was going to write the biography of the bright flame, whom you all knew to be bisexual, and probably a rapist to boot. Now it turns out that the bright flame was snuffed out by your mother.'

'Not proven,' Matthew snapped.

'I'll give them a bucketful of DNA and so will Betty if it will make you admit the truth for once, Matthew.'

He blenched, but replied calmly enough, 'Why don't we go to the pub while they're waiting for the next stage?'

Molly looked undecided, but Georgia took her arm and led her back to the crossing stones to join Peter and Mike. Molly grinned at her as she thanked her. 'Don't say life must go on, will you, Georgia?'

'I promise.'

In fact, once they were established in the warmth of the King's Head, it was Molly who reverted to the practical approach. 'Assuming what we've just seen are indeed Roy's remains, I suppose we need to decide pronto what's to happen about the launch of the arts centre and whether we do want reprints available.'

Matthew answered her stonily. 'The centre will go ahead, as arranged, of course.'

Georgia was as taken aback as Molly clearly was. 'Just like that?' she asked. 'But there's no legend left to promote.'

'I think you'll find there is. The legend, as you rather scornfully refer to it, is that my mother was in love with Alwyn and he with her. Has that been contradicted? No. There is nothing in my book about the plagiarism – or otherwise – of *The Flight of the Soul*, merely a passing reference to both poets having been involved in it. That could well be true. No mention of Jenny Baker's rape either. Roy's death occurred during an air raid. True enough, even if the raid were not the cause of it. I have dealt in *my* book with the artistic achievements of the Five. I suggest we leave it at that.'

Georgia glanced quickly at Peter, and then spoke for them both. 'You can leave it where you like, Matthew. Marsh and Daughter won't. Your book skims over the surface.'

'There is no need to tell the whole sordid story . . .' Matthew began.

'There is,' Molly said flatly. 'Believe me, Matthew, this time there is. We do tell the whole story. If we don't, others will sensationalize it.'

Georgia was appalled. 'Peter and I won't do that . . .'

'I'm sorry.' Molly looked aghast. 'I should have said the whole story must be told by you, not by the tabloid press. We have six months, we can do it.'

'Including the truth about Roy?' Georgia was astonished at Molly's turnaround.

'Yes,' Molly said. 'There's no way I can do a biography of Roy now that the poor devil has been deprived of his life and his reputation.'

'The poor devil you refer to raped Jenny Baker,' Georgia retorted.

'True.' Molly looked worried. 'What do we do about the Bakers, Matthew? They'll have to be told.'

'The advantage of having been a businessman,' Matthew said wryly, 'is that one learns to move forward with the tide. In this case, with our friends the Marshes so heavily involved, I suggest there is only one way out. Everyone concerned takes a seat at the table to sort out the mess.'

Molly looked pleased. 'That's a brilliant idea, Matthew –

provided you make sure the meeting comes to some agreed conclusion. We can get Great-Aunt Betty and Birdie in on it. If we all work together we could get the whole story out at once and have a tremendous opening.'

Peter had been silent for too long, Georgia realized, but now he said his piece. 'Aren't you overlooking something? We haven't got the whole story. You're forgetting Alwyn.'

'I'm tired, Georgia,' Peter said wearily as she drove them back to Haden Shaw.

'Take the rest of the day off, come to us,' she urged.

'Not physically. I'm mentally tired of never having enough answers.'

'You're thinking of Rick again,' she said gently. 'You can't do that. That's our personal problem. You've had no answers to the advertisements?'

'No. Still early days, I suppose. But it won't lead anywhere and I know that. We'll never have the answer, just as we won't about this case. I'm on the point of giving up.'

'Don't,' she said firmly. 'You know the solution is there waiting for us.'

He sighed. 'I suppose Alwyn Field *is* the key to this, not Roy. He almost has to be. We think we know Roy's story, but it's led us nowhere. If Clemence and Damien were killed because of their knowledge of Roy's murder, then it would surely have led us onwards, but it hasn't.'

'Matthew – Ted,' she began hopefully.

'We don't believe that, do we, Georgia? Not deep down. I wish we did.'

'No. Apart from Scatty Betty, whom I presume we can discount, who hated Alwyn sufficiently to want to murder him?'

'There's only one answer to that, isn't there?' Peter said.

She looked as if she had been expecting them. Perhaps she was, as there was no Christopher here today. Birdie's bright eyes were cold like a bird of prey's; she was sitting erect, no blanket around her, just a frail and very old lady. Frail in body perhaps, Georgia thought, but, like Clemence, not in mind. Birdie said nothing, but kept those cold eyes on Peter, which made it all the more chilling as he said flatly:

'You killed Alwyn, didn't you, Birdie?'

For Georgia, murder by a frail old woman had seemed unbelievable. Now looking at those stony eyes she knew it was the truth. Of course, Georgia and Peter had reasoned, Birdie hated Alwyn. Her brother or not, he had seduced her beloved Roy away from her. She had never forgiven him for it. Or Elfie for telling her after Roy's death that Roy and Alwyn were lovers. That's why Birdie had invited her to live at Shaw Cottage, so that Elfie should suffer every day. She knew Elfie hated the place, although Birdie assumed this was because her beloved Alwyn had spurned her love here. It had been Birdie's revenge. She had turned on the messenger, not the culprit. She didn't know that her Roy lay there dead all that time, not until after Elfie had died. The stories she had told them about Elfie and Alwyn at Shaw Cottage were malicious lies. The trust and Birdie had different interests, the trust determined to protect the secret of Roy's murder – a secret Birdie couldn't reveal after she knew about it, lest investigation opened up the matter of Alwyn's death again.

Georgia waited for Birdie to speak but she did not. Peter repeated the question and this time Birdie did reply.

'I was away,' she said indifferently.

'You planned it,' Peter said. 'Perhaps you drugged Alwyn and Joe Baker carried the deed out, after you had told him that Alwyn had raped Jenny. Falsely of course. And with your artistic skills you copied all Alwyn's poems into Roy's handwriting, and faked suicide notes in Alwyn's. Tell me, Mrs Atkin, why didn't you destroy Alwyn's original manuscripts of the poems? Did you see a chance of using them in some kind of blackmail, hurting Alwyn even more by letting him think that Elfie had been the forger in revenge for his not loving her in the way she wanted? Is that why he left nothing to her in his will?'

A laugh, still in a monotone as though these were matters of complete indifference to her. 'The bitch needed a lesson. All "darling Elfie" and "how clever of you, Elfie". I needed to keep an eye on her, so I told her we could mourn Alwyn together if she came to live with me. I took my forgeries up to the manor saying they were files Roy had left at Shaw Cottage when he died, and I pushed one or two of Alwyn's originals plus one or two forgeries in Roy's handwriting into

Elfie's papers, hoping Gavin might find them and think she'd done it. He never did, and she never found them. So I put the rest of them into her junk when she moved in with me. Insurance policy, as I saw it. They're always saying we should have something in the bank. I could shut Gavin up if he ever suspected there was more to the suicide than met the eye.'

'And the rape of Jenny Baker? That was Roy, wasn't it?'

She shrugged. 'Rape? The girl was always throwing herself at him. Why shouldn't he take her? He loved me, not her. Easy enough to make Joe think it was Alwyn and talk him into the rough music and then into killing him. I made it easy for him. I left some pills dissolved in his whisky, and then went off and left things to Joe. Alwyn was a fool, he always was.'

Peter glanced at Georgia, who nodded. They needed the whole truth now. It was Peter who put the question. 'And Clemence and Damien Trent had to die for that?'

Her face went blank. 'I'm tired,' she complained.

'Then the police will have to come.'

The eyes grew cunning. 'I'm an old woman.'

'Not too old to murder.'

'Who says I did?'

'We will, and they'll believe us,' Peter said matter-of-factly. 'Damien came to see you. He told you all about Roy being his father, and not Alwyn. You were afraid that he'd spill the beans, and that it could lead to the discovery that Alwyn's death wasn't suicide, but that you murdered him. Did he suspect the truth about Roy's death too? You wanted your moment of glory at the opening, not to have the past dragged up in front of you.'

Georgia was afraid they'd gone too far, for Birdie made no reply, or gave any sign that he had spoken. But she wouldn't stop now.

'And then Clemence came to see you,' Georgia said. 'She told you we were working on the theory that both Alwyn and Roy were murdered. You couldn't kill both of us, but you could get at Clemence. She *knew*. She was the last one of the Five. And if we discovered through her about Roy's murder, sooner or later we would link you with Alwyn's death, as well as Damien's.'

Birdie was quiet for a while, with her head nodding gently.

Then she turned on them. 'You fools don't understand,' she screeched. 'If they knew about Roy, they'd know *why* that woman killed him. I couldn't have that – Roy loved me. *Only* me. Not Alwyn, not Jenny, not that woman. Not Elfie Lane.' Her voice was rising, and Georgia half rose. But Birdie grew quiet again, her eyes glittering.

'We were in love, Roy and I,' she crooned to herself. 'He loved me. He came to me in flower time, put a rose in my hair and his kiss on my cheek. He touched me so gently. "My Birdie," he said, "my gentle, gentle Birdie. We'll fly together, you and I, not in my Spitfire, but on the wings of love. When the war's over we'll marry – all the poems of the world I will lay at your feet, my Birdie, my Dorinda." We walked by the stream, we walked in the fields. We picked primroses together. He bound them in my hair, a garland of flowers. For *me*. Mrs Roy Sandford . . . After the war, after the war . . .'

She was still burbling, still rambling on, as they left.

'When we came for him,' Mike told them, 'he was sitting stuffing a dead squirrel. Seemed more important to him than what we were saying. Disgusting. Said it was his father's hobby and he'd ordered him to carry on. He's as potty as his mother. He said he had to kill Damien Trent and Clemence Gale. No emotion. Talked of the squirrels with more feeling. "I had to protect Mum," he said. "She told me to do it, so I did it." He said he knew that Sean's gun was in that shed, and he'd had army training in his youth. He told Trent that the footpath was a short cut to his cottage, and he was inviting him back for a drink after taking him to see Shaw Cottage. Trent, being a stranger, believed him. He's a weirdo, all right. Seemed to think there was nothing much wrong in murdering two people.'

Georgia shuddered, remembering Christopher's words. 'Oh, yes,' he'd said, when she'd asked if he knew who had killed Damien. If she had persevered, would he have admitted that he was guilty? She doubted it. Christopher was the perfect carer. His job was to provide Birdie's comforts, and the two murders were on her list of needs. That was enough for him.

'We've enough DNA to hold him on,' Mike told them. 'Clemence had plenty on her. I doubt if Birdie's caught up with the DNA generation. Meanwhile he's blandly confessed to both Damien and Clemence's murders, both the planning and the execution unfortunately. Birdie will deny everything, of course, and she's unfit to plead anyway. We'd have a job holding her on Alwyn Field now. What's that poem about cats?' he asked out of the blue.

'Eh?' Peter recovered quickly. '"Macavity the Mystery Cat" maybe?'

'Yeah. He wasn't there. That's Birdie for you.'

'And top of it all, there's Christmas coming up,' Georgia pointed out to Luke as she finished bringing him up to date.

'Don't mention it, please. I'll be busy reprinting poetry collections.'

'Oh, good.' Georgia was pleased. 'So you're back in favour again. Including *The Flight of the Soul* under Alwyn's name?'

Luke grinned. 'Yes.'

'You'll need me to put my house on the market to pay for it.'

He stared at her in amazement. 'You're serious?'

'I'll do it in the spring.' Seeing his look of disbelief, she added, 'But I'm getting the seller's pack ready. Honest.'

'Would you like an engagement ring for Christmas?'

'Why not?'

A startled silence, then a crash as the pile of advance copies Luke was unpacking fell to the floor.

'Didn't you mean it?' she asked politely.

'Yes, but . . . No bloody buts. Of course I meant it!'

'Then so did I.' A pause while she looked at him, highly pleased. 'We'll tell Peter on Christmas Day.' She'd been meaning to tell her father that they were expecting him to spend Christmas with them as usual, but so far she hadn't had a chance.

'Good idea.'

Celebrating took some time, and the phone call to Peter was never made. Better, Georgia decided, to tell him the news in person at Christmas.

To her surprise, Peter looked taken aback when she invited him the next morning. 'Christmas Day?' he queried. 'Could we make it Boxing Day?'

It was Georgia's turn to be taken aback. Peter *always* spent

Christmas Day with her and Luke. 'Of course. But why? You're
not being a burden, if that's what worries you.'

Peter looked shifty. 'As a matter of fact, I have a date
already.'

'With Gwen?' His sister lived not far from Dover.

He looked smug. 'No. With Janie.'